# Redeeming The Time

## Faircourt Friends Series
## Book One

# Alexandra T Armstrong

PARABLE PRINT

This book is lovingly dedicated to
April Wong loi Sing
Twilah Copeland
and
Karen Chadwick
who have been my steadfast friends for lo, these many decades.
Thanks, girls.


Look carefully then how you walk, not as unwise but as wise, making the
best use of the time, because the days are evil.
Ephesians 5:15-16 (ESV)

# CHAPTER ONE

Ava's eyes widened, and an audible gasp escaped her throat, visceral and uncensored, as her daughter, Marit, emerged from the bridal store dressing room and stepped onto the viewing stage. Marit twirled before her mom and three accompanying bridesmaids, a delighted, full-faced smile crinkling the corners of her eyes. *This is a joke. She's pranking me,*" Ava hoped, relaxing the shoulders she had reflexively tensed.

Marit turned to examine herself in the dress before the 180-degree mirror at the back of the platform. Barely visible bands of nude organza over each shoulder supported a low-cut bodice of white brocaded lace that clung to the torso and bum tighter than the grip of a frightened toddler. At mid-thigh, the dress inflated in volume into scattered lace patches on sheer white organza that fanned into a wide circle train edged with heavy brocade. Underneath the sheer organza peeped an underskirt of nude-colored silk. White pearl buttons ran the length of the back of the dress, which, due to the deep back plunge, began nearly at the waist.

The dress made a statement. To the mother-of-the-bride paying for the dress, the statement was: "Here comes the Vegas showgirl wanna-be."

A gray-haired bridal consultant with a fine-tuned sense of impending drama, passed a hand mirror to the bride-to-be and fled to the safety of the dress racks behind the platform.

Marit gathered her mid-back-length raven hair with her other hand,

and with a deft twist of her slender wrist, piled it on top of her head to accentuate the deep back plunge of the dress.

"Isn't it glamorous, Mom?" she gushed, more statement than question. "This is the one!"

Marit sought neither bridesmaids' nor her mother's approval. As the baby of the family and accustomed to her mother's unfailing support, she was not concerned that her mom would respond with anything other than affirmation and compliments.

Ava, distressed by the choice, which appeared to be authentic now, pasted on a smile and brightly encouraged Marit to keep looking. A flash of disbelief stamped Marit's face. However, she remained resolute. This immodest, flamboyant mermaid gown would be her wedding dress.

Ava was not prepared, nor did she want, to share her honest thoughts with an audience of bridesmaids, shop employees, and another nearby bridal party. There was no need for the spectacle of a public disagreement with her daughter. So as casually as she could muster and with her checkbook snugged safely in her purse, Ava breezed toward the shop's front door saying, "We'll talk about it, honey. It seems we're all done here, so I'll see you at home!"

Home was a small, post-World War 2, three-bedroom, one-bathroom brick ranch in Bloomington, Illinois, which Ava and her husband, Marcus, didn't own though they'd lived there for 35 years. It was the parsonage of Delaware Street Community Church located next door.

When Marit showed up there later that afternoon, fortified with her bridesmaid's assurances that her chosen dress was indeed stunning, she lit into her mother, who was tearing lettuce leaves into a salad at the kitchen counter.

"Why would you embarrass me like that in front of my friends?" Marit demanded, hands on hips.

"That's exactly was I was trying not to do, sweetie," Ava replied. "I didn't say anything negative about the dress for that exact reason."

"You make your opinions known very well without words, Mother. We all knew you hated it. The girls knew. The bridal assistants and their manager knew. Even the flower girl from the other bridal party knew. So you didn't like it, and you just walked out. You never told me I needed your approval for my wedding dress."

Ava was flustered by her daughter's unfiltered critique of her behavior, critiques which had been more frequent in recent weeks. She meant to explain the dress's shortcomings rationally, but at the moment, she wasn't clear-headed enough to temper her words. They poured out bluntly as she threw lettuce at a bowl.

"What do you think a dress that leaves so much uncovered and so little to the imagination says about you? And what does it say about your father and me if we approve of it? Are we really that trashy?" Ava blurted.

"You thought I looked *trashy*?" her stunned daughter asked with angry tears gathering. "You thought I looked *trashy*?" Marit repeated, unable to get past the adjective.

Ava knew it was the wrong word to use as soon as it left her mouth. But there it was, a disaster hanging in the air like a blimp on fire. She tried to navigate around it.

"Poor choice of words. I just meant to ask if you're so focused on your new life with Robby that you've forgotten Dad and I will continue to minister here. And escorting you down the aisle in something that looks like lingerie will create a scandal he'll bear the fallout of. You don't have to care what people think of you, but you should care what they think of Dad. I thought you did."

"And there it is! Don't say this, don't do that, don't have a life because your dad is a minister. Well, Mom, my husband will not be a minister. My husband is a pharmaceutical sales rep. And my first decision as the wife of a pharmaceutical sales rep is to wear a dress for our wedding that he will like - whether you and Dad pay for it or not, and whether Dad walks me down the aisle or not!"

Marit stomped to her bedroom down the hall, slamming the door for emphasis.

Ava sighed and wondered what had happened to her formerly easy-going and manageable daughter. Until her engagement, Marit enjoyed a confidential and playful relationship with her mother. Now their bond felt stretched, and instead of springing back with resilience, it hung uncomfortably loose.

As Ava's thoughts acknowledged this, her gray-blue eyes gathered tears that spilled down freckled cheeks that flushed so easily. She cried at the realization she'd wounded herself by embarrassing Marit in the bridal shop. She cried because of her lack of verbal discipline. And she cried because she was not the parent she promised herself she would be.

Marcus made parenting look easy, no matter the season of life. He didn't fail their daughters – Marley Marie, 38; Mia Louise, 37; and baby Marit Anne, now 27. Marcus was the parent who let his toddlers paint his toenails Easter egg colors when his leg was in a cast, did The Worm at their 5th grade Father/Daughter dance, and pranked his high-school girls with tattoo sleeves and a magnetic earring.

By contrast, the trajectory of Ava's early parenting style indicated she would be a cranky old woman shouting at kids to quit running through her yard. She thought the baby she had at 39 would give her a second chance to implement more of the parenting approach she'd seen in Marcus' example. The regular reminders of their father's profession, which Ava had used to regulate the behavior of Marit's older sisters, had not been used to control Marit despite her appropriated memories from hearing her sister's complaints. Ava had not expected her youngest daughter to spend her childhood living as a moral example for other children.

But now, she wanted to be proud of Marit's decisions as an adult, and it was becoming increasingly difficult. The dawning realization of a correlation between Marley and Mia's stricter childhoods and their ability, as grown women, to be prudent and considerate in their decision-making added to Ava's sense of parental guilt. Perhaps she had over-corrected with Marit and failed her in that way.

Ava dabbed her tears with a corner of her homemade apron and abandoned the salad. She grabbed her cell phone and retreated to her bedroom to call Marie, her childhood friend and the namesake of her firstborn daughter. In trying times, Marie was a reliable fount of sensible counsel.

Ava's tears flowed anew as she described Marit's tasteless choice of a wedding gown and how she'd taken her leave to avoid a public scene and endured a private one instead.

Marie listened to her frazzled friend and responded pointedly. She reminded Ava that her daughter was an adult who dressed herself. She told Ava to get used to keeping her mouth shut in the affairs of adult children when the consequences of their decisions weren't life-threatening.

Ava rolled her eyes, unseen by her friend. She could have gotten that kind of canned, knee-jerk response from a stranger on the street.

Marie continued, "I know you know this. You've already practiced this with the older girls." And then, she caught herself. "No, you haven't. You didn't have to, right?"

"Not really, no," Ava affirmed. "Marley and Mia have so much sense."

"And Marit?" Marie asked to draw out her friend's thoughts.

"Marit thinks with her emotions," Ava blurted. "Wow, I don't think I've ever verbalized that so succinctly before this minute. But it's true. She doesn't use a lot of other information available to her. Instead, she leans into her feelings to make decisions. And here's the worst part, Marie:

That's got to be my fault. Every child starts out ruled by emotions, and a good parent corrects it, not caters to it. I'll admit I did more catering than correcting her. But I wanted a turn to be Marcus."

Ava's last statement stunned her ears. It was transparent and selfish, and accurate.

"Ava, girl," consoled Marie. "You're not the first mom who wanted her turn to be the good cop, the fun one."

"Yeah, but a good parent does what's best for their child even if it doesn't make them the favorite."

"You're a good parent, Ava. So, you're not a perfect parent. There's never been one."

"But what do I do now? Do I look away and whistle "Dixie" because she's an adult?

"Yes, you do. You and Marcus have done your best as her teachers. Now let Providence have its turn with her. She'll learn emotions aren't trustworthy guides. In the meantime, tell it to Jesus, girl!"

Ava put the phone in her apron pocket and returned to salad-making in the kitchen. As she chopped radishes, she mentally prepared to accept the floozy wedding frock.

# Chapter Two

Ava waved goodbye to Marit and Robby as their rented limousine pulled away from the downtown Bloomington hotel reception venue. Hers was among the waving arms of a dozen friends of the bridal couple who stayed to party until the DJ announced the last dance of the evening. The friends promptly dispersed toward their own vehicles before the limo reached the next block.

Ava raised the hem of her royal blue gown, chosen to highlight her blue eyes and the red hair she vigilantly maintained against ever-encroaching white roots, and walked on tired feet back inside the hotel. Inside the ballroom, where the catering staff was boxing up leftover cake and counting wine bottles, Marcus was bent over one of the DJ's speakers, using it as a desk to write out a check for the balance payment of his services. Ava pulled off her silver dressy heels and headed to join the real wedding diehards collecting unclaimed, monogrammed soap table favors. These were her and Marcus' dearest friends, Grant and Marie Renniger and Elodie Ford.

"I'm sorry, but that boy has biscuits for brains," Elodie said as she placed soaps in a cardboard box scavenged from the hotel kitchen. She said it fully aware this was already the settled opinion of Ava and Marcus regarding their newly minted son-in-law. They'd figured out quickly that Robby got by on his good looks and charm, not his common sense.

Marie tried to sanctify the criticism. "Well, at least you can bless his heart if you're going to put it out there that way," she reminded.

With the precision timing of a gold-medal synchronized swim team, Elodie, Ava, and Marie raised their right hands and intoned, "Bless his heart."

"I did apologize before I said it," Elodie clarified. "But he had no business leavin' Marit after the cake-cuttin' to go smokin' those cigars with his groomsmen in the parkin' lot. And then that mess! It's gonna be awhile before that bridesmaid recovers her right mind after gettin' a lap full of his vomit. Should probably just throw the dress away." She hesitated a minute and added, "Think the photographer got *that* picture?"

"If he didn't, I did," Marcus answered as he joined them. He reached in the breast pocket of his tuxedo jacket for his cell phone and asked, "Anyone care to relive da moment in all its digital glory? Got his mother's reaction in da shot, too!" His Caribbean accent melted through his words.

Grant groaned and shook his head with a pained expression. He added his soaps to Elodie's box and moved to sit down at the table Marie was working. In just another minute, their task was complete. All sat, chairs askew, around the table. Marie and Elodie followed Ava's example and removed their shoes. Marie put one bare foot in Grant's lap, hoping for a foot rub. He loosened his tie and shirt collar and gamely obliged her.

"Well, Van Zants, that's the last of your three girls married - for better or worse," Marie addressed Ava and Marcus. "What's the next chapter going to be?"

"Dat's our Marie, always looking forward to da next ting while da rest of us are still trying to catch our bret from da last ting!" Marcus chided her. He sat back in his chair and laced his fingers behind his head, which sank into his curly hair, now a 70/30 mix of black and white. His trim goatee,100 percent white, contrasted vividly against his cocoa skin.

"Guilty. I allow the comment to stand unchallenged," Marie admitted with spunk.

Ava exhaled and looked up at the ceiling chandeliers as if she was assembling a further answer from the dimmed bulbs and dusty crystals. She looked to Marcus next, who nodded a wordless consent and folded his arms across his chest.

"Ok, actually, change is in the air for us," Ava began. "Last month, the Chairman of the Deacons told Marcus it was time to retire. They want a younger man in the pulpit. Someone closer to 40 than 70. He said that!" Tears gathered in her eyes but did not spill. "It's all being done so badly," she lamented.

"I'm so sorry, man," Grant offered his condolences to Marcus, who gazed stoically at his wife.

Ava continued. "The thing is, we're not financially prepared for this. Our investments comprised three girls, three sets of braces, three college educations, and three weddings on a preacher and preschool teacher's salaries. We thought we'd have some time to catch up a bit – we're both healthy enough to keep working. This isn't how we imagined our ministry would end there after 35 years. The wedding preparations absorbed the initial blow these past few weeks, but now we have to face it."

"We'll be ok," Marcus offered earnestly, reaching for Ava's hand. He knew it took more than optimism to soothe Ava's anxiety about their retirement prospects, but without a concrete plan, it was all he had to offer.

Emboldened by Ava's candor, Elodie spoke up. "Girl, I'm not ready for any next chapter either, even though my eyesight is gonna force me to quit workin' sooner than later. Gonna be hard livin' on Social Security and the little I've got put away, but I can do hard. What's scary is doin' by myself. At least you all have each other and your kids. I'm the only black woman I know who doesn't have family to fill a country church. You know my parents were both only children, so there were no aunts, uncles, or cousins, and my little brother passed at 16. So now, it's knowin'

I'm growin' old alone that's keepin' me up at night and prayin' till I fall asleep."

Marie shot a glance at Grant, who did not catch it. He was feigning unusual interest in the foot he was massaging. Conversations that expressed vulnerability made him uncomfortable. Even conversations with these friends he'd known for years upon years. He knew, however, that his wife delighted in this kind of relational intimacy with her friends. Marcus, too. He was worse than Marie. Marcus would joyfully plumb the depths of their souls with provocative questions. Grant did not enjoy soul-plumbing, neither his own nor being witness to anyone else's. He thought himself a simple man who enjoyed simple conversations. Grant braced himself for an awkward, complicated one.

"El, you know we're family," Marie reassured. "After nearly 50 years of friendship and fusses, we're sisters. Ava and I won't let you be lonely. Didn't we completely forgive you after you nearly killed us and our families with a bad batch of oysters that Thanksgiving? We could have had you locked up for attempted murder. Nobody but family gets away with that." Marie's brand of comfort was often passive aggressive. She believed it lightened the mood.

Elodie understood Marie's intent, but instead of offering her usual deadpan look over the top of her glasses in response to her friend's playful jab, she drew a deep breath. She'd started out being honest about her fears, and she'd continue that course.

"First off, I thought we were not talkin' about the oysters anymore. Second, are you gonna be in my apartment in the middle of the night if I have a stroke like my Momma, and there are eight minutes to get me help before I'm a total vegetable? Who's gonna know if any bad stuff happens to me livin' alone? You're both hours away. Look, you're both my sisters, and maybe your ugly husbands are my brothers, but none of ya gonna be in my apartment, and that is facts."

Cued for his role in any discussion he felt called for further investigation, Marcus ignored Elodie had referred to him as ugly for the thousandth time since he'd met her when he began dating Ava. Instead, he inquired: "So El, if you could draw up a plan to solve your problem, what would dat look like?"

Elodie pretended to hesitate. She pushed her teeth into her lower lip as if thinking on the fly. The truth was, she'd been drawing up such a plan in the wishes of her heart for over a year but was not about to admit it. Finally, she answered Marcus but looked toward Ava and Marie as she did so. "I'd live in a big ole house with my friends. And it could solve your problem too, Marcus."

# Chapter Three

Grant and Marie sat at the breakfast table in their retirement patio home, which still smelled like new construction. They blew over the steaming mugs in their hands: his black tea with honey; hers, creamed coffee with honey. It had been a long day at Marit and Robby's wedding, made later by the post-reception discussion of their friends' potential scheme to buy into a communal retirement house.

Neither Grant nor Marie had anything of substance to contribute to the discussion since they had implemented their own retirement plans six weeks ago. They could have gotten on the road home an hour earlier than they did. Instead, they stayed to listen and give their support. At least, that's what Grant thought they were doing.

Marie feigned sleep during the entire 5-hour drive home to Lansing, Michigan, while her mind raced with possibilities. Unbeknownst to Grant and even her friends, she'd been having nagging buyer's remorse for settling into a retirement home so far away from the Bible Belt, where both of their twin sons lived and were likely to remain. She regretted their choice to stay in Michigan.

It was 1:30 pm, and the usual early birds were just starting their day at the kitchen table. Both were still wearing their pajamas or what passed for pajamas. Marie loved the classic matching floral pajama sets and robes she ordered from a country store catalog. She wasn't a shoe or a perfume girl; she was a pajama girl with at least a dozen sets to her name. On the other hand, Grant picked up a pair of flannel night pants from a national discount chain once every few years and paired it with whatever t-shirt was on top of the stack in his chest of drawers. Regardless, neither wore their bedtime outfits into the afternoon unless they were sick. But at ages 68 and 62, Grant and Marie discovered they no longer bounced up from late nights that stretched into wee morning hours.

Marie swept her middle fingers underneath her frameless eyeglasses and rubbed the corners of her hazel eyes. Then she raked her fingers through her salt-and-pepper shoulder-length hair and gathered it into a messy bun at the back of her head with a claw clip she discovered in her bathrobe pocket. Unsure of what to do next, she studied the squirrel raiding the birdfeeder by the window while carefully sipping the hot coffee. Marie was determined not to speak before Grant was ready. She'd learned early on in their marriage not to crowd her husband when she wanted something. If he didn't have time to mull over a new idea, his spontaneous response would be "No."

For his part, Grant knew precisely what Marie was thinking. He hadn't lived with this woman and loved her wholeheartedly for 39 years without learning nearly everything about her. Every passion of his heart was wrapped up in her and her happiness. Nine times out of ten, what made Marie happy made him happy too, but not this wild plot. Grant was traditional, conservative, private, and pragmatic. This plan was none of that for him.

Though he knew Marie was giving him space to consider what she hadn't verbalized or needed to, he didn't like the distance between them. It felt uncomfortable. The sooner he waded into the subject they were both evading, the sooner they could put it behind them and resume life the way they'd planned and prepared. Besides, while she'd been pretending to sleep on the ride home last night, he'd been formulating his plan to shut down their participation in this hippie commune scheme gently but effectively.

He drew a deep breath and dove in. "You want to talk about it, Baby Doll?"

Marie turned her attention from the window to look at her husband, noting his normally clean-shaven head sported a five o'clock shadow in the early afternoon. It was she who'd talked him into shaving his head when he confessed his thinning hair horrified him. She convinced him it would complement the rest of his robust features: thick eyebrows that were still dark, large brown eyes, and a Roman nose. After he worked up the courage to shave it for the first time, they both agreed it improved his appearance. Over time, Grant saw the look as an enhancement to his persona. He felt nearly as confident as he looked.

Marie looked demurely through her eyelashes and offered him a little grin.

"I love that you know me so well and that there's nothing we can't talk about – eventually," she answered, setting her mug to the side of the table. "I have more questions than answers about Elodie's suggestion about all living together, but something about the idea hits my heart with this wildflower mix of emotions: excitement, compassion, gladness, peace, and security. And before you say it, I know we don't arrange our lives around emotions. That's why my head is spinning with questions like, how would this even work with finances and dividing responsibilities, and how do we incorporate all our styles into one house? The only thing I'm sure of is that we've known these people longer than we've known our children. I've known the girls since I was a child myself! And I love them. And you love them, too."

Grant was ready with his objections. "I'm glad you recognize I know you well. But sometimes I wonder how well you know me. And I wonder if my feelings matter to you because in my emotional flower garden, as you call it, are anxiety and...," he hesitated momentarily as he searched his emotional vocabulary, "...and don't-want-to-do-it!"

His emotional vocabulary wasn't extensive. He pressed on.

"And I think about questions like, what financial sense would it make to consider moving again when we only bought this retirement home six weeks ago? And why would we give up our own space and privacy? Honestly, there's no possible benefit for us in this. It's my job to look out for us. So, it's not selfish to stick with our plan and let Ava, Marcus, and Elodie do their thing." Now that he'd spoken his mind, Grant lowered his gaze from his wife's face and into his mug.

"Of course," Marie responded gently, "it's not selfish to stick with our plan. I agree it wouldn't make financial sense to pay a selling commission and probably lose money on the sale of this place. Undoubtedly, we wouldn't have the same privacy as in our own home. All that is true. But there is, actually a benefit for you in this."

Grant doubted it, but his large brown eyes rejoined Marie's.

"You've worked as a CPA your entire adult life, taken good care of the boys and me, and you've been generous to the church. But I know a part of you was open to a path on the mission field. You've always had a heart for that – as long as you could still speak English and eat the foods you like," she interrupted herself to tease him.

"So, what if God is giving you that chance in this opportunity for missional living with our friends? Last year when we were making retirement plans, we didn't realize our friends needed help to make it through theirs. Now we know it. Jesus said his disciples would be known for their love for one another. Yes, we can love our friends without moving in with them. But wouldn't it be both ministry to them and a public witness of how God loves and cares for His people if we did? And you might find fulfillment in that vocational ministry space in your heart without getting a seminary degree or acceptance to a mission board. Grant, we could both invest the remaining years of our life – redeem the time, as it were – in sacrificial, Kingdom purpose."

Grant sighed deeply. Marie agreed with nearly all his objections, so there was no need to reinforce his position. She'd found the vulnerable part of his tender heart and addressed the area without exploiting it. He knew she genuinely wanted the best for him. Maybe a mission field was a possibility for him after all, even at this late stage, but differently than he'd ever imagined - missional living, Marie called it.

Grant remained at the kitchen table after Marie went upstairs to shower and dress for the late lunch he promised her at the local Mexican restaurant they both enjoyed. He recalled the sermon their pastor had given just two weeks previously – a sermon Marie had evidently forgotten, but that was coming back to his memory clearly.

"Run the race God gave you and finish strong!" their pastor implored the congregation. Grant assumed he was giving particular attention to those nearest the finish line, like himself, and felt a bit tweaked. After 45 years of a secular career, he planned to finish with a golf handicap lower than his younger brother's. He'd somehow derived from his pastor's exhortation that his goal was insufficient. He'd been subconsciously unsettled since. Now he was consciously unsettled.

# Chapter Four

Elodie woke up to a whirring sound she instantly recognized. Marcus was roasting coffee beans in a hot air corn popper he'd converted for that purpose. She'd spent the night at the Van Zants' home in the "Elodie Room," as their guest room had been dubbed for as long as they'd lived there. Though many others were accommodated in the parsonage guest room over the years, Elodie was its most frequent occupant. It had even been decorated to suit Elodie's restrained bohemian style and in her favorite color combination: lilac purple and periwinkle blue.

She smiled slightly at the sound of the whirring roasting beans and inhaled deeply through her nose in an attempt to draw the aroma from the kitchen to her bed. Marcus made coffee that tasted like a symphony. He imported raw beans from Ethiopia, roasted them in the modified corn popper just before grinding them, and then poured hot water over the grounds until the coffee bloomed in appearance and flavor. There were dozens of flavor notes in each sip. Adding cream or sugar to such artistry would be a vulgar crime.

As she wrapped herself in her robe and slipped ashy feet into a pair of open-toed slides before going to the kitchen/coffee paradise, Elodie recalled a Labor Day weekend several years ago that the Rennigers also spent at the Van Zants' home.

One morning, Marcus thought he might convert confirmed tea drinker Grant into a coffee connoisseur with his special pour-over brew.

He spent 20 minutes making the perfect cup only to have Grant take one sniff and say: "It still smells like coffee. Smells like Starbucks, and I hate that smell!"

Marcus was incredulous. "Den leave my house right now!" he ordered Grant, flinging a pointed finger toward the front door. But of course, no one took him seriously, and Grant made his usual tea with honey.

The memory made Elodie's heart flush with happiness. She loved those old goats and would keep that to herself.

When she reached the kitchen, Elodie greeted Marcus, Ava, and Marley, who'd also spent the night with her folks. Though she lived just half a mile away with her husband and 8-year-old boy, Marley wanted to spend as much time as possible with "Auntie El."

Of course, she'd known Elodie all her life. Auntie El was the refuge she needed during difficult high-school years when she could not confide her teenage anxieties to her mother for fear of how Ava might manage them. Auntie El would always listen and usually laugh at her until Marley learned to laugh at herself. For that life skill alone, she was indebted to her mother's friend, who became her friend too.

As Marcus brewed the coffee, Ava pulled pumpkin pecan scones from the freezer and defrosted them in the microwave.

"So, Miss Marley," Marcus addressed his daughter as he customarily called her, "guess what kind of scheme your Auntie El has cooked up now."

"There is absolutely no telling!" Marley declared with conviction while patting the chair beside her at the kitchen table for Elodie to sit in. Elodie obeyed, giving her a little playful pinch on her cheek as she sat.

"Auntie El thinks it would be a good idea if we retired together and lived in the same house," Ava informed her.

Marley responded by raising a single, perfectly arched eyebrow and asking the only question she cared about: "Where?"

She hoped it would be in Bloomington and not five hours away in

Columbus, Ohio, where Auntie El lived. She knew her sister, Mia, would also share that hope.

It wasn't merely because they depended on their parents for regular babysitting respite; they both enjoyed warm adult relationships with their aging parents, and neither had ever lived more than 10 miles away from them. Marley and her husband, Adam, would have offered her parents accommodation in their finished basement. They'd discussed several times what a benefit that arrangement would be for their only child, Ethan. But that would leave Auntie El out in the cold. Occasionally, Marley could be selfish, but she was never heartless.

"We don't know the answer yet, honey. We're just kind of wrapping our heads around the idea of it. Seems practical, though," Ava offered in explanation.

Marley understood her parents' financial dilemma without having it spelled out. She was observant and connected dots. She wouldn't embarrass them with questions to make them spell out or defend their need to be "practical."

"Well, I think it's a marvelous scheme," Marley cheered, swallowing her disappointment. "I'll always get two-for-one when I visit your house!"

Elodie pressed the gas pedal of her white SUV and tried to make up time on the highway from Bloomington to Columbus. It was already one o'clock in the afternoon, and she needed to get home before dark, though the GPS indicated that was not likely. A triple threat of glaucoma, macular degeneration, and early-stage cataracts plagued her dark brown eyes. So, she didn't drive at night if she could help it because she could barely see the lane lines. Knowing she would run out of daylight before she reached home, Elodie repeated aloud a phrase she'd learned as a child from her God-fearing mother: Pray, don't panic.

And so, she prayed. First, she thanked God for her lifelong girlfriends, Ava and Marie, and for the continuing ministry of Holy Ground Camp, where she'd met them when they were all young teenagers. "Ho-G-Ca!" she said out loud in remembrance of the shout that concluded every meal in the dining hall. She laughed and congratulated herself for remembering that tidbit of trivia from so long ago. Next, she took herself on a mental walking tour of the camp's enormous log chapel, the sandy lake-front and wooded trails that led to chalet-style cabins, and the Snack Shack at the edge of the baseball field where she bought cherry snow-cones for a quarter. She delighted in visualizing the pastoral mountain scenery that surrounded it all. Then she apologized to the Lord for letting her mind wander when talking to Him.

Refocused, Elodie prayed for the newly-wedded Marit and her knucklehead, Robby, that their first year would be lived sacrificially for each other as she'd advised them in a private moment before the ceremony. She asked God to help them when they couldn't help themselves because, like her, they were also selfish sinners. Next, she boldly asked for her heart's desire, that God would provide her a home with Ava and Marcus and meet their needs for financial relief and companions.

As the miles passed and the horizon swallowed the sun, Elodie tightened her grip on the steering wheel, her dark skin taut over flexed forearm muscles. She continued to pray.

She confessed her fear of her failing eyes and asked God to help her reach home safely, sure that He could. She thanked Him for the daylight hours when she could drive confidently. Finally, when she got to her parking space in the apartment complex lot and turned off the ignition, she thanked God for watching over her and for a godly mother who taught her to pray when she was scared.

# Chapter Five

The Renniger condo kitchen was a hive of post-Thanksgiving meal activity. Grant packaged the leftover turkey into two vac and seal bags and transferred them to the freezer while Marcus dried the pots that Elodie hand-washed. Marie pre-treated spots on the table linens, and Ava wiped the counters clean.

"I had my doubts about smoking the turkey, Marcus. But you were right. It's the only way to do it from now on. Believe me, there wouldn't be any leftovers if my wife had let me keep eating," Grant congratulated him.

"I'm glad I've converted you to my turkey even if I couldn't convert you to my coffee," Marcus accepted the compliment. "And smoking is safer den deep-frying!" They all chuckled at the reference to last year's deep-fried fiasco.

Last Thanksgiving, they were at Grant and Marie's former subdivision house. Grant learned his neighbors were going to New York City for the long holiday weekend to see their son march with his high school band in the Macy's Parade. So he asked to borrow their turkey deep-fryer. He'd heard from guys at church that deep-fried turkey was what they served in Heaven and thought he'd treat his friends to a preview.

But in Heaven, they probably don't over-fill the fryer with peanut oil. And in Heaven, they probably don't place the fryer close to a giant white pine tree. Grant did both. And when he lowered the turkey into the fryer, the peanut oil spilled over the sides and ignited when it hit the burner below. The flames shot fifteen feet into the air, and a sap-laden branch above their heads caught fire. Grant and Marcus shared a moment of horrified expression and frozen panic before rushing to extinguish the growing blaze. Marcus thought to turn off the burner but was unable because peanut-oil-fueled flame engulfed the valve. Grant ran to the side of the house to turn on the water spigot and retrieve the hose that was, fortunately, still connected. He directed a steady blast of water at the tree limbs and, by the grace of God, extinguished the pine tree. But water and burnt needles fell directly below into the turkey fryer, displacing even more oil onto the burner. Grant continued to douse the overhead limbs until the fire below burned itself out.

They only noticed the women standing on the back deck watching them when Elodie could not stifle her laughter after the danger had passed. All agreed they would not try to salvage the turkey. They had enough food without it.

"I hope the newlyweds are still happy. Been married a whole month now, right?" Elodie commented as she dried her hands on the hem of her colorful flowing skirt and inspected the crown of graying braids on her head in the reflection of a glass-fronted cabinet.

"Yeah. Marcus and I are giving them space to settle in the big new house they bought," Ava answered.

Marie and Elodie glanced at each other. Ava had answered a question not asked in a tone that sounded defensive.

Elodie shrugged and changed the subject. "Grant, I can't thank you enough for almost burnin' down your neighborhood last year. You gave us a new Thanksgiving near-tragedy to reminisce about in place of the oyster poisonin'."

Grant headed toward the family room, and as he passed Elodie, he gave her a fist bump and said humbly, "I do what I can."

He joined Marcus, who had already made himself comfortable on the couch in front of the television. Grant picked up the remote and scanned the stations to find the Cowboys game. They both hated the Cowboys and made it a point to watch every year to root for the opposing team, whoever they were. When Grant located the station, he handed Marcus the remote. Marcus was a militant commercial muter. He hated commercials. He even refused to make allowances during the Super Bowl, though Grant explained the entire rest of the world considered them part of the event. It was the first and last time Grant and Marie visited the Van Zants on a Super Bowl weekend.

"Come here, girls," Marie whispered to Ava and Elodie in the kitchen. She tossed the pre-treated linens into a basket in the adjoining laundry room and beckoned the ladies toward the small home office.

"Look what I found!" she said as she sat at a small, modern desk and opened her laptop to reveal a real estate website page with a picture of a large 2-story, gray stone house. Marie scrolled through the interior and exterior photos of the property.

"It's ideal!" Ava squealed.

"Oh, my goodness! It's so beautiful inside," Elodie gushed.

"I know, right? I just love it!" Marie matched their enthusiastic volume.

"What are you girls all excited about?" Marcus asked as he and Grant wandered into the office, holding unopened cans of soda they'd retrieved from the fridge to encourage a pressure-relieving, post-Thanksgiving meal belch.

"Must be commercial time," Marie remarked in a tone she hoped sounded nonchalant. Internally, she panicked as Grant walked around the desk to see what had captured the ladies' attention. He had not given Marie his consent to participate in what he'd been referring to alternately as "the hippie commune" or "the socialist project." Now she was caught with her hand deep in the house-hunting cookie jar. Marie began to babble words.

"I've been looking at houses online – just trying to help. I saw a beauty that I wanted to show the girls. It might work for them." Marie tried to exclude herself and Grant from the picture but stopped herself. Grant was no fool, nor should she play him for one. She turned away from the computer screen to face him.

"No. I know this is too much for them. It's just so pretty and perfect," Marie's shoulders sagged, and she lowered her head. "I'm sorry, I rushed ahead of you. Please forgive me."

Grant offered no response.

Marcus stepped forward to look at the computer screen in which Ava was still keenly interested. Marie, embarrassed, rolled her desk chair out of his way. He bent over the laptop, placing his hand on the mousepad to scroll through the pictures. Grant looked over his shoulder. They studied the screen silently until Marcus noted the location aloud: "Faircourt, Kentucky?"

Grant whistled when they arrived at the listed price.

It had been a month since the idea of the communal household was floated. Grant knew his wife favored it, and as the idea marinated in his mind, he was growing more curious. Grant couldn't say he completely hated the possibility anymore. Worse, when he prayed about it, he wasn't getting the definite "No" that would settle it for him. And now, like the others, Grant liked this house on the computer screen. The pictures added vivid details he couldn't imagine without them.

Without taking his eyes off the screen, he remarked evenly: "We're going to need another financial contributor to this hippie commune to make it work if this is the house you want."

Then he turned toward Marie and gave her a not. With that understated gesture, Grant and Marie officially committed.

# CHAPTER SIX

306 Cedar Street occupied the corner of Cedar and Tamarack Streets in the small town of Faircourt, Kentucky. It was an American foursquare house built in 1920 from cast stone. The stone was actually concrete, formed on-site with a cast iron molding machine and a half dozen various faceplates to mimic the look of chiseled limestone. A four-sided hip roof capped the house in original slate shingles and was detailed with eyebrow windows on each side, naturally lighting the attic space.

Across the entire width of the front façade ran a 10-foot deep covered front porch supported by six white columns – three on either side of the center entrance. The front porch was designed to be the home's warm-weather gathering place and could comfortably accommodate seating eight to ten people and a smattering of dogs. It perfectly suited the hospitality style of the original owners, Mr. and Mrs. Theron Frye, who had often welcomed neighbors for spontaneous Saturday evening conversation and cream gin cocktails on the porch wicker suite.

The house was situated on a large lot that sloped gently to the rear of the property so that the area of visible basement foundation, a smooth concrete painted white, gradually increased from front to back. The rear wall of the basement foundation had three evenly-spaced windows, too small for egress but large enough to provide the unfinished basement with a sufficient amount of natural light to see one's way around.

The original building lot was increased in 1949 when a fire destroyed the house at 502 Tamarack St and took the life of two young brothers. The boy's parents were not inclined to rebuild on the site and sold it to the Frye's unmarried daughter, Miss Bermuda Frye, who had inherited the adjoining property when her parents passed. The double lot was just over an acre in size and boasted a 50ft magnolia that scented the entire block when it was in bloom. Mature boxwoods, which miraculously escaped the blight that overtook most others in the neighborhood in the late 1980s, surrounded the front porch as casual witnesses to the comings and goings. They were neat but not sculpted. A paved driveway to the left of the house led to a detached, white-painted clapboard, single-bay garage with a potting shed behind it. A row of lilacs was meticulously pruned along the left side of the driveway to keep from reverting to bush form. On the right side of the driveway, between the driveway and the house, was a perennial shade garden running the length of the house. It was filled with hostas, lily-of-the-valley, astilbe, bleeding heart, coral bells, and foxglove and was a beautiful legacy from the labors of Miss Bermuda, who passed in 1993.

There had been a large garden in the backyard at some point in its history. Now filled with grass, a narrow brick path that outlined its perimeter and divided it into four quadrants was all that remained to testify it had existed.

In 1979, Miss Bermuda had a two-car garage built at the end of the driveway that belonged to 502 Tamarack Street, which she rented out before public storage units became widely available. It matched the home's primary white clapboard garage with the addition of a farm-style floodlight mounted at the roofline between the double set of doors. Additionally, two small casement windows on the upper back side of the garage provided good airflow when the garage doors were open.

Without a doubt, the exterior of the house made a good impression. It was traditionally styled, well-maintained, and heavy on curb appeal.

But it was the interior features and craftsmanship, cost-prohibitive to reproduce in new construction, that drew in everyone who appreciated vintage detail.

Upon passing through the original oak door with an oval inset of beveled glass, one entered a spacious hall with a ten-foot ceiling that ran from front to back of the house. To the left was a large living room with two sets of pocket doors - one set off the entrance hall and one set connecting the living room to the dining room beyond.

To the right was a room smaller than the opposite living room. It was lined from floor to ceiling on one wall with unpainted oak bookcases and a rolling library ladder to access the upper shelves. Just past this door was the bottom of the wide staircase that led to the second floor. The staircase was also oak and surrounded by raised oak paneling. A runner of black carpet sprinkled with tiny gold fleur de lis covered the center two-thirds of each stair and riser. Tucked under the staircase was a half bath not original to the house but added with thoughtful respect to the 1920 era. It had a high-tank pull-chain toilet and matching porcelain sink with exposed pipes and an antique mirror with age blemishes in its silvering.

Past the half bath, on the right side of the hall, were a set of 15-pane glass doors covered on the inside with cream silk curtains on brass rods mounted to the door. These doors were the entrance to a first-floor master bedroom and bath, which had once been the kitchen.

At the back of the hall was the entrance to the new kitchen. It had originally been an enclosed porch that ran the entire width of the house. But when the Estate of Bermuda Frye sold the house to Jeff and Michelle Scott in 1994, the Scotts converted the porch into their dream kitchen with an island cooktop, Sub-Zero fridge, and a breakfast area. A door on the left-side wall, covered by a small roof-ledge outside, led out to the driveway.

The house's second floor had five gorgeous 6-panel oak doors, with transom windows above, off a wide central hallway. There was a main bathroom and four generously sized bedrooms – two of which were connected by a small Jack and Jill bathroom between them. This bath was added, with much difficulty and swearing by the plumbing contractor, during the 1994 Scott renovation.

The Scotts raised three children in the home – a son and two daughters. All three had been academic and track stars at Faircourt High School and then at the University of Kentucky. Jeff and Michelle were selling to downsize into a patio home near their son, who had settled in Charleston, South Carolina.

The summer before they sold the home they respectfully referred to as "The Old Girl," they selected a flawless magnolia blossom from the aged tree in the yard and preserved it in acrylic as a keepsake.

# CHAPTER SEVEN

It was a warm mid-March afternoon, and the Rennigers, Van Zants, and Elodie stood on the front porch of the Cedar Street house, keys in hand, ready to step into their retirement adventure.

"There's no goin' back now," Elodie shouted gleefully. She wore one of her many colorful flowing skirts and a purple sweatshirt, sleeves rolled up. She'd wrapped her braided head in a fuchsia-colored cotton scarf, ready to work.

"There was no going back when I sold my condo," Grant muttered in response. He was not looking forward to the work ahead: fussy house cleaning and precise organization of household goods to Marie's exacting standards.

The women, on the other hand, were positively gung-ho. They'd worked out whose furniture would go in common areas and appropriated the best of their combined appliances, dishes, flatware, and cookware. Everyone would use their own bedroom furniture and linens. To maintain cohesion to the disparate assembly of furnishings, it was decided the entire house would be painted in a light, neutral beige - Sherwin Williams' "Patience," to be exact. To be more exact, Marie decided it. Insisted, actually.

Bedrooms were the exception – a kaleidoscope of personal expression in the private rooms. Elodie would paint hers Rhapsody Lilac; the Van Zants chose Kind Green; and the Rennigers, Banana Cream. The fourth upstairs bedroom, designated as a permanent guest room for visitors, would be painted Charming Pink.

The wildcard, for the moment, was what color the Shermans would paint the first-floor master suite when they arrived to take up residence in a week.

Calvert and June Sherman were the key to making the house affordable for all in equal shares. Marie and Grant went to lunch with the Shermans after church one early December Sunday to break the news to their good friends that they were moving away and why. They expected Cal and June would be saddened, but they did not expect them to be intrigued.

The Shermans, a matched set with light blue eyes, white/blonde hair, and plump figures, had been unable to have children in their young adult years. Unbeknownst to their friends, they felt increasingly vulnerable in their post-retirement years. Cal had been facing health challenges in increasing frequency and severity, and June bore the responsibility of caring for him alone. Although they'd been close to several young nieces and nephews, those relationships eroded with distance and commitments when the children were grown. This was a particular and burdensome loss for Cal, who worried about June having little to no long-term support after he passed.

"Tell us about your other friends. Is it a single-level house? What is your timeline? Are there solid churches nearby? Will the house be full? Do you mind if I ask what's the buy-in?" Cal asked in brisk succession as he poured four packets of Splenda into his unsweetened iced tea.

While Marie answered the questions, Grant stirred his cola with a straw while mentally vetting the Shermans as the additional hippie commune residents they sought. He wondered how he'd overlooked this couple. Grant knew Cal had beaten cancer twice and put it in the rear-view mirror. He looked healthy, having gained back the 40 pounds he'd lost during the last treatment cycle. Grant was vaguely aware Cal had occasional aches and pains here and there, but didn't they all?

What fired up Grant about their potential were Cal's strengths. The man was as handy as a Swiss Army knife – plumbing, electric, carpentry, welding – he did it all. Whereas Grant thought a charge controller was the limit on a credit card and Marcus thought a miter was a hat worn by a bishop, Cal had practical knowledge and abilities regarding household maintenance. This was a weighty factor toward acceptance.

Also working in Cal's favor was that he liked NASCAR and Southern Gospel music. Marcus was not a fan of either and mocked Grant for his pedestrian tastes. Having a like-minded brother who supported and joined him in these pleasures would be refreshing. Furthermore, June, who hid her ample figure in black leggings and long tunics, was a fantastic cook, a passionate baker, and a gifted pianist. She needed no other qualifications, although she had one. Grant and Marie agreed they knew of no woman with a sweeter disposition than June.

As Grant considered these attributes, he sold himself on Cal and June joining their tribe. After an hour and a half video chat the following evening, the others were sold on them, too.

Transition into a consolidated household moved like a hungry dog through his dinner. The Van Zants had no real estate to sell. Elodie's landlord hadn't asked her to sign a lease in years. And the Rennigers received a cash offer on their patio home just 8 hours after they listed it. Grant took charge of setting up the trust and working through the closing process of the Faircourt house.

The Shermans listed their home and hired an estate liquidator to downsize 40 years of collected possessions. They would be just a week behind the others who pulled up stakes, at warp speed for older adults, to secure the house they'd fallen in love with online.

The first-wave residents stepped through the doorway carrying buckets of cleaning supplies, brooms and mops, and a 3-step ladder. Regardless of the fact the Scotts had left the house spic and span and even went so far as to repair nail holes from picture hangers on the walls, they would clean the entire house again.

Marcus and Grant, accidentally twinning in gray sweatshirts and blue jeans, balked when they saw the shiny sinks and crumb-free cupboards. Why should they re-clean what was already obviously clean? But the ladies were insistent.

Marie schooled them. "We don't know that some little man from a discount relocation crew didn't take off his sweaty t-shirt, shine the faucets, and wipe the counters willy-nilly. If you don't see with your own eyes that clean sponges and Lysol disinfectant are used where our belongings are to go, then we all might as well start a course of antibiotics right now!"

And so, cleaning commenced. Of course, it would all get dirty and germy eventually, but it would be their dirt and germs. So, while the ladies roamed and cleaned the rest of the house, Marcus and Grant tackled the kitchen cupboards and appliances.

"I'll be back in a sec," Grant hollered over his shoulder and went out the back door.

Quick as a thief, he returned with a small wireless speaker he'd retrieved from his car and set on the counter. Instantly, the Gaither Vocal Band was blaring in the kitchen and wafting through the house. Grant was happy now and cleaned the appliances double-time. Then, when he finished with the oven, he crowed to Marcus, "Look at the shine inside that baby!"

"Great," muttered Marcus. "Now I can feel good about turning it on and sticking my head inside." He finished wiping out the last cupboard and walked out to the front porch to breathe in some Gaither-free air.

Marcus spent the next few minutes in open-eyed prayer, taking in the new neighborhood. He asked God to help him find a place of ministry in Faircourt and for common ground to bond with Calvert, the incoming stranger to him. He also prayed for grace to acclimate to increased exposure to Southern Gospel music.

He prayed until a movement in a window across the street caught his attention. Someone had been watching him and darted away. A woman, maybe?

# Chapter Eight

As expected, the Shermans and their belongings arrived at the Cedar Street house the following week. A two-man crew quickly unloaded a small moving truck of what remained after an emotionally brutal purging of their possessions. The more significant items consisted of bedroom furniture and a baby grand piano, their sole contribution to the community furnishings. June had given scores of children lessons on the piano over 40 years, and it might yet provide a source of income, if needed, in Kentucky.

The Jennings Family Painting team, which they'd all contributed to funding, had just completed painting every room, including the Sherman's first-floor en suite. Marie talked June out of the dark teal "Mariner" color she initially selected for their bedroom because it matched their teal and brown bedding.

Marie was sure at least 50% of all frat house bedrooms were painted "Mariner" based on knowledge gained through her own sons' college experiences. The muddy-sea color disturbed Marie because she imagined jagged-toothed sharks and hideous giant octopuses lurking in the wall under the thin layer of paint, poised to snatch the unsuspecting to a watery grave. At least, that's what she told June, who relented and went with Barely Brown instead.

As Cal and June toured the rest of the downstairs, they noted with amazement how much had been accomplished. Pictures hung on the walls, and even the bookshelves in the front study had been filled and organized save for a shelf reserved for June's collection of Southern Living cookbooks. Ava had her extensive, eclectic cookbook collection arranged on three more shelves and would make the combined cookbook section nearly a quarter of the bookshelf real estate. One partial shelf was occupied with Marie's gardening books, and all Marcus' theology and Bible reference texts occupied the rest.

Added amongst the books were a smattering of sentimental knick-knacks and tokens from his years of ministry, including a 12" silver loving cup commemorating his 25th anniversary at Delaware Street Community Church, which Marie convinced Marcus to display.

"I know the end was painful," she sympathized with him. "But don't let it erase all the previous years of fruitful ministry. Choose to remember those when you look at this cup," she encouraged.

So he agreed. And to further furnish the study, Marcus added his antique double-pedestal desk and white leather wingback swivel office chair. He positioned these on a gently worn, 12' X 9' brown rug he found at a Goodwill, with the chair's back against the front windows and facing the bookshelves.

Marie contributed two colorful crewelwork-upholstered rocking chairs to the study furnishings. Between the chairs, she added an antique pie-crust table that had belonged to Grant's grandmother, and a modern mercury glass lamp with a tan linen shade sat upon it.

"Wow, you all must have worked day and night to get this house so far along and put together," June gushed, clearly impressed. She sat on one of the rocking chairs, tired of standing on bunioned feet.

"You're welcome to see our upstairs rooms," Elodie offered and turned to the staircase to lead the way. It didn't register with her that June had just sat down.

June gamely stood and followed, with Marie and Ava following be-hind her. Cal stayed downstairs with the men. Unfortunately, Cal did not have the knees for stairs, which was why he and June had been awarded the downstairs en-suite.

"We'll be right back, Calvin," Elodie hollered over her shoulder.

"It's Calvert. And take your time. I'll be staying," Cal responded with a slight smile. "Since I'll be staying," he turned to Marcus and Grant, "I guess I better start unpacking." And off he shuffled to his room.

"He has no books," scowled Marcus after Cal was gone. "How does a man improve himself without books?"

"I have no books," Grant stated as a challenge to the theory.

"Nor improvement!" Marcus retorted and gave him a soft elbow to the ribs. "Let's go poke around da kitchen and see if we can find someting to snack on while da girls aren't looking."

"Maybe we should help Cal instead," Grant suggested. When he saw Marcus's pained expression, he offered an alternative. "Or, we could ask him to join us in the snack search. Let's not leave him alone until he feels part of things here."

"Well, I've had my fill of unpacking and am more amenable to da cupboard ransacking option," Marcus pushed for his preference.

On the way to the kitchen, Marcus stepped inside the open door of the Sherman's bedroom.

"Our ladies went shopping yesterday, and Grant and I carried da grocery bags. We know dere's a bag of Doritos squirreled away somewhere in da kitchen cupboards. Do you want to help us find it while der backs are turned?"

Cal dropped an armload of his signature Monday - Saturday wear, blue jean overalls, on the bed. "I could eat," he said, joining them.

A ransacking proved unnecessary. Cal walked to the oven and opened the warming drawer, where he was sure he'd find two things back in his old house: baking pans and goodies. He pulled out the Doritos bag and raised it triumphantly over his head.

An astonished Marcus proclaimed, "You're a bloodhound, man!"

Grant could only shake his head and laugh.

"Not really. That's where June "hides" things," Cal explained with finger quotes. "I know it, and Marie knows it, too. So, I figured Marie might borrow June's hiding place, and I got lucky."

He opened the bag and set it on the island while Grant retrieved a 2-liter of cola from the fridge. It took only one wrong cupboard guess for Marcus to locate the glasses. The men set upon their illicit snack like locusts. There was no conversation, just the sound of munching. In under ten minutes, they devoured the bag while the ladies dawdled upstairs.

"Let's make this look like it never happened," Cal suggested mischievously.

Grant took the empty chip bag outside to the big trash can on wheels next to the garage. Cal washed the glasses and wiped up incriminating crumbs from the counter, and Marcus dried the cleaned glasses and returned them to the cupboard.

When the ladies completed giving June the tour of their upstairs rooms, including a peek in the attic, they found the men in the Sherman bedroom. They appeared engrossed in pulling winter coats out of a cardboard wardrobe and adding them atop a mound of church dresses and dress shirts on the bed.

"What have you gentlemen been up to?" Ava inquired.

"Not much," Marcus responded, trying to sound bored.

He was trying to come up with some details to add when Grant accidentally released a belch he'd worked up from wolfing down the chips and soda. Marcus shot him a sideways evil eye like he'd just ratted them out for dealing drugs to minor girls. Cal was on the verge of herniating something from stifling a belly laugh and spontaneously produced an erupting noise of his own from a lower region.

"We got the wrong room! There are no gentlemen in this one!" Elodie turned with a huff and marched down the hallway.

Marie and Ava followed and closed the door behind them, leaving the men with their hands cupped firmly over their mouths to silence their laughter. When they'd regained their composure, Grant and Marcus left Cal to work on unpacking with June.

"I believe he feels a part of things here now," Grant speculated to his friend as they parted ways in the hall.

# Chapter Nine

T he Shermans had their room organized and decorated five days later. It had only taken the other household members seven days to complete that task for their rooms and all the communal rooms as well. Time management was the first area to become apparent where all would have to make adjustments. Some (Grant, Marie, and Ava) operated on hyper-drive, some (Cal, June, and Elodie) on a mosey setting, and one (Marcus) somewhere in between. They'd have to find a pace for their community that worked for all. Not for all the time, but for when they needed to work together.

Nobody wanted hurt feelings. Nobody wanted tension. They all agreed that communication was the key to heading that off. Because the first one happened to be on a Thursday evening, Thursday Meeting was instituted – the weekly household meeting.

They'd already worked out community finances before moving into the house. The couples contributed an equal amount to purchase the property in the name of a trust – Faircourt Friends Trust. As a single, Elodie contributed the same amount as the couples since she would have her own room. However, she contributed half of what the married couples contributed to the monthly expense budget since she consumed half of what they did. Theoretically. The woman had a healthy appetite.

After nearly three weeks in the house, the first Thursday Meeting commenced. Marcus tried to usher them into the dining room to sit around the table, but the ladies walked past him and took places in the living room instead.

The first rule was wordlessly implemented: Marcus was not their boss. The ladies weren't trying to make that point, though they made it. They simply wanted their discussions to have a more informal feel. It would be less intimidating and less confrontational to have their meetings without the barrier of a substantial table between them.

June sat on a corner of the couch, wearing her black leggings with a knee-length tunic printed with tiny pink roses on a black background. Then, reaching into a large wicker basket next to the sofa, she picked up a cross-stitch project to work on while the others took their seats.

"What do you have there?" Ava asked as she leaned over to see June's design. It was a Bible verse worked in many shades of gray on white fabric that said:

> *Even to your old age, I am He. And to gray hairs I will carry*
> *you. I have made, and I will bear; I will carry and will save.*
> *Isaiah 46:4*

Around the elegantly lettered verse was a stitched trellis frame with flowers and vines twining throughout.

"It's almost finished and ready to be framed. I started it nearly a year ago before we thought about moving. I had the perfect spot for it in our old house, but I don't know where to hang it now," June furrowed her eyebrows, making creases on her forehead.

"I hope you'll put it somewhere that we can all enjoy it – maybe in the center hall or here in the living room. It's going to make wherever you put it beautiful!" Ava complimented her.

"You ladies have made dis place look like a beautiful home already." Marcus saw his opportunity to get down to the business at hand. "So, let's talk about how we want life here to function."

"Let's talk about mealtimes!" Grant interjected. Meals were a particular concern to him because, as he readily admitted, he was fussy.

Grant loved salads and could eat them every day. However, if a salad contained nuts, berries, or fruit of any kind, he dismissed it as a "feminized" lady's salad and would reject it outright. He thought vegetables were best eaten raw except corn and potatoes - but the potatoes were only allowed in mashed, baked, or French fry form. Grant could not abide the deviant incarnations of hash browns or tots. He was a fan of medium-rare red meat with a palate open to most origins, including lamb and bison, and he loved "guy food," which meant wings, pizza, and pasta. Treats were lobster, sushi, and salmon. And every tooth in his mouth was a sweet tooth. He loved desserts, especially fruit pies.

Grant wanted the women to know his tastes, to be sympathetic to his choices, and to prepare his preferences with the skill of a four-star chef. Based on past dining experiences with his new female roommates, he believed these might be reasonable expectations. They were all excellent cooks who enjoyed and excelled at it. Although he adored his wife, Marie was a B+ cook on her best day. She never aspired to a higher grade, wanting to keep his expectations of her culinary abilities low.

"Grant, don't worry. We'll take care of you," assured Ava.

The promise relieved Grant's concern, and he sat back in his chair, visibly relaxed.

"Well, what time do we eat?" Cal wanted to know. 72-year-old Cal had several medications that needed to be taken on a schedule and with food. He was the medically fragile one of the group with two bad knees, one kidney, no prostate, diabetes, and poor iron, He liked to point out that his heart was healthy as a horse, though.

Elodie spoke up while distractedly rubbing the side of her jaw where a tooth had been bothering her. "Here's my suggestion, Calbert. I think we eat breakfast at whatever time suits us. Same with lunch since some of us might have weekday obligations. But how 'bout we all eat dinner together at 5:30?"

"It's Calvert – a family name on my momma's side - and could you all work with 5 o'clock instead?" he countered with some irritation that she couldn't seem to get his name right.

Everyone nodded their agreement about the 5 pm dinner. They worked out that Ava, June, and Elodie would rotate cooking duties. Cal and Marcus would team up to clear the table and load the dishwasher after dinner; Grant would empty the dishwasher every morning, and Marie would do the weekly grocery shopping and kitchen floor mopping. On Saturday mornings, everyone would pitch in for half an hour to dust, vacuum, and clean bathrooms.

"Everyone's doing their own laundry, right? Please tell me the only man's underwear I have to be familiar with is Marcus'," Ava nearly pleaded her request. She wished to remain blissfully ignorant regarding intimate aspects of cohabitating with men who were not her husband.

"Agreed!" Grant and Cal were quick to respond in unison.

"Now, there's one chore I'd like to claim for myself," Grant added hurriedly, eager to get off the subject of men's underwear. "And you all know what it's going to be."

"Mowing!" they shouted in unison.

They all knew Grant loved making straight lines on a lawn. It was a metaphor for his life. He was a boy scout, a rule-keeper. Grant colored inside life's lines.

"Have at it, pal," Cal responded happily. He had tolerated mowing since he was a teenager responsible for his parents' yard and his grandparents' next door.

"It's all yours," encouraged Marcus. "Ava and I intend to revive da garden ruins in da backyard. So, dis summer, we'll all be feasting on home-grown tomatoes, peppers, onions, zucchini, corn, cucumbers, snap beans, and whatever else we can fit in dere."

"I'd like to know where we'll be going to church," June quietly interjected. "I mean, we're all going to the same place, right?"

Like all of them, June's faith was central to her everyday life. She wasn't a Christian only on Sundays, but Sundays were important. Being part of this household of faith found a context in being part of the larger Body of Christ – the church. June was eager to join and become an active member of a local fellowship of believers. It was a good question, and after June asked it, there was a moment where they all looked from one to another.

Grant rubbed his smooth head and spoke first. "I think it'd be nice if we all went to the same church – like family. It's not a big town. Maybe we visit the four or five options and see if God gives us agreement on one of them."

"Dat's what I was tinking we should do," Marcus agreed, sorry that he had not taken the lead in this discussion area. However, he was quicker on the follow-up. "Grace Fellowship" is just tree blocks away. What if we try dat one dis Sunday? We could even walk if it's not raining."

Cal shot a glance toward his wife at the suggestion of walking. Cal's knees and June's dessert weight preferred to drive.

Marie considered the church matter settled for now and was eager to move to an issue of importance to her.

"This is such a lovely house; I think it should have a name. I've always wanted to live in a house with a name."

Marie watched little television, but what she did watch was primarily British period dramas in which houses had names. Ava had long teased her friend that she dressed as if she lived in a British period drama set in the 1930s–40s because of her affinity for shirtwaist dresses and blouses with belted, wide-leg trousers.

There was silence as the group considered Marie's suggestion.

Finally, Grant suggested, "Why don't we just call it 306 Cedar Street? It fits in with the other houses' names on the street."

"Precious husband, you have zero imagination," Marie exhaled a sigh and picked a piece of lint off her brown, lightweight wool trousers.

"Maybe we could call it Green Acres," Marcus suggested in a nod to his vegetable garden aspirations and his affinity for nostalgic programs.

"We only have one full acre. So, it would have to be Green Acre," corrected Grant.

"How 'bout we call it Tooth Acre," Elodie suggested, again rubbing her jaw. June chuckled out loud.

"I can see you're all taking this seriously," Marie was indignant.

Trying to soothe her friend's feelings, June suggested, "What if we name the house in honor of the woman who lived here so long? What was her name?"

"Bermuda, wasn't it?" Ava guessed.

"Yes!" exclaimed Cal slapping a bad knee and wincing. "Let's call this place the Bermuda Triangle!"

Marcus and Grant began to chuckle.

"And if we're raptured into glory, our heathen neighbors will say we disappeared because we lived in the Bermuda Triangle," Elodie joined in. She often joined Marcus and Grant, and now apparently, Cal too, in their man-humor. She was unreliable like that, though she never let go of her dignity as the guys did.

She wasn't finished. "And when we're too decrepit to do our chores, we'll call it the Wreck Tangle," she laughed at her own joke.

Grant nearly slid out of his chair, and Marcus' eyes filled with hysterical tears at the sophomoric humor. They were having a bona fide laughing fit.

"Oh, stop! I need a breath," Cal gasped, trying to calm himself.

"I guess we're through here," sighed Marie. She got up and headed upstairs to her bedroom. Once she cleared the living room doorway, she threw a "Goodnight, all" over her shoulder.

Ava caught up to her. "The dynamic's changed, hasn't it?" she observed as she climbed the stairs with her friend.

"It certainly has. Adding one more man in the mix has turned them into a pack of savages. And when El goes feral and joins their tribe, they're uncontrollable!" Marie griped.

"It might be cute now, but I hope it doesn't get on our last nerve," Ava sighed.

"Time will tell," Marie said, shaking her head.

# CHAPTER TEN

"Good morning, Calcutta," Elodie greeted Cal as she entered the kitchen just a few steps behind him.

Cal, dressed in his weekday uniform of a white tee shirt under blue jean overalls, turned around and gave her a look that was part bewildered and part hurt, which made her laugh. Then it dawned on him. She had been saying his name wrong on purpose. Teasing him.

Not knowing how to respond, he simply nodded and said, "Alright, then."

With wordless efficiency, they coordinated the preparation of a simple breakfast. Cal filled the coffeepot with grounds and water while Elodie retrieved bran cereal from the pantry and set the table with mugs, bowls, and spoons for them both. Once seated at the table, she watched him pour milk into his bowl and add the bran flakes cereal on top.

Incredulous, she stated, "I've never seen anyone make a bowl of cereal backward! Did I say 'backward'? I meant 'wrong.'"

"It's not wrong. It tastes the same either way, girlfriend."

"Oh, you did not just call me 'girlfriend'!" Elodie was mockingly indignant.

Pre-caffeinated, Ava and Marie shuffled into the kitchen. "What are you two squabbling about?" Marie wanted to know as she tied the belt of her bathrobe.

"Nothing," they replied in unison. Both continued their breakfast with a half-smile on their faces for having gotten, playfully, under the other's skin.

"What's everyone's plans for today?" asked Ava, grabbing a mug from the cupboard. She was unsure whether she should inquire but still curious. There were still so many little dynamics to work out in this unusual household. But she had no doubt Marie or El would tell her if it wasn't her business.

"Well, Grant's been up and gone for a while. He's hoping to find a part-time job as a starter at an area golf course to make a little money. But mostly, he wants to play for free," answered Marie. She opened the dishwasher to make sure he'd emptied it before he left, as she'd reminded him. "Um, good," she noted as she closed it again.

"As for me, once I eat breakfast and get out of these pajamas, I'm going to get my hands in that side flower garden, clean out the dead leaves, and see what's what. I noticed there's new growth poking up."

"I'm looking for a dentist today and hope to get in to see one," said Elodie. "It's my only goal."

At Cal's turn, he said, "I noticed the front porch light fixture is hanging a little wonky, so I thought I'd straighten it up. And Marcus says the door to the half-bath sticks at the top. So, I'll take a look at that too."

"Cal, if you're on a ladder today, just be careful, alright?" cautioned Marie, who was genuinely concerned for him. Then, afraid she'd sounded like his mother or wife, she turned her attention back to Ava. "And what about you, girl?"

"Well, whenever Marcus emerges from the study, he and I will shop for a lightweight rototiller for the backyard garden. There's no way we can dig that grass out by hand with a shovel. I hoped to find something gently used online, but nobody's selling when it's time to be tilling. So, we'll go see what Farm Supply has that's affordable."

Ava was already dressed for Farm Supply and rototilling. She wore a long-sleeved, light-yellow t-shirt, olive-colored overalls, and red-brown garden clogs. A light-yellow bandana scarf with little blue flowers and leaves the color of her overalls loosely encircled her neck. Her wavy, shoulder-length bob was pulled back in a stubby ponytail at the nape of her neck. It was a cheerful, youthful look for her, but not in the mutton-dressed-as-lamb way some senior women, desperate to appear young and relevant, dress.

June, a breakfast skipper, began playing *When I Survey The Wonderous Cross* on her piano in the living room. She played softly in consideration of Marcus, who brought his coffee into the study and read most mornings. Of course, he told June her playing wasn't a distraction to him with the study door and living room pocket doors all closed, but still, she tried to be thoughtful.

Playing hymns was an act of worship for June. She could be so absorbed in the music she offered to God that she'd forget others were nearby. Once in a while, her worship became boisterous, and when she'd realized it, she was self-conscious and apologetic. She wasn't ashamed, but she missed the privacy of her former home with Cal in those times. But since it was not an option for her to give up her method of worship in her new living situation, she adapted as best she could with the effort to play softly.

Cal dutifully rinsed his breakfast dishes, put them in the dishwasher, and headed out to retrieve his toolbox from his truck.

When he and June arrived at the house a week after the others, he figured out Elodie had taken the single space in the original garage, and the Rennigers and Van Zants parked their vehicles in the second garage on the Tamarack Street lot. He could park his truck behind any of them and constantly move it to let others out or park on the street in front of the house. He preferred and adopted the latter.

Cal hobbled slowly out to his truck and grabbed his toolbox from the locked storage bin in the bed of his white F-150. When he turned around, he was face-to-face with a petite woman dressed smartly in a cream silk blouse, cream cashmere cardigan, and black tapered slacks that touched the top of her ankles. Long strands of light blonde hair were swept up neatly in the back, and her makeup was subtle and classy. Nevertheless, by the thin skin around her sharp blue eyes and spotted decolletage, Cal guessed she was in her mid-seventies.

Startled by her sudden appearance, he didn't think to extend a greeting before she snapped at him: "Do you have to park this old wreck in the street every day and bring down the entire neighborhood?"

Cal was not usually quick on his feet to respond to surprise attacks, but this lady had besmirched his beloved F-150 work truck and struck a nerve in his base nature. He reacted without thinking.

"I don't have to, but I get to. And for the record, this truck is only eight years old, which is a lot newer than those age spots you ain't quite covered up," he retorted defensively.

The woman's lip-tinted mouth tightened, and her voice deepened. "I can see neither you nor the other residents of the old folks' home you have going here care about the welfare of the community you've invaded. So be it! We'll see what my brother has to say about this."

She turned on her stylish-not-sensible shoes and walked up the porch stairs of the house directly across the street, pausing to scold the yard maintenance man who had been spraying chemicals on her pristine lawn.

"Mind your own business and get back to work!" she barked.

Once she was in the house, the man looked at Cal and gave him a sympathetic shrug.

# Chapter Eleven

Grant closed his eyes as he savored the last bite on his dinner plate of Elodie's Cajun Mac & Cheese with Shrimp and Crab. The dish hadn't suffered in the least for substituting imitation crab. He'd skipped the roasted broccoli the others enjoyed, which was fine because the women on the cooking rotation never included him in their serving calculations for cooked vegetables. They economized by forgoing name-brand ingredients and waste but were lavish with flavor and variety. Grant had never disparaged Marie's cooking, but he was undoubtedly enjoying the upgrade of culinary talent in his new situation.

Just as the dinner conversation was trailing off and they were ready to clear the table, Cal captured everyone's attention by clearing his throat and making the announcement he dreaded: "I met the woman who lives in the white house across the street."

Although they were eager for the opportunity, they had met none of their neighbors yet. The only person they'd all spoken to at least once was Will, their mailman. Being a vintage neighborhood, all the houses had either a mailbox on their porch or a slot in their front door, giving everyone ample opportunity for acquaintance with their mailman. But aside from friendly Will, no one else had introduced themselves to the new residents.

"I tought I saw a young lady in da window when we were moving in," said Marcus, pleased that he was correct.

"What's her name, and what's she like?" Marie asked excitedly.

"Oh, she's not young by any stretch of the imagination, likely a little older than us but dressed fancier – like well-to-do. Colors her hair blonde. And we didn't trade names," Cal replied.

"Cal forgets to get people's names. And sometimes, he won't remember them when he's told them. I told him my grandmama's name was Opal, and he called her Ms. Pearl for the first year we were married," June explained. Her husband's inability to gather this singular piece of basic information about their neighbor slightly frustrated her.

"Well, you said you met her. What did she say to you if she didn't tell you her name?" Marie questioned further.

"I learned she doesn't like my truck being parked out front and takes us for an old folks' home. She said she's going to run her mouth to her brother about it – like I care. That ole girl is mean as Satan in lipstick, I'm sorry to say."

The group released a small collective groan.

"So, what did you say to her?" Marie continued pulling bits of information from Cal like pulling a stubborn splinter from his palm.

"I believe I pointed out her age spots were older than my truck," Cal muttered as he lowered his head.

This time, the group released a giant collective groan. This was not the start they'd hoped to make with any of their neighbors. Their plan was to be a lighthouse of the love of Jesus – offering friendship, hospitality, and the good news of forgiveness for every sin by repentance and faith in Him. This interaction with the neighbor woman across the street was a severe and unfortunate setback to that plan.

There was no need to brow-beat Cal about how he'd handled himself. It was clear he knew he'd done wrong and regretted it. Besides, they all knew Cal truly loved three things: God, June, and his F-150. They also knew, every one of them, the embarrassment of letting their mouths run ahead of their sanctification. What was done was done.

Marcus had an idea. "I tink we should all tink about dis and discuss what we should do about it next Tursday Meeting."

"That's all fine and dandy," Cal started slowly. "But I'm going out to move my truck right now. Is everyone okay if I park off to the side of the driveway below the garbage bin? That way, Elodie could still get out of the garage. I'll figure something out to deal with the ruts it'll make in the grass."

Though the thought of ruts in the grass he took such pride in gave Grant a pang, he encouraged Cal, "That'll be fine. And if you use the back door, it'll be closer for you than parking out front, anyway."

Heads nodded in agreement all around. At least this would be a step forward in appeasing their disgruntled neighbor.

As she stood to help clear the table, Ava remembered: "I saw some neighbors, too, today. I was reading on the porch this afternoon and saw the school bus drop off a boy and a girl who went into the green house next door. The boy looked about 13 or 14, and the girl about six. We didn't speak, but I did wave to them. Funny, now that I think about it, I know they saw me – we made eye contact – but they didn't wave back. So, we might be zero for two on the neighbor scorecard."

Marie rolled her eyes, and Marcus shook his head sadly.

"If we find out who lives in the dark house across the street, maybe we can find a way to make them hate us, too," Elodie muttered as she left the kitchen.

Since they'd moved in, they hadn't seen a single light on in the yellow house on the corner lot across Tamarack Street. There was no FOR SALE sign posted, but the first-floor blinds, as well as the detached garage, remained closed. The grass was past due for its first mowing of the Spring.

Just yesterday, Elodie had invited Ava, Marie, and June – whose eyes were all sharper than hers – to look through her bedroom window, which faced the house's upper, unshuttered windows. Through squinted eyes, Ava believed she saw furniture in an upstairs bedroom.

"Either they're away, or our neighbor is an energy-saving hermit," June concluded.

"That would be interesting. I've never met a hermit," Marie mused to herself, hardly aware she'd spoken the thought out loud.

"Nobody meets hermits. That's their point," Ava chided, prompting a quiet chorus of muffled titters from Elodie and June.

"Well then," Marie said as she turned to leave the bedroom. "I may make it my life's goal to bring home a hermit for dinner one evening and share my accomplishment with you all."

# Chapter Twelve

It was early Saturday morning, and Cal had his navy Carhart jacket on as he shuffled into the kitchen and poured coffee into his thermal mug.

Elodie was finishing her coffee and a blueberry muffin. "Where you off to so early, Calorie?" she asked.

Without a flinch at the misnaming, he answered, "I'm goin' to the Man Mall for some paver stones."

"Man Mall?" Elodie repeated with a quizzical expression.

"I'm goin' to Home Warehouse – otherwise known as the Man Mall. Gonna' get some 12″ X 12″ pavers and bags of gravel and sand to make myself a parking pad for my truck."

"Boy, when you get an idea, you're on it like white," Elodie froze before finishing her sentence.

"Ha! You were gonna' say 'like white on rice,' weren't ya? Go ahead. Nothing wrong with that. Rice is white. I'm white. My truck is white. And I'm a grown man who's pretty secure with all that. I don't get touchy about colors – mine or anybody else's. But since we're on the subject and don't know each other well, how do you feel about being black?"

Elodie put an index finger to the corner of her mouth and pretended to ponder, looking at the ceiling for several seconds while absent-mindedly scratching at the neckline of her peacock blue linen top with her other hand.

"I believe I'll be used to it in another month or two," she replied with straight-faced sarcasm.

"Well, you'll have that to look forward to, then. Glad we got it sorted out."

"Yup. Glad we did too. Good luck with your project today."

Cal added creamer to his coffee, twisted the lid on his thermos, and grabbed a muffin from the counter before heading out the door. Then, he stuck his head back in the door and asked, "Did you ever see a dentist?"

"No, but I found one takin' new patients, and I have an appointment for Monday mornin'. Hate to wish away the weekend, but relief is in sight."

"Good." And Cal was off.

Elodie finished her breakfast and headed upstairs to read her Bible in her room. She met Ava and Marie on their way down the staircase - already dressed for their day. Marie wore wide-leg blue jeans, a red pullover sweater, and her everyday makeup: silvery taupe eyeshadow, black/brown mascara, and a hint of crème blush. Her hair was piled high on her head, fastened by a gray claw clip somewhere underneath a puffy spray of tendrils.

Ava wore her green overalls with a pink tee shirt underneath, her hair in a loose ponytail, and zero makeup. God had blessed her with beautiful pink skin sprinkled with copper freckles, which gave her a natural, healthy-looking color. Aside from the monthly application of dye to maintain her formerly natural red hair, at 63, Ava was still effortlessly pretty, even with a few laugh lines.

"Do you know I'm just about used to bein' black?" Elodie said to Marie and Ava as she passed them and continued her ascent on the stairs.

Marie and Ava stopped and looked at one another in confusion.

"Glad you took your time and thought it through," Marie yelled after her, mixing a laugh with her words.

"What was that about?" Ava wondered aloud.

"There's no telling with that one," Marie answered, shaking her head.

Marcus and Grant were chatting in the study when their wives passed the door and invited them to come to the kitchen for breakfast. June, they'd all learned, was a sleeper-inner. While they were all up and at 'em by 7 am, June did her best to see the sun by 8:30 am. Cal had warned them, "If you like to see June shine, you'd better give her time to rise."

After their coffee/tea and muffins, the Rennigers and Van Zants headed to the backyard to make progress on the gardens. This morning's plan was to remove the dried grass clods from the previous day's tilling and add soil amendments, including compost, manure, and worm castings. In another week, cool-weather vegetable plants would be available in Kentucky stores, and Ava wanted to be ready. She planned to put broccoli, cabbage, onions, and lettuce in one of the four garden quadrants. And since there was still a chance of frost till early May, she'd install arching bands of ½" PVC pipe across the bed and drape clear plastic sheeting over the top to make a little greenhouse for the young plants.

While they were preparing the garden beds, Cal returned with his supplies and started installing the parking pad for his truck. His design was simple. He'd have two rows of paving stones placed 63" apart, on-center, with a grass median between them. He'd lay the stones flush to the ground with a layer of gravel and sand underneath to keep them level. Nice and tidy. No ruts. The most challenging part of the job for Cal would be digging out the sod before he could lay his materials. His burden was considerably eased when Grant and Marcus left their ladies to the soil amending and came, with their shovels, to help Cal with his project.

"As my mother always says, 'Many hands make light the work,'" Grant quoted as he pulled up the sleeves of his black sweatshirt and dug his spade into the sod.

After her morning worship, June started her day by getting the evening meal in the crockpot. They'd have open-faced Mississippi pot roast sandwiches with gravy and French fries. She noted the activity in the backyard and took her coffee to sit for a few minutes on the front porch and watch the robins hopping around the front yard.

She wasn't seated on a rocking chair a minute before a little girl appeared between the budding lilac branches that formed an open, airy hedge at their base until they leafed out about four feet from the ground. The girl wore blue jeans that sparkled and a pink hoodie with the cuffs folded over like it was bought a size too large for her. Her straight sandy hair was more or less center-parted and un-brushed. She swiped at her overgrown bangs that fell over her round green eyes.

June smiled at her and said, "Hi. Do you live in that house next to me?"

The girl nodded.

"My name is Mrs. Sherman. What's yours?"

The girl stepped through the hedge onto the driveway and answered, "Lovie. I'm in first grade. I have a brother who's in 7th grade. His name is Chase. My daddy works in an office, and my mommy is an angel now. And I have a loose tooth on the top." She pointed to her mouth.

June left her seat and coffee on the porch and joined Lovie on the driveway. Although there was so much information in Lovie's extensive response to the little question, June spoke to comfort her motherless young neighbor rather than satisfy her curiosities. Now that she was closer, she noted Lovie's face testified she'd recently eaten strawberry jelly.

She knelt to speak face-to-face with the child. "I'm so glad you told me you have a loose tooth. Do you know, I've had a loose tooth for years and years, and I keep it mostly a secret."

In the most casual way the thing could be done, June popped out a false front tooth and held it in front of the wide-eyed child before popping it back in the hole in her smile.

"You don't have to wait to grow the new one!" laughed Lovie, impressed with the trick. "I've had two come out from my bottom teeth, and I had to wait forever for the new ones to come in."

"It was that way for me, too, when I was your age. But as a grown lady, I had an accident and hit my front teeth. One stayed in, and one fell out. So, the dentist ordered me this one to take its place. And do you know what? It felt like it took forever for this one to arrive too."

Lovie lowered her head and, after a few seconds, looked at June through her dark eyelashes and said, "My mommy had an accident, and now she's an angel far away, and I can't see her, but Aunt Shelby says she can still see me. Is that for real? Do you think she can see me?"

Though June never had children of her own, she had definite views about raising them. One of these views was that one should never lie to them. She didn't know the exact answer to Lovie's question, and she thought the idea that people become an entirely different spiritual species in Heaven was shady theology, so she said what she knew for sure.

"I'm not 100% certain, sweetie. God gave us a book called the Bible that tells us a lot about Himself, angels, and Heaven, but it doesn't tell us everything. It tells us that God sees everything we do. But I haven't found where it exactly says anyone else can see or not see us from Heaven. So maybe we shouldn't know it."

"Why," Lovie's innocent voice questioned.

"Well, what if Mommy could see you were afraid, sad, or needed help? She would want to help you with all her heart, but I'm not sure she could. So, it's good to know that when God sees we're afraid, sad, or need help, He can certainly help because the Bible promises He can. All we need to do is ask Him for help."

Lovie's attention was engaged. "How do people talk to God when Heaven is so far away?"

"Would you like me to show you?" June offered sincerely. It would be much easier to model prayer than to explain it.

"Ok," Lovie answered softly and nervously.

"Can I hold your hand while we talk to God together?" June asked permission. Lovie held out a hand that also had a trace of jelly on it.

And on the driveway of 306 Cedar Street, June prayed:

*Dear Father in Heaven, thank You for my new friend, Lovie. I'm so glad she's my neighbor. And I thank You that You see the smallest people and hear the smallest voices. You know how many hairs we have on our heads and how many teeth are in our mouths. So, Father, I ask you to help Lovie grow a new, pretty tooth to replace the loose one. And I ask you to help her when she misses her mommy. Help her when she's sad. And help her be glad again, too. Amen.*

"God could hear that?" Lovie's little voice asked.

"He sure could. He can even hear what we say in our hearts when we don't speak any words out loud at all," June assured her.

Just then, Chase's voice called harshly from their front porch. "Get in here, you little toad! You're not supposed to be outside when Dad's not home!"

Lovie looked stricken and turned to go. She hesitated and turned back to June to ask, "How did you know I missed my mommy?"

"Because I still miss mine," June, who'd lost her mother nine years ago, replied honestly.

# Chapter Thirteen

Marie rubbed Grant's tired hands as they sat on the front porch glider after the delicious dinner prepared by June. She'd also baked an apple tart that looked styled for a food magazine cover. But Grant and Marie, already stuffed, decided they'd save their servings of the tart for a Sunday evening snack. On Sundays, the big meal of the day was after church; in the evening, everyone made do for themselves.

"Wonder where they're off to," Grant mused as they watched Marcus and Ava drive down the street in their black minivan.

"No need to wonder. Ava said they're going to Big Mart to look for garden seeds and plants."

"Oh, ok."

"Have you noticed they don't seem like the same old Marcus and Ava since we've been here? Actually, before we moved here. They're sad, and I'm pretty sure it has something to do with Marit, but they're not ready to talk about it yet. El and I have been praying for them."

"Yeah, Marcus hasn't been running his mouth like usual. I just thought he finally ran out of things to tell me I was doing wrong. Well, I'm sorry if there's trouble for them."

"Yeah, me too. So how's the job search going?" Marie asked, sensing trouble on that front too.

"It's gone, Baby Doll," he shrugged. "I've been to all four golf courses in the area, and they have all the old starters they need. It's a popular job for retired guys – we all want to play golf for nothing. So, I'm going to have to wait till someone croaks. I left my name and number everywhere. Ow! Watch out for the blisters," Grant yelped after Marie rubbed a painful spot.

"Sorry," apologized Marie. "I didn't even see the one on your thumb. You've definitely got working man's hands now. And bicep muscles, too!"

"Really, you think my biceps are bigger?" Grant asked, inspecting them and forgetting about his aching hands.

"They are definitely bigger and more defined than when you were fifty, dear. Physical labor looks very nice on you," Marie was intentionally gushing. She believed a man needed to hear his woman gush about him now and then.

"Thank you for that," Grant said as he settled back into the glider and put his arm around his wife. "Digging out a parking spot for Cal wasn't on my to-do list today, but I couldn't watch him struggle to do it alone. I sure hope that's not a strategy he takes up: start a project so Marcus and I will finish it."

"Well, is that something you've seen him do before in the years we've known him?" Marie asked in defense of their friend.

"No."

"His health didn't get bad overnight, you know. Every project he's done for years, he's struggled to do alone unless he was coming over to help us with our projects - which he did more times than you or I can count. But you think now is when he might start running his game, huh? Even if he does, don't you think we owe it to him? And when I say "we," I mean you. You owe him, Grant."

"I don't know why we didn't send you to law school, Marie. Your talents were wasted as a kindergarten aide."

"Lawyers don't get summers off to raise their boys. Maybe we should have sent you so you could learn to defend yourself," she countered with a chuckle.

Grant returned to Marie's point. "I just get mad at myself that I don't always see situations the way you do. And then when you point it out, I feel dumb because it should have been obvious, and I missed it because I'm selfish."

"Grant Renniger, you are the least selfish person I know or have ever known. And I say this while sitting on the porch of a beautiful house we bought with our friends because of your unselfishness. So who cares if you don't see the whole situation in the first pass? What matters is that you always do the right thing when you do see it – or I help you to see it. That's what makes you the man of integrity that you are. And that makes me so grateful to God that you're mine."

Her respect and encouragement brought a smile to Grant's face. It amazed him how God used the wife he adored to break and rebuild him, usually in the same conversation.

"Can we glide on this thing? It glides, you know," Marie asked to give Grant some emotional breathing space. Then, without waiting for an answer to the rhetorical question, she proceeded to glide them.

"Mentioning summers off with the boys makes me think of them. Have you heard from David or Daniel lately?" she wondered aloud, reaching up to hold Grant's hand draped on her shoulder.

"Neither one," he lamented with a heavy sigh.

It wasn't unusual for them to go for a month, though rarely more, without hearing from their sons. David was the actual attorney in the family. He had recently made partner in the firm he'd started with right after passing the bar exam. His wife, Liza, was a nurse practitioner. Grant and Marie loved her to bits – probably more than David, they teased him. The couple had given them a succession of rescued grand-dogs over their 12-year marriage but no grandchildren.

David's twin, Daniel, owned a sizeable insurance agency. He was dad to Grant, 16, and Georgia, 14, with his first wife, Ruby, with whom he shared amicable custody. Daniel was married to his second wife, Andie, for over a year. She was eleven years younger and, in Grant's estimation, more high maintenance than a grand piano in a traveling show.

Their boys were successful and busy. So very busy.

Illumination from streetlights replaced the evening sunlight on Cedar Street. The air had grown chillier, and Marie pulled her sweater tighter around her.

"Don't look now," Grant advised, "but Satan in Slippers across the street, or whatever Cal called her, is watching us from an upstairs window."

"Will told me her name is Christine Williams. Maybe we should wave to her. Or would calling her out for watching us make her mad – rather, madder? Perhaps we should give her something to look at," Marie giggled at the suggestion.

As far as Grant was concerned, he'd been given an invitation. He guided Marie's chin with his hand, turned her face to his, and kissed her lips. Then, knowing Marie's eyes were closed, he mischievously waved a hand to his neighbor, who turned abruptly away.

# CHAPTER FOURTEEN

They'd planned to walk the three blocks to Grace Fellowship Church if it wasn't raining, but it was, so they car-pooled instead. They'd also intended to disburse themselves among the congregation, but that didn't work out either. At a serious-faced usher's direction, they ended up seated in a single row, making a concentrated target when the pastor instructed members to greet any visitors they saw. Furthermore, they planned to visit the Sunday morning service of this church and then others. But this one hooked them before that could happen.

Pastor Jonathan Jefferson was born and raised in Faircourt, Kentucky, as were his parents and grandparents. He'd moved to Louisville, just under 20 miles away, to get his undergraduate education at Boyce College and seminary training at the affiliated Southern Baptist Theological Seminary. Then, Jonathan came home to accept the call as Pastor of the struggling little Grace Fellowship Church. He'd been there for twelve years now. In that time, he married his high-school sweetheart, Kesha, and produced four sons: Kayne, age 9; Taj, age 7; Dakari, age 5; and Jalen, age 2. And in that time, the church grew numerically. But more importantly, it grew spiritually healthy and strong.

Naturally, Marcus dialed in to the young preacher's sermon that morning. He listened for the three things he considered most important: Gospel-centricity, hermeneutical integrity, and the two-sided character coin of boldness and humility. It was no good to have a pastor who could deliver a technically sound sermon without a man behind it who possessed both a backbone of resolve and awareness of his vulnerability. He'd seen too many pastors destroy churches for lack of one or the other. Marcus himself had nearly been one of them.

In his early years as a pastor at Delaware Street Community Church, Marcus focused on growing his congregation numerically with pragmatic sermons designed to meet their felt needs. He preached to make them better spouses and parents, to develop character and refine flaws, and even to increase Biblical literacy and promote discipline. It was what other preachers were doing, and it filled the pews. It filled them, that is, with self-centered, self-sufficient, self-satisfied members who were a blight on Christ's reputation. That was the unintended consequence of following the pastoral fad de jour. When you preach to people for years about themselves, you teach them where to focus. Themselves.

One day, in private study, Marcus was challenged by the Apostle Paul's statement to the Corinthian church.

*For I decided to know nothing among you except Jesus Christ
and him crucified. (1 Corinthians 2:2)*

Marcus questioned its practicality. He questioned its potential for monotony. He laughed to think of how his congregation would receive such a ministry. However, through his questioning and by the grace of God, he realized he'd pastured his flock in barren fields. He admitted to himself the anemic state of the congregation he'd been entrusted to shepherd and was ashamed.

Marcus suffered a long and dismal season of depression upon his realization, but this, too, was grace. A depressed man has nothing to lose. He trimmed the fat from his preaching and gave his congregation the lean meat of the Gospel: their sin, God's justice, Jesus' sacrifice and resurrection, and a call to repentance. A few people quit the church and disparaged Marcus on their way out. But most stayed and were transformed by the repetition of the simple message, including Marcus. The preaching of "Jesus Christ and him crucified" sufficed to make mature believers who glorified God, and Marcus never left the subject.

There were, however, at least three 20-year deacons of Delaware Street Community Church who clung to numerical growth as a barometer of spiritual vitality. They were the reason that today, Marcus was listening to preaching instead of doing the preaching. He was still adjusting to that reality.

Pastor Jefferson began his sermon this morning by relating his counseling experience with a young man. The guy's fiancé had called off their engagement, and he was crying, bent over like a fiddlehead fern in a chair in the Pastor's office. Pastor Jefferson's advice to the distraught man? "Quit sniveling and sit up like a man before I puke!"

The friends looked at each other up and down their row. Pastor Jefferson continued his sermon with the text at the conclusion of the Apostle Paul's first letter to the Corinthian church:

> *Be watchful, stand firm in the faith, act like men, be strong. Let all that you do be done in love.* (1 Corinthians 16:13-14)

He expounded on Paul's example, of Christ's ultimate example, and how believers are strengthened to obey Scriptural commands through the Gospel message of Christ. He explained that biblical love isn't one-dimensional and flat. It doesn't always look like a warm hug. Sometimes love looks like rebuke and exhortation – and Scripture records Jesus giving more of the latter than of the former. Marcus wore a big, silly grin through it all.

Their discussion was lively once the friends were back at home and gathered around the kitchen island, assembling turkey sub sandwiches and adding low-sodium potato chips on their plates.

"I'm glad to hear an older man will still tell a younger man to act like a man!" said Grant.

"He didn't short-change da gospel!" enthused Marcus.

"You don't know you've been hearing weak messages until you hear a strong one," Cal remarked.

"I could grow at a church like that," said Elodie.

"If Pastor Jefferson has Marcus' seal of approval, he's got mine too!" offered Ava.

"He had me at the clarification of biblical love," Marie chimed in.

"He had me at 'before I puke!'" declared June.

Everyone stopped what they were doing and stared at her.

# Chapter Fifteen

There were lights on in the house at 400 Cedar Street. There hadn't been an interior or exterior light in it since the friends took up residence in 306. Marie recently learned from Will, a paragon of postal discretion who gave up very few details to the newcomers, that this neighbor's name was Bobby McBride. He was not a hermit.

As soon as she noticed the lights, June got to baking. Cal would go with her to take a pound cake with bourbon cream sauce over to Bobby tomorrow to introduce themselves and welcome him home. They hoped it might also help make up to their housemates for Cal's awful start with the angry lady across the street, Christine Williams.

Elodie appeared in the kitchen doorway, beckoned by the wafting smell of vanilla-scented heaven from the oven.

"Hey, Calamari," she nodded to Cal, seated on a stool at the island and licking the spoon his wife had used to stir the bourbon cream sauce.

"Hey yourself," he responded cheerfully as any man would be who'd been given the spoon to June's specialty sauce.

"It smells like God's own bakery here," Elodie complimented June.

"Thanks. It's a pound cake for the neighbor in the dark house across Tamarack. There are lights on tonight! We're going to take it over and introduce ourselves tomorrow afternoon. Want to come?"

"If there's a 5% chance he'd ask us to share a slice of that cake, I'm down!" Elodie exclaimed. "Do we know anything about who lives there?" she continued.

"Will told Marie it's a man named Bobby McBride," June replied.

"Ok, Irish dude," Elodie shrugged. "Just hope he's the kind of guy who shares his cake."

Elodie didn't see Cal at the breakfast table the following day. They usually fired up the coffeepot together in the morning. At about nine o'clock, she heard June playing *I'd Rather Have Jesus* on the piano. She waited until the music stopped before entering the living room to inquire about Cal's absence.

"Missed that ugly old man of yours at breakfast this mornin'. He ok?"

"He had a miserable night and didn't sleep much. He takes so many medications, and sometimes he has, let's say, 'side effects.' He'll be fine, but he needs to lay low today. So I guess it's just you and me to carry the pound cake to the neighbor this afternoon."

Elodie left the house for her 10 o'clock dentist appointment. Ava, Marcus, Marie, and Grant – because he was not fast enough with an excuse to get out of it – headed to the backyard to work the garden in the beautiful sunshine. Ava gave Grant a brush and a bucket of bleach water to scrub the moss-covered bricks that outlined the garden beds. The others tried their best to stay out of his way while they planted spinach, broccoli, cabbage, radishes, onions, Brussels sprouts, cauliflower, zucchini, tomatoes, and sowed corn seeds. One entire quadrant was planted with young strawberry plants that wouldn't fruit till next year. Then, they'd have strawberries by the bucket.

Two and a half hours later, Elodie returned home with a brand new ceramic filling in her formerly painful tooth. She volunteered to hose the garden tools while her exhausted housemates went inside to wash up and prepare lunch.

"Well, that was a productive morning," Ava said, standing shoulder to shoulder with Grant as they scrubbed their hands in the kitchen sink.

"I have to agree. The bricks look great, don't they now?" Grant asked to highlight his contribution to the effort.

"Clean bricks are da critical element of every successful garden! It's in all da books," Marcus retorted with good-natured sarcasm.

"We can stop buying these salad fixings in a few weeks," Marie declared brightly as she gathered store-bought produce from the fridge to make a big Cobb salad for them all. "And wouldn't it be great to have chickens so we didn't have to buy eggs either?"

"Like a tiny farm!" June enthused. "We could have a stock tank, too."

The others looked at her, and Marie spoke their collective thought: "Chickens don't drink from a stock tank. Too big."

"It's not for the chickens; it's for us! Kind of like a kiddie pool but for adults and with a farmhouse feel. I've seen them done up online. But free-range chickens would look sweet walking around it; I have to say."

"No chickens! We can't keep chickens!" Grant was emphatic about this idea he had not been primed for.

Ava gave Marie a side smile unseen by Grant. She knew if Grant shot down an idea of Marie's with an emotional reaction instead of a rational explanation, there would eventually be the thing he said there would not. Ava had seen this play out too many times before. Grant had said there would be no St. Bernard puppy, no trip to India, and no hot tub before all these things made their way into Marie's life. So, based on history, she was reasonably confident there would eventually be chickens on the property. It was allowed by the village, and it made sense for the household. Marie noted the smile Ava gave her. She was glad to see that smile again, if only for a moment.

June joined the others, squeezed in around the kitchen table, and was as surprised as everyone else to see Cal shuffling into the kitchen, apparently feeling slightly better. He'd even made an effort to change from his pajamas into a tee shirt and overalls.

"Hey, Cal, would you mind sticking your head out the door and hollering for El to come in," Marie asked as Cal was about to pass the doorway.

"No problem," he replied.

He opened the door, leaned out, and shouted, "El!" And with just a half-second hesitation added, "Com-in-o!" Then, he repeated it more fluidly, "El Camino!" He started laughing so hard June rushed to his side to support him.

"Dat's a good one, Cal!" Marcus laughed.

"El Camino!" they whooped in unison when Elodie entered the doorway.

"Ain't funny," she deadpanned at their mirth.

"Um, it seems pretty unanimous dat it is funny," Marcus rebuffed. "I tink Cal's got a nickname for you now!"

"I thought he was sick or somethin'," she shot Cal a look over her glasses.

"I'm feeling better now!" he responded as he regained composure and his balance.

Laughter was good medicine for Cal. Still, he returned to bed after eating his lunch of boiled eggs and toast instead of the communal salad.

# Chapter Sixteen

June held her pound cake, and Elodie pushed the doorbell as they stood on the porch of 400 Cedar Street to meet Bobby McBride.

"I thought the Irish were fastidious," Elodie said as she surveyed the grimy window in the door, the crispy leaves from last fall that lay scattered on the porch's floor, and the dingy yellow siding that could use a gentle power wash.

"Give him some grace," June urged. "He just got home yesterday."

Through the window, they saw a figure approaching the front door. Elodie just had time to whisper, "He doesn't look full-blooded Irish!" before the door opened.

"Hello, ladies, how can I help you?" said the attractive black man, with more white hair than black and a mega-watt smile, who greeted them wearing a light purple, short-sleeved, button-down shirt and dungarees.

Elodie looked him up and down, noting he was slightly smaller than she – about 5'8" and 170 lbs if he had a full belly. He had several years on her, too. A lifetime of living as a single woman had instilled the habit of evaluating potential threats. She decided she could take this one down with little trouble if needed.

"We moved across the street into the Scott's former house last month. We saw lights on in your house last night and thought we'd come by to welcome you home and introduce ourselves. I'm June Sherman, and this is Elodie Ford," said June. And then, holding out the cake platter, "And this is a pound cake with bourbon crème sauce. We hope you'll like it."

"I'm Bobby McBride, and I never met a cake I didn't like," he said eagerly, accepting the cake from June's hands. "Will you come in?" he motioned for them to follow him as he carried the confection through the house to the kitchen. June and Elodie accepted the invitation and entered their neighbor's home.

It was from the same 1920s era as their 306 Cedar Street but in the bungalow style. It had the same thick baseboards, original glass doorknobs, and plaster walls; but fewer built-in woodwork features, lower ceilings, and less square footage. Natural light streamed in through windows covered with half-drawn matchstick shades, and the light bounced off the white-painted walls throughout.

They walked down a narrow hall and passed a living room with a jute rug covering most of the hardwood floor. A modern navy sectional sofa was situated on the carpet and faced a wall with an enormous television mounted to it. Below the tv was a low console cabinet with electronics and a row of DVDs arranged behind glass doors. A 1980s-era fixture in the center of the ceiling was the only supplemental light source. There was nothing that hinted at a feminine touch to the décor. No plants. No pillows or blanket throws on the sofa. No pictures adorned what could be seen on the walls from outside the room. It had a minimalist bachelor vibe. Not so the kitchen.

If the living room was bare and austere, the kitchen at the end of the hall was well-appointed and infused with life. The first thing that caught the women's eyes was the enormous 7-burner gas range with dual ovens. It was a stunning emerald green enamel with brass knobs and oven handles crowned by a matching and equally impressive range hood. Neither June nor Elodie had seen anything like it in person and were awed.

Bobby set the cake down on a corner of the white quartz countertop, and the ladies drew their gaze away from the stove and took in the rest of the room. A large single-bowl porcelain sink was stationed below two casement windows with diamond-shaped mullions. Oak-paneled cabinets covered two walls and concealed a refrigerator and dishwasher amongst them. Two open shelves with cookbooks and a few stoneware bowls were arranged on a third wall above a small bistro set that would seat four but was set for one. A pile of letters, catalogs, and advertising flyers sat on one chair. Near the back door, a small bowl and water dish sat on a red mat with the word "Meow" printed in white letters and tiny printed paw prints scattered haphazardly all over it. Above the cat dish, on the wall, was an oak-framed corkboard with a picture of a young family in front of a house with palm trees and school pictures of two smiling girls with braids and braces.

"Your oven is the stuff of my dreams," June couldn't help gushing. "Can I take a closer look?" she asked.

"Help yourself," Bobby beamed in appreciation. "My wife ordered it from Italy. I had to work a lot of overtime to make the payments, but she wanted it, and I couldn't refuse her."

"Is your wife at home?" June inquired as she grazed her fingers against the brass oven handle.

"My Julia's at home across town in the Faircourt Memorial Cemetery. Seventeen years now," he answered as the smile disappeared.

June's eyes swept Elodie's face as she turned to Bobby. Elodie hadn't spoken a word so far during the visit and didn't look likely to start.

"I'm truly sorry for your loss, Bobby. However, I'm guessing she was a wonderful cook, and you still miss that, along with a hundred other things about her."

"Every day, Miss June," he replied somberly. "So don't you know how glad I am to see a homemade cake coming my way borne on the wings of neighborly angels," he brightened, and the smile returned.

June noticed a slight smirk cross Elodie's face as she lowered her head. Still, she said nothing.

"I don't know about angels, but there is more living in our house than Elodie and me. There's my husband, Cal, our good friends Grant and Marie, and our new friends, Marcus and Ava. We all went in on the house together for our retirement years. We're just a month in, but so far, so good."

"Well now, I'm looking forward to the pleasure of their acquaintance too. It's just me and Rover rattling around this place," he said, nodding toward the dishes on the floor.

"You have a dog; I'd guessed a cat."

"Oh, you guessed right. Rover's my cat. But he's a rover if there ever was one. He goes all over this neighborhood hunting for mice or birds to bring to the back porch. You'll know him if you see him 'cause one side of his face is black, and the other is tan. Split right down the middle. Everybody around here knows Rover. Might be a little different having a cat named Rover, but it suits him."

"Good to know we have a mouser worth his kibble in the neighborhood," June responded. "And if I had to make another guess, I'd guess those sweet girls in the pictures are your granddaughters." She was pressing for more information to bring back to Marie and Ava.

"You're right again. The older one is Fendi, and the younger one is Prada." And before the ladies made the connection, Bobby added defensively, "What can I say? My daughter was going through a luxury brand phase when she had them. But they sure have their Granddad wrapped around their little fingers. There's none smarter or prettier, and I'll fight anyone that says otherwise," he concluded with a little laugh. "That's where Rover and I've been for the last eight weeks. I spend all my vacation time in Florida with those girls and their parents. And old Rover hunts lizards instead of mice when we're there."

He looked directly at Elodie as an invitation to comment, and she declined the invitation. So Bobby turned to the cake on the counter, lifted the foil covering it, and sniffed. Now, his eyes smiled with the rest of his face. "I don't know how much longer I'll be able to resist this magnificent cake. Would you ladies care to join me for a slice?"

"We can't stay," Elodie answered too abruptly. She turned and started heading back down the hall to the front door.

June did not see that coming. She recovered, shrugged her shoulders, and whispered to Bobby, "She's a little shy."

She turned to follow Elodie, then paused and offered the necessary departing courtesies. "Guess we'll leave you to enjoy your cake. It was nice meeting you. I hope we'll see you again soon." They let themselves out the front door.

"Okay, then. More for me," Bobby decided as he turned his full attention to the confection on the counter.

# Chapter Seventeen

"What just happened?" June quizzed Elodie as they walked back home. "I thought you were there for the singular purpose of putting cake in your mouth."

"Not with that man. Don't have time for him."

"What? Why? What?" June flustered in disbelief.

"I've seen his type a hundred times - all smiles, charm, and flattery. When someone don't know you and calls you an angel, that's some shifty talk. I 'bout laughed in his face."

"I didn't read him that way at all. I thought he was nice, not over the top. So, I will give him the benefit of the doubt."

"I realize I don't know you well, June, but I believe you might like the benefit of that man's fancy stove."

June laughed. "I will not deny my attraction to the man's to-die-for Italian stove. But, you know, there's something strange about it. Didn't he say his wife wanted the stove? Well, that stove has never been used. When I looked at it up close, I saw shipping packaging in the burner wells and protective tape around the oven seals. If his wife never got to use the stove, why wouldn't he sell it or use it himself if he put so much blood, sweat, and tears into buying it?"

"See, that's the thing about his type; you can't trust what they say either," Elodie advised.

They reached the walkway to their front steps nearly simultaneously with Will. He was sorting out their mail from the stack in his hand as he walked and almost ran into them.

"Oh, sorry," he apologized. "Wasn't looking where I was going. My feet know the route, so I just let them go while I figure out what goes in your mailbox. Let me see if I can guess right: you're June Sherman and E-lo'-die Ford. Am I right?"

"You're two for two," Elodie answered. "But it's pronounced El'-o-die. Rhymes with melody."

"Got it. It usually takes me only a week to learn the household members of my new customers, but the gang in this house is a challenge. I like a challenge," he chirped. "Here's your mail." He handed them a small stack of mail and spared himself the walk up the porch steps and back. "Have a nice day. It sure is a pretty one."

The ladies entered the house's foyer and saw Marcus and Grant in the living room watching a rerun of Hogan's Heroes. Marcus was raised on the Antillean island of Aruba, an ethnic mix of African and Dutch, with a dab of Asian. He didn't come to the United States until he started college. So, what was a corny, nostalgic rerun to Grant was whimsical, novel entertainment to Marcus. He loved old shows from the 60s.

"Mail call!" Elodie bellowed into the living room.

Marcus was engrossed, so Grant responded. "Just toss what you don't want here."

Elodie did a quick shuffle, handed June a doctor's bill for Cal, and stuffed her auto insurance invoice in her skirt pocket. She gave the rest to Grant and sat down to join the guys for the remainder of the show.

"Well, I've got nothing else to do till dinner time. It's Ava's night to cook," said June as she sat.

Grant handed Marcus a letter from Grace Fellowship Church. "Welcome letter, I'm guessing. That was fast," he commented.

While the others chuckled at the shenanigans between Hogan and Colonel Klink on the television, Grant opened a letter addressed to the Faircourt Friends Trust from The Law Office of Luther Hall. The color drained from his face as he read it. He folded it, returned it to the envelope, and placed it on his lap. It took a few minutes for the others to realize Grant was not engaged with them. Marcus noted it as he muted the tv for a commercial.

"Someting wrong, Grant?" he asked.

Grant held up the letter. "It says we're operating an unlicensed care facility, and we have 30 days to vacate the premises or face a lawsuit from the Village of Faircourt."

Marcus stunned, turned the television off completely.

"Is that what we are? Are we a care facility?" asked June with a sudden rush of self-doubt.

"No! We're just friends who bought a house to share. People do that all the time," Grant insisted. Though, now that he thought about it, did *seven* people do that?

Elodie physically wilted in her chair. "I have no Plan B," she said faintly. "I've no idea what I'll do or where I'll go."

"None of us do," said Marcus.

"Well, we're going to fight this," Grant was adamant. "I have no intention of just accepting this absurdity. It's completely ridiculous!"

"We can't tell Ava! We can not tell Ava while we fight dis. Promise me none of you will tell Ava," Marcus was begging. Then he was sobbing. A dam had broken, and there could be no more polite pretending nothing was wrong.

June, Elodie, and Grant circled their figurative wagons as literally as possible and drew up close to him.

"Where's Ava now?" Grant asked, calmly controlling the emotionally charged situation like he was born to manage drama.

"She went for a walk, and Marie is wit her. To da big cemetery, I tink," Marcus answered.

"Okay, so she's out of the house, and we can talk," Grant reasoned.

"Tell us what's going on with Ava."

"I don't know where to start. So much has happened, and it's overwhelmed her. In our 41 years of marriage, I've never seen her like dis. And as hard as I try, I can't help her. I'm afraid of what might happen if one more ting is added to stress her."

"We had no idea, Marcus. Marie and I just thought she was sad. Both of you, actually. I just figured sometimes change is hard for a while. So, it's more than that. What's happened?" Grant asked in a tender tone, usually reserved for Marie.

"It's more dan one ting, but da main ting is neider Mia nor Marit is speaking to us. Dey haven't for months now. In a nutshell, Marit and Robby can't start a family because we've moved away, and dey assumed we'd always be dere to care of a baby as we did for her sisters. Marit has to work to help pay da enormous mortgage dey took out and is stuck and angry about it. Mia has been struggling in her marriage in recent years. We saw dat happening but didn't know how bitter her heart had become. She said we were selfish to move, proving dat we always were. From dere, it was a short jump to da conclusion dat we're selfish people who are a terrible influence on grandchildren. Not only are we not allowed to see dem, we understand dey've been told Ava and I are not even real Christians. It's like she's settling some score we weren't aware of. Dere's got to be more going on dan we know, but dis is where we're at. Dey refuse to speak to us to work it out.

Ava feels like an utter failure as a mother, which, you know, is foundational to her identity. She left dem both voicemails begging for mercy and dey sent her a joint email mocking her. She can't find relief from her anguish over der blind-siding abandonment. When I led a church, she buried many hurtful things because she felt she had to as a pastor's wife. But dat constraint isn't dere anymore, and she doesn't know how to handle da hurt of rejection now dat she has no excuse to stuff it. She's cried every day for months. I mean, *every day*. Marley tried to explain to her sisters how painful it was for dere mom, and dey used it against Ava. Dey said it proves she's unstable and unhealty for da kids to be around. So, we've been blocked from der phones and social media accounts.

If dis wasn't enough, Ava's under incredible spiritual attack. The Enemy doesn't care if we're in a bad spot. He kicks us when we're down. And he doesn't care dat our women..." Marcus' frail composure began to fold, and his voice cracked as emotion tightened his throat. "...he doesn't care dat our women are delicate when vulnerable. He beats dem like he would any man. Nuting I say to her helps – so, a lot of good I've been."

And then, to give them an idea of what it was like, Marcus added, "She says dat God is hiding from her, and she hears Him laughing at her from His hiding place."

The words hung in the air like a puff of noxious gas that emotionally choked them all.

Elodie responded first. She spoke softly as she processed her dear Ava's grief. "Five minutes ago, I thought the worst thing I could hear was that I'd have to move."

All Grant could manage was to shake his head and make a sound: "Um, um, um."

June offered a suggestion. "This is too big for us," she said. "We need to pray."

They reached for one another's hands in their tiny huddle, and June prayed:"

*Father, how glad we are to come to You knowing we don't need to explain what's happening or our helplessness. We love imperfectly, but You love perfectly and steadfastly, and You've promised You always act for our good. None of this looks good to us, Father. But our view and our knowledge are limited, and Yours, limitless. By faith, we trust Your word above our perceptions. May that be for Your honor and our sanctification.*

*We ask that You encourage Ava through this heartbreaking trial by helping her discern Your truth from the Enemy's lies. Your word says Your laughter is for the wicked, but You sing over Your own. Father, let her hear Your song. And when she is overcome with weakness, show her Your strength is perfect and your grace sufficient. You have not lied to us. We know that trials are necessary and produce maturity. Thank you that Jesus endured hardships and gave us an example to follow so we do not have to flail about without a guide. But it is useless to have an example if we do not have the strength to follow. Please strengthen Ava and Marcus for this challenging road.*

*Father, I also pray for Marcus and Ava's daughters, who have turned their backs on their parents. Your word says You discipline Your own; if You do not, they are not Yours. So, we ask for Your hand of discipline in their lives to prove they are Yours and for a harvest of righteousness in their lives as a result. We remember that we, too, are prone to turn our backs on You. We long to extend the same mercy to repentant children that You have extended again and again to us and for which we thank You, in Jesus' name. Amen."*

# Chapter Eighteen

"Pass the salt, please, Calico," Elodie requested after tasting the homemade tomato soup Ava had prepared for a household whose majority was limiting their sodium intake.

"I live to serve you, El Camino," Cal replied with a grin.

Dinner was conversationally subdued other than the good-natured name-calling of these two. Everyone seemed to be engaged in private contemplation. Even though they all tried their best to eat their hot soup with decorum, slurping was the overall ambiance around the dining table. The quiet ticking of the center hall clock was not much competition.

Grant and Marie finished their meal, cleared their dishes from the table, and excused themselves to their room for the evening.

Their room was a private haven decorated to straddle a delicate design tightrope between cheerful and calm. The walls were Marie's favorite color - buttery yellow – and decorated with muted-hued artwork with frames of faux gold leaf. Four windows, two looking out on the front yard and two overlooking the left-side yard, filled the room with natural light. The windows were functionally covered with white, two-inch blinds that could be opened for light or closed for privacy. On each side, strictly for decorative purposes, hung nubby linen drapes Marie constructed herself. The nightstands and triple dresser were intentionally mismatched but shared the same aged maple and brass hardware tone.

The bed was brass, with ornate flourishes and swirls in an antique finish. It was trimmed with a bed skirt patterned with cream ribbons in loose, diamond shapes on a background of pale yellow. A queen-size silk damask-textured duvet covered the bed, ornamented with Euro-shammed pillows in the yellow bed skirt fabric. Marie had campaigned to have a king-sized bed, and it was a rare loss for her. Grant insisted there would be too much room for her to "run away" from him. He liked to sleep close to her. She didn't think she should begrudge him this and abandoned her crusade.

Grant, especially, often retreated to the privacy of this room to recharge his social battery or to watch his guilty pleasure on television: a show about Tennessee mountain folk who made bootleg liquor. He confided to Marie that he found the characters intriguing because their lives seemed so opposite to his. Grant also claimed to be learning a life skill since everyone would need a barter item in the Last Days when one couldn't make purchases without the Mark of the Beast. He tried to convince her that watching these moonshiners was the act of a forward-thinking man. Marie humored him in this. It amused her that her rule-keeping man had a secret attraction to outlaws.

Husband and wife changed into pajamas and robes and settled in their matching cream-colored, leather rocker recliners that sat, near the foot of the bed, on an oriental rug with a floral pattern of yellows, browns, and greens on a creamy background. Grant flipped on the 6-in-1 modern Victrola on a low table between their chairs. The FM station was tuned to the local Christian radio station, and R.C. Sproul was preaching the doctrine of election. Grant lowered the volume so they could hear each other speak above him. Just.

"I've something to tell you," they said in unison as they settled in for a conversation lacking at the dinner table.

"Ladies first," said Grant.

"No, mine can wait. I want to hear what's on your mind first."

Grant began with a sigh, and this was a terrible sign to Marie. She mentally braced for impact. He told her about the letter from the attorney, which claimed they were running an unlicensed care facility and the threat of a lawsuit if they didn't abandon ship. Marie was as incredulous as he had been when he first shared the news with Marcus, June, and Elodie that afternoon.

"That's nonsense," she responded. "We'll fight this!"

"Of course it is, and we will. I just wonder who this attorney is and how he's privy to the situation under this roof. We purchased the property in the name of our trust, so who knows how many people live here, and why do they care?"

Marie thought for a minute, and then she remembered. "Didn't Cal say the lady across the street, the one he made mad, didn't he say she called us an old folks' home? And didn't she say she was going to tell someone?"

"That's right! I forgot about that. I bet that's who's behind this. But in a way, it makes me feel better to know it's just that little old biddy being crazy. We can handle her."

"Shouldn't we start by not referring to her as 'that little old biddy'?" Marie asked with a raised eyebrow.

"Yes, dear," he said, slightly ashamed. And then, to change the subject, he added, "But that's not the only news of the day. Marcus was freaked out that we'd tell Ava about the letter. He told us Marit and Mia refuse to speak to them and have cut them off from seeing their grands. He said it's been happening for months, and Ava is distraught. Marcus also said she's been having a terrible spiritual struggle on top of it. He doesn't think she could handle any more stress and asked us not to say anything about the attorney's letter to her."

"Well, that explains a lot. We knew something was wrong. But the poor girl! I know her heart is broken. I wish she'd told Elodie and me when it all started. But knowing Ava, I bet she was trying to spare the girls' reputations by not letting us know they were behaving so ugly and ungodly. The more you let it outside the family, the more real it becomes, and the more people can ask you about it."

"How was your walk around the cemetery with her today?" Grant asked.

"It was good. It reminded us both of when we were kids, and we'd walk through our neighborhood cemetery looking for headstones that had our birth dates on them or names we'd consider naming our future children. We didn't discuss anything more current than 50 years ago until..." Marie's voice trailed off. "That brings me to my news and what I wanted to talk to you about."

"Ok, what's your news."

"I took a phone call on my cell while Ava and I were walking home. It was David."

"Oh good, how's he doing?" Grant jumped in, eager to hear news of how the partnership was going.

It was Marie's turn to sigh. "Liza has ovarian cancer."

# Chapter Nineteen

There was a lot to discuss at Thursday Meeting. Grant, Cal, and Marcus hadn't heard the details of June and Elodie's reconnaissance visit with cake to Bobby McBride's house across Tamarack Street. The guys were told only facts they would care about in descending order of certainty: Bobby's marital status (widowed), employment status (had a job, not sure what it was), and did he golf or garden (no clue). The men were satisfied with this skeletal information.

"So, have we settled on returning to Grace Fellowship Church, or are we trying somewhere new dis Sunday?" Marcus asked the group.

"I don't need to look anymore," answered Elodie.

June and Cal looked at each other. Then finally Cal answered for them as a couple. "Don't know what we'd be looking for that Grace Fellowship doesn't have."

"I'd be happy to stay there, too," said Grant.

"Ava and I feel da same," said Marcus.

"It's unanimous then," said Marie, adding, "Only I won't be joining you all this Sunday."

Marie, restlessly toying with a gold chain bracelet on her left wrist, shared her daughter-in-law's cancer diagnosis and the fact she had already arranged to fly on Saturday, to David and Liza's home in Atlanta. She'd be there for the scheduled surgery and first chemotherapy treatment and would help with household jobs. She would also try to soothe David's guilt for not being able to assist with the latter tasks because of the new demands of the law firm partnership.

Marcus kept his eyes on his wife's face as Marie talked about Liza and her husband, the boy she'd known all his life as the serious, inquisitive twin. In their early years of motherhood, Ava and Marie had girlishly fantasized about arranging a marriage between their David and Marley. They didn't account for the fact the two would grow up thinking of one another as brother and sister and often fussed with each other as such. Ava was still very fond of David and was sorry for his trouble, but her countenance remained steady. Marcus was relieved.

"Does anyone have an idea of how we can make a positive connection with Christine Williams across the street?" Grant asked without mention of the letter they'd received.

Cal slumped a little in his chair and lowered his eyes like he wished to disappear altogether. He felt awful about his sassy outburst and the trouble it had caused.

"We know nothin' about her," said Elodie.

"We know she keeps a lovely rose garden in her side yard," Marie offered.

"Do we grow any roses in our yard?" Marcus picked up on the idea.

"We, meaning me – the one who tends the flowers, do not! They're high-maintenance. Pests and diseases love roses," Marie answered quickly, regretting her input had put her on the defense.

Cal couldn't help himself. He chuckled and muttered, "High maintenance. That suits her."

"But haven't you always wanted to learn how to grow a prize-winning rose?" Marcus asked in a singsong tone, suggesting it should be Marie's answer rather than his question.

"Ah, personally, no. But if that's all we have for ideas on how to reach out to her, I'll think about it."

June glimpsed something out of the corner of her eye. "Gotta go!" she said, jumping from her seat and heading toward the front door. "Lovie is crying on our porch. Pray for me."

They all turned to look out the living room window; indeed, the little girl was standing on their porch. Tears streaked her dirty face. June unhurried her pace as she opened the door and stepped outside to greet the upset child with calm.

"Hello, Lovie sweetheart, what's the matter?" she asked as she stooped face-to-face.

"Chase punched me in the back, and it hurts. He's so mean," she whimpered.

"Oh, I'm so sorry that happened. Is your daddy home from work?"

"Not yet. He had to stay late today."

"Ok then. This is what we're going to do. We'll go and sit on your porch until your dad comes home. You go and wait for me. I have to go inside and get something, and I'll be right there. I promise."

Lovie nodded and walked back toward her house. June dashed back inside and headed toward the kitchen.

As she went, she hollered, "Cal, I need your help. Grab our jackets and come with me next door."

Cal did as she asked. While he was getting their jackets, June grabbed a wet paper towel and gathered the cooling cookies she'd baked before Thursday Meeting onto a plate. June and Cal headed out the front door as the others watched from their seats.

"Aww, not the cookies," Grant groaned as he watched them disappear. Four sets of raised eyebrows in the room sent him a wordless rebuke.

Lovie, reluctant to walk back to her house, was waiting at the end of the driveway.

June whispered staccato sentences to her husband before they reached her, "Brother hit her. Dad's not home. We'll wait for him. Don't know if brother will come out. Be gentle. You haven't been a dad, but you've been a boy. Try to remember."

"Lovie, this is my husband, Mr. Sherman. And these," she said, lifting the plate she held, "are cookies that I just baked. Do you like cookies?"

"I used to make cookies with my mommy. We liked peanut butter with chocolate chips."

"Those sound delicious! I never thought of putting chocolate chips in peanut butter cookies. I'll have to try it. These are just regular chocolate chip cookies."

They settled on the broad steps of the blue-green two-story house's porch since it had no other seating accommodations.

"Here, Lovie, do you mind if I help you clean your hands and face before we dig into the cookies?" June asked as she produced the wet paper towel.

Lovie held out her hands, but June went for her face first. She wanted to erase the signs of drama before her father came home. June's intuition told her their initial interaction with him would be more soothing if there weren't emotional triggers blaring like a child's tear-stained face.

Cal decided to wade into the conversational water with his little neighbor.

"Lovie, Mrs. Sherman said you took a wallop from your older brother. My little sister used to get into my stuff all the time and make me mad. Did you get into your brother's stuff?"

Lovie took a cookie and shifted a little closer to June.

"I did not. He gets mad all by himself and comes lookin' for me," she answered.

"Oh," said Cal, retreating from his investigation and grabbing a cookie for himself.

June took over. "Lovie, does your daddy work late a lot?"

"No. But sometimes. Chase gets mad when he does. But Chase can make eggs and toast or spaghetti for us. Once, Dad had pizza sent to our house. Just one time. It costs a lot."

They were all still on their first cookie when Cal noticed Chase looking out the window at them. He motioned for him to join them. Chase saw the cookies in their hands and ventured out. Lovie moved another inch closer to June.

"Hey buddy, we got cookies. Want some?" Cal offered.

Chase reached wordlessly toward the plate, over his sister's shoulder, and picked up three cookies in his hand.

"We're Mr. and Mrs. Sherman, your neighbors next door. Do you want to sit here and visit with us? We're just getting to know your little sister," he followed up.

Chase turned, went inside the house, and closed the door.

"Man of few words, I guess," muttered Cal.

"Daddy!" yelled Lovie as she jumped up and ran to the minivan pulling into their driveway.

Out of the silver minivan stepped a man who looked to be in his early 40s. He was taller than most, at least 6'2" but on the thin side. Cal sized him up. He thought the man could stand to put away a few bacon cheeseburgers and fries. June's first take was that his expression looked a little lost. Then she noted his sandy hair, green eyes, and fair complexion dotted with freckles. His daughter favored him, she thought.

He scooped up Lovie in his arms and headed toward the strangers picnicking on the steps of his house.

"Daddy, this is my friend, Mrs. Sherman. She lives next door and made cookies. Chase hit me again."

The man's expression turned from smiling to weary with the last revelation. Then, as Cal and June stepped forward to meet him, he put Lovie down and held out his hand to Cal.

"Micah Norman, pleased to meet you," he said, replacing the smile on his face.

"Cal Sherman. And this is my wife, June," he replied as they both extended their hands, in turn, to shake Micah's.

"We're your neighbors next door," June reiterated, pointing toward their house. "Well, we're part of the contingent, anyway. I met your daughter last week. She came over this evening, but I thought it best to visit outside on your porch since she said you weren't home and she couldn't have gotten permission to be at ours. She mentioned a bit of a fuss with her brother."

Micah hung his head. "Lovie, please sit on the porch and wait for me there."

The little girl did as her father asked and procured another cookie from the plate as she sat down.

"Thank you for being so kind to her. My wife – their mother - passed in a car accident a little over two months ago," he explained.

June gasped involuntarily. "I had no idea it was so recent when Lovie told me! I'm so sorry for your loss."

Cal nodded in agreement.

"We're trying to find our new normal, but we're all still grieving differently. My son, Chase, is very angry. He's lashed out at his little sister before, and I've warned him about it. But he blames her for their mom's death.

My wife, Dahlia, was driving to the grocery store to get Lovie's favorite stuffed bear she had dropped when they were there earlier in the day. I was home, so she left the kids with me and went by herself. They said an aneurysm burst in her head. She ran off the road and hit a tree. Died instantly. It wasn't Lovie's fault, but Chase doesn't know who to blame.

My sister came to stay for the first two weeks, and then I had to go back to work. There are two hours between when they get home from school and I get home from work. But then there are days like this, maybe once every other week, that I have to work late. If there's trouble, that's usually when it happens. I asked them about getting someone to come in after school, but Chase threw an absolute fit over the idea. He said no one would replace his mom. He's old enough to look after Lovie but not settled emotionally enough. I feel damned if I do and damned if I don't."

June felt no conflict about what Micah should do, but she knew better than to blurt it out. So instead, she offered sympathy and an invitation.

"That's completely understandable in such circumstances. I have an idea! Tomorrow's Friday. Would you and your children be available for supper at our house? Then you could meet the rest of your next-door neighbors, and so could Lovie and Chase. It might be helpful for you to have another set – or seven sets – of eyes around when you're at work. We're all grandma and grandpa age and love kids, but you should still do your due diligence and check us out," she added a laugh at the end of her offer to add lightness to the heavy circumstances.

Micah hesitated and glanced Lovie's way. She was happily devouring who-knows-what-number cookie.

"Um, Okay. That would be nice, I guess – something different for the kids," Micah gradually decided. "I'll be home at 5:30 if that's not too late."

"Five-thirty is perfect," agreed Cal, who readily sacrificed his negotiated 5 o'clock dinner schedule.

# Chapter Twenty

The doorbell rang at 5:35 pm. Cal and June greeted their neighbors at the front door and welcomed them inside. Lovie was wearing a blue Cinderella-princess dress and a plastic silver tiara on her head. Her blond hair was askew from the school day and several repositionings of the tiara. Chase wore blue jeans, a green t-shirt with an image of the Incredible Hulk, and a scowl on his face. Micah wore his business-casual work clothes: navy Dockers and a grey/navy striped golf shirt.

"Welcome to our home," June said as she ushered them in.

"Hello again," said Cal as he extended his hand to shake Micah's.

"I'm so delighted to see we have royalty joining us for dinner," June remarked to Lovie with a warm smile. Lovie moved to June's side and placed her small hand in June's.

"We're just about to get dinner on the table. So let's go in the dining room so you can meet everyone else before we eat," said June, who led the way, walking hand-in-hand with Lovie.

"Everyone," she announced to her friends, "these are our neighbors, Micah Norman, Chase, and Lovie." Then, she introduced each member of the household in turn.

Grant identified the Marvel character on Chase's shirt. He approached the boy, flexed his shoulders, and growled, "Hulk, SMASH!"

Chase laughed contemptuously at the older man, though Grant didn't recognize it as such. He thought his effort genuinely connected with the boy.

Micah jumped in. "It smells amazing in here!"

"June is a wonderful cook, and we hope you'll enjoy more meals with us in time to come," said Marie. "She's made one of her specialties tonight, lasagna."

Chase's countenance brightened. He loved lasagna and hadn't had it since his mom passed.

"That's one of our favorite meals," Micah replied with genuine gratitude.

Marie guided the guests to the added chairs around the dining room table while June and Elodie brought in salad, lasagna, and toasted garlic bread. The small guest's eyes widened at the sight of the garlic toast.

"Everyone, eat up! There's another pan of lasagna in the kitchen. But save room for chocolate cake," June advised.

Chase and Lovie looked at each other at the mention of chocolate cake. They were amazed that Mrs. Sherman had made all their favorite foods. How did she possibly know what they were?

For her part, June had never known a child not to like pasta, garlic toast, or chocolate cake. She'd been to a lifetime of church suppers and seen these items regularly set upon by children like pack wolves. So, it was a can't-miss menu from the get-go.

"We give thanks before we eat. Will you join us?" Cal invited his guests.

"Um, sure. By all means," Micah replied as he folded his hands and indicated to his children they do likewise as Cal began to pray.

*"Gracious God, we thank You for your watch care over us this day and for this food provided. Bless it to the nourishment of our bodies. And bless our guests around this table this evening. May they enjoy friendship and fellowship in this home. We ask this in Jesus' name. Amen."*

Chase hadn't expected to like the "old people's food." In truth, he didn't want to enjoy it; but he jettisoned his obstinacy for the satisfaction of his palate, eating his food with enthusiastic abandon. But perhaps, a tad too much abandon. When he reached for his second piece of garlic toast, his knuckles knocked over his untouched water glass and emptied it on the table. His previous too-cool-for-school demeanor gave way to abject mortification. He looked to his father with pleading eyes that said both "I'm sorry" and "Help me!"

Before Micah could gather the napkin on his lap to assist his son, Marcus reached for the salt shaker and spilled his water glass. It drew every eye his way.

"Really, Marcus! Monkey see, monkey do? Children are expected to have a spill, but you're a grown man," Ava scolded her husband as he would expect her to do for the boy's sake.

"Sorry," he apologized. "It's only water, right, Chase?"

Chase returned a grateful smile.

Ava, Marie, Elodie, and Grant cleaned up Marcus' spill while June quietly wiped up Chase's.

"I didn't spill, Mrs. Sherman," chirped Lovie.

"Not so far. But there's always next time," June said with a smile, yet tamping down the little show of pride in her young friend. She briefly touched Chase's shoulder as she walked around his chair to reach for another napkin on the buffet. It was two seconds of connection. Two seconds of kindness and affection. Chase subconsciously let out the slightest sigh, and a touch of heart-heaviness left with the air he exhaled.

"Would our guests like to step outside for a game of cornhole while da ladies clear da table and set out dat chocolate cake?" asked Marcus.

"Ha! I haven't played cornhole in forever. I don't think the kids have ever played," answered Micah. "Come on, kids. You'll like this," he encouraged.

The men led their guests to the backyard, where the cornhole game had been set out just beyond the garden. Marcus got them organized.

He explained to Chase and Lovie, "We play wit two-person teams, and we have enough for tree teams here. I propose each team must have players from both households and da teams wit a child on dem play each other first. Den da winner of dat round plays da team wit dere dad. I further propose dat my teammate is Chase. No one can argue. I've called first dibs on him."

"My teammate is Lovie," Grant said quickly. "Guess that means you've got Dad, Cal."

Marcus offered the young players a quick explanation of the fundamental objective and rules. But, unfortunately, his description was met with quizzical expressions that indicated less than complete comprehension.

Micah simply added, "I'll keep score. You guys just try to throw your bean bag in the hole, ok?"

"Ok," they responded with nods and went to their places next to their teammates.

"Let da games begin!" Marcus intoned with an official voice.

Chase threw his first bag directly into the middle of the hole he'd aimed for. It didn't even skim or slide.

"Are you sure you've never played dis game?" asked Marcus in amazement. "Maybe you should be teaching me!" He offered his teammate his fist, which was met with a grin and a bump.

Lovie threw her first bag, hitting her father in the head. He was standing behind her.

Marcus and Grant's first throws landed on the board, but Grant's fell off.

On Chase's second throw, his bag landed half in and half out of the hole.

"I'm thinking about quitting right now," Grant moaned. "You've got a ringer!"

Chase beamed.

Lovie's second throw went forward, which was progress. But it landed about four feet short of the board. And, about that much to the left as well.

Marcus knocked Chase's hanging bag into the hole on his next throw. Grant's next bag flew over the board entirely.

Nobody's play degraded or improved much through the remainder of the game. It was a short match. Marcus and Chase moved on to play Cal and Micah. Finished clearing the dishes, June, Marie, Elodie, and Ava came out to watch. They brought three large quilts with them for the spectators to sit on. Lovie plopped herself in June's lap and adjusted her tiara.

The contestants took their positions.

Micah told his son, "Boy, you have a hidden talent for throwing bean-bags in a hole. But you haven't seen what your old Dad can do with a beanbag!"

Cal's eyebrows shot up on his face in surprise and expectation. He'd thought they were doomed, and hoped Micah was more than trash-talking. They were playing against a child, but Cal was still in it to win it.

Chase threw first and landed on the board very close to the hole. Micah threw next, and it was an ace – straight down the hole. He gave his son a sideways look with raised eyebrows and a grin that wordlessly said, "That's right. I did that."

Marcus threw his bag, and it slid into the hole. "Doesn't matter how it gets in long as it gets in," he said. Then he turned to Chase and whispered, "We're not scared, right?"

"Right!" the boy whispered back. And he beamed some more.

Cal threw his first bag and missed the board by just an inch. "Little rusty," he muttered to Micah.

Chase threw his second shot, and it slid off the board. He stopped beaming and frowned.

"Dat's ok," encouraged Marcus. "Happens."

Micah followed his first with a second ace. Marcus aced his second throw as well.

"Calculus, you put that beanbag where it belongs!" Elodie cheered as Cal stepped up to throw his turn.

If there were balking in cornhole, it would have been called. Cal had to step back and regroup. He threw Elodie a side-eyed glare, making her and the other women laugh.

"If you don't mind, ladies," he scolded them. "This is a serious competition."

The women did their best to temper their behavior with sobriety.

"Cal is short for Calculus?" Micah asked, trying to hide his amusement. "Was your mother a math teacher?"

"My given name is Calvert. But, for reasons known only to the voices in her head, Miss Elodie calls me everything but Calvert or Cal."

Cal threw his bag, and it missed the board by a lot.

"My sister can do better than that!" Chase taunted gleefully.

"Hey, partner, dat was harsh," Marcus admonished in a whisper.

Chase hung his head. "I'm sorry, Mr. Sherman. I shouldn't have said that," he apologized. Then, Chase looked to his dad, who gave him a thumbs up.

"I forgive you, son," Cal responded. "You're up next."

Chase threw his beanbag, and it slid off a second time. "Stink!" he said, slapping his leg.

Micah ended his tiny streak of aces with a bag that landed just next to the hole. Marcus' next throw teetered on the board's edge and fell off.

"That's ok. It happens," consoled his young teammate. Marcus smiled down at him.

Cal decided he needed more muscle on his throw and pitched his bag with extra oomph. It didn't go in, but it did knock Micah's edge-sitting bag in, turning that one point into three.

"Great throw, dear!" June hollered.

"Cal has cheerleaders," observed Marcus.

"I'm the only one who needs them," replied Cal, laughing at himself.

After a few misses on the board, Chase found his game and his beaming smile again. He and Marcus didn't win, but it was a respectably close game against Mr. Sherman and his Dad - 18 to 21.

They finished just as the sun's evening rays were fading. Then, finally, everyone returned to their seats at the dining room table and enjoyed a piece of June's chocolate cake with a glass of milk.

At 8:30, Micah noted his daughter had already yawned twice. He thanked his neighbors for their hospitality and said he'd better get his sleepy girl home to bed before she dropped right there. Everyone exchanged "Good night." Micah carried Lovie home in his arms. Her head rested on his shoulder with the tiara perched at a precarious angle. Chase had energy to spare and ran rabbit trails before arriving at their front door. Micah wondered if letting him have sugar so late was a mistake. But the boy was more engaged and animated than he'd been in the weeks since they'd lost Dahlia. Naturally, what made Chase happy made him happy too. No, Micah decided, it wasn't a mistake. It was medicine.

# Chapter Twenty-One

The bedroom was quiet except for the sound of Marcus' haphazard snoring. He wove a discordant melody of heavy breaths, throaty exhales, lip puffs, snorts, and occasional coughs. Every night of their marriage had been a new verse of the same song. Fortunately, it had become white noise to Ava. It did not bother her the way Marie admitted she was bothered by Grant's nocturnal serenade and who had invested, over the years, in all manner of gadgets meant to curb it. These included a gadget worn on the wrist that would give a light shock to the wearer when it detected snoring. But, like all previously tried methods, it failed. There wasn't a setting high enough to wake Grant from his dormancy. Marie swore Ava to testify in her defense if she ever smothered Grant in his sleep, and Ava worried her friend was a tiny bit serious.

Tonight, Ava lay on her back next to Marcus, intentionally listening to the sounds he made while silent tears ran down the sides of her head and into her ears. She was learning to control her crying and not let it run amok until it descended into heaving sobs that Marcus expected himself to calm. Ava figured out he couldn't be her rock during the day if he couldn't sleep at night. So she must give him that.

She sat up a little to dab at her eyes and ears and looked around their room. It was illuminated by a nearly full moon shining in one window through blinds she'd intentionally left open. The light was weak enough to muddy the light green walls into a shade of gray but good enough to identify every object in the room.

Across from her, between the room's two windows on the far wall, was the old mirrored chifforobe that cost them nothing but the fortune they paid to ship it from Marcus' parents' home in Aruba to their parsonage in Bloomington. Her mother-in-law offered it to them on a visit to her island home, recalling how 2-year-old Marcus could be persuaded to nap if she convinced him the lower section was a fort, not a blanket chest. The sentimental trap was set, and Marcus took the bait. He insisted he recalled sleeping in the piece and had to have it, so now it resided with them.

The nightstands on either side of their bed came from the estate sale of a woman who'd been a member of their Delaware Street Community Church for 65 years. They were art deco waterfall-edged beauties with single drawers and large, ornate brass handles. The handles were inset with white and orange variegated Bakelite made to resemble a scalloped shell, which also reminded Marcus of his island homeland. They'd only paid $30 for the pair, and Ava decorated their room to highlight the seashell motif they both loved.

Their bed was a recent upgrade when they moved into this home. With the retirement love-gift the church gave Marcus, they purchased a badly needed new foam mattress set and the first headboard they'd ever owned. Ava selected a tufted headboard upholstered in a textured linen fabric that resembled burlap. There was enough left over from the gift to buy two sets of drapes for the windows and a large painting from a national-chain decor store for an empty wall. The picture was a modern, abstract piece with shades of green, cream, gold, and just-the-right touch of muted orange that matched the nightstand shells.

The bedding was not brand new, but nearly so. The sheets, 750 thread count white cotton, had an 'MVA' monogram in tan silk on the top sheet and on each pillowcase. They'd been a gift from Marley just two Christmases ago. The comforter was smooth cotton, unquilted except for a single flange. It was just a shade darker than the headboard and separated from it by two Euro pillows in soft coral orange. A hope chest, given to Ava as a high school graduation present from her grandparents, did double duty at the end of the bed as a bench.

The new bed, drapes, and artwork made this the prettiest bedroom Ava had ever slept in. Anywhere. She was so thankful for it. She tried to remind herself, as Marcus had tried, that she still a lot to be grateful for.

But the unrelenting cruelty of Marit and Mia, who refused to converse with their parents about their grievances, was an Excalibur sword firmly fixed through her heart. She was shocked her girls were capable of such brutal callousness, much less that they would aim it at their parents. She was angry at herself for her own failures. Ava was jealous of Marcus, who could handle it much better than she could. She was troubled that she couldn't tell if the vengeful thoughts that came to her were arrows of the Enemy or the impulses of her own heart. Most of all, she was frustrated that she couldn't stop the obsessive thinking about it all, though she desperately wanted to.

She prayed for God's peace, but her prayers seemed to stick to her bedroom ceiling and went unanswered. The only respite she found was in sleep, but too often, it eluded her. She tried to help herself with over-the-counter sleep aids, herbal relaxers, and melatonin. Tonight, she was at the end of her tolerance for herself. She opened her nightstand drawer, found the small bottle of generic sleep aid, and washed down a handful of the pills with a sip from her nightstand water glass. She didn't care if she slept through the next day or never woke up. It still took an hour, but she finally fell asleep.

She woke up at 7 am the following day as usual. Her first thought was of the missing pieces of her life.

# Chapter Twenty-Two

"Good mornin', Calamity. Good mornin', Marcus." Elodie greeted the guys as she joined them in the kitchen. She wore a roomy gold linen dress, over which she donned a cross-back, purple-flowered apron she retrieved from a cabinet drawer. It was her day to cook supper, and she wanted to get the chicken thawing and the coleslaw made so it could sit awhile before she served it. Because of course, nobody should eat just-made coleslaw. She took the family-size package of drumsticks out of the freezer and set it on the counter, where she discovered an open box of donuts. She helped herself to a cream-filled Long John.

"Where'd these come from?" she asked, taking a seat at the breakfast table.

"Grant picked dem up after he took Marie to da airport at dawn o'clock dis morning," answered Marcus.

"God bless, Grant," she praised, sinking her teeth into the donut.

"He's going to bless you right back when he sees you're making your amazing fried chicken tonight."

Elodie smiled. It was a lot more work cooking for six housemates than just for herself. But she considered it no bother to contribute a skill that was appreciated – not just by Grant but by everyone in the house. Furthermore, being in a rotation schedule with Ava and June for meal preparation spurred her to locate the single competitive bone she had in her body. She wanted to take her cooking game to a new level.

While June and Ava had honed their culinary skills from cookbooks collected over the years, Elodie seemed to be a natural cook – like she'd teethed on a spatula, as Marie once remarked. She just put ingredients together and made deliciousness.

In reality, Elodie had handwritten recipes on yellowed and stained 3" X 5" cards that she kept in a tin recipe box in her nightstand. Most of these were handed down from her grandmother and mother, which she had memorized long ago. She had some standout gems, to be sure. These included her crab cakes, spare ribs, potato salad, banana cream pie, corn casserole, and fried chicken. Naturally, the household was especially delighted when she made her potato salad and fried chicken. But she needed to expand her repertoire.

One night, when everyone had gone to bed, Elodie crept down to the library like a teenager coming home after curfew. She closed the door, felt for the light, switched it on, and sat on the floor in front of the lower bookshelves containing June and Ava's cookbooks. Elodie looked through several of them before settling on one written by a celebrity chef with a tv show on the Food Network. She tucked it under her arm, turned off the light, and scurried back to her room with her "borrowed" booty.

Tonight, not only would they devour Elodie's fried chicken, but they'd enjoy the best coleslaw they'd ever put in their mouths thanks to the pirated cookbook no one suspected she'd consulted.

As she started gathering ingredients for the slaw, Marcus and Cal finished their coffee and donuts and took their leave of the breakfast table. They headed outside as Grant, marching through the kitchen, followed them.

The guys headed to the Tamarack Street garage, as they'd come to refer to the second garage, utilized initially by the Rennigers and Van Zants for housing their vehicles. But it had become something of a man cave. Grant and Marcus would back their cars into the driveway, which opened up space to set up canvas outdoor folding chairs and, sometimes, a folding table if they wanted to play dominoes, cards, or a dice game.

Today, Marcus and Grant were "supervising" Cal as he worked on a project at the workbench set up in a corner. He was making a 3-drawer, dresser-top jewelry box for June's birthday. Unfortunately, neither Marcus nor Grant had any expertise to offer Cal, a talented woodworker and craftsman. Their "supervising" consisted mainly of distracting Cal with their chatter while he was making measurements or cuts with the band saw. It took him twice as long to make progress on the project than if he'd been left to himself, but Cal didn't mind. He'd come to love Grant like a brother over their shared years in Michigan, and Marcus was growing on him.

Cal sat with the guys while he sanded drawer fronts by hand. They discussed last evening's dinner with the Norman family and their hopes for future opportunities to bless Micah, Chase, and Lovie and share the gospel with them.

"Makes no eternal impact to feed or entertain dem or even to soothe dere pain. All dat's good, but temporary. Dey need Jesus for dis life and da life to come," Marcus reasoned to the nodding heads of his friends.

"Look at that!" Cal interrupted, pointing with his sanding block to something behind Grant.

A cat with a face half black and half tan walked into the open garage like it expected to be as welcome as a hundred-dollar bill that blew in. However, Grant was allergic to cat hair and dander and was not about to roll out the red carpet to this animal. Nevertheless, he didn't move to shoo it away since both garage doors were wide open, and it wasn't like any of them would try to pet it.

"God's creation sure has some strange to it," Cal said, intrigued by the striking critter. He reached down to beckon it toward his hand so he could pet it.

Grant rolled his eyes and scooted his chair farther away from Cal. Fortunately, the cat had the good sense to ignore Cal and keep moving. It made a wide circle through the garage to survey the contents and walked back out, never altering its casual pace.

"Did you see da name on its collar?" asked Marcus. "It said 'Rover.'

"Who in their right mind names a cat 'Rover'?" laughed Grant.

"Well, I mighta had a beer or two under my belt when I came up with it," said the man standing right outside their garage, who they hadn't noticed for watching the cat. He was holding a familiar plate in his hand.

Grant and Marcus jumped to their feet, and Cal followed as quickly as he could with achy knees.

"I'm sooo sssorry," stammered Grant. "I didn't realize..." he abandoned elaboration.

Marcus took over for his friend and met the situation head-on. "A beer or two can cloud a man's good judgment. But we'll never forget your cat's name. I'm Marcus," he smiled and held out his hand.

"Bobby McBride. I'm your neighbor across the street," he said, accepting the outstretched hand and jutting his chin toward the yellow house across Tamarack Street. "

"Dis is Cal, and dis is Grant, who also may not be in his right mind at da moment," Marcus laughed at his friend's expense.

Bobby shook Cal's hand and then Grant's, saying, "A man can say anything in the privacy of his own garage. I didn't mean to sneak up on you. Sorry about that."

Grant gave him a relieved smile.

"I was headed to your house to return this plate that Miss June and Ms. Elodie brought over. But then I saw you all in the garage and thought I'd come on this way instead since I'd already met the ladies." He handed the plate to Marcus. "Had a pound cake on it when they gave it to me. Had to wrap up half and put it in the freezer before I ate it all in a single day. Sure was good!"

"June can make a pound cake better than Timex can make watches. She's my wife," Cal beamed with pride.

"What are you making there?" Bobby asked, noting the wood and sanding block in Cal's hand.

"Jewelry box for June's birthday."

"Oh, when's her birthday?"

"August 4th," Cal answered with a straight face, thanks to years of practice. Then, after a second, he corrected, "No, just kiddin', June 4th. I only got a couple of weeks left to get this finished."

"Well, I'll let you get to it. Just wanted to introduce myself and return the plate," Bobby turned to go.

"Hey, do you play cards or dominoes?" asked Marcus without pausing for an answer. "Dat's usually how we entertain ourselves on Friday evenings here in da garage while our ladies have dere little hen party in da house. We welcome you to join us since dere are four places at da table and only tree of us. We need to find anoder man because Grant's wife, Marie, treatens to come out here and play wit us. She's cut-troat and zero fun."

Bobby laughed. "Well, it's been a while since I've played any games, and I might be rusty on the rules, but if you're willing to refresh me, I could join you. Yeah, I'll be here Friday evening. I'll just watch for the garage doors to come up." Bobby turned to go. "See ya later."

He walked across the street and through his back kitchen door, smiling that big smile to himself while his back was turned from his neighbors. He was thankful for the invitation. The time was right for him to be social again. He knew many people in Faircourt, having been born and raised here, but he'd withdrawn after all the drama with his son, DeShawn. When his wife passed two years later, he never looked for company. The isolation served as insulation.

But in the long months between his trips to Florida to visit his daughter's family each holiday season or Spring, he'd begun to feel differently about keeping so much to himself. He was coming to terms with acknowledging his loneliness and the approach of his seventieth birthday. Hanging out once a week to play games with guys who didn't know his business was a tolerable way to stick his toe in the social waters again. Best of all, he figured guys don't care to be up in one another's business. At least, that was his experience.

# Chapter Twenty-Three

"Where ya'll goin' all dressed up?" Lovie wanted to know. She was sitting on her porch steps petting Rover when the Van Zants, Grant, and Elodie walked by her house on their way to Grace Fellowship Church.

They all stopped, and Marcus answered, "We're going to church. Have you ever been to church?"

"Yes!" Lovie answered triumphantly. "I was a flower girl at a wedding once, and it was at a big church." She noticed her special friend was not among them and asked, "Why don't Mrs. Sherman and her husband go to church too?"

"Oh, they'll be along, but they drive to church," explained Ava with a friendly smile.

"Your daddy know you're outside this early?" Elodie inquired. She saw the van in the driveway but wanted to ensure Micah knew his young daughter's whereabouts.

"Yup. He's in the kitchen making us pancakes like always on Sundays. Momma used to do it."

"Ok then." Elodie was satisfied, and the group continued on their way.

This week the friends would try out a Sunday School class in addition to the church service. They did not, however, want to be a contingent that would appreciably change the dynamic of an existing class. So, they decided the men would go to a men's class and the women to a class for women.

A woman with a name badge that said "Sarah" was working at the Visitor Center desk in the vestibule. She directed the ladies to a room directly behind her desk where the senior women's Sunday School class met. She flagged down a deacon to escort the guys to the men's Sunday School class. He explained it was a multi-generational group – open to men over 25. Marcus liked the sound of that. Grant and Cal were apprehensive but willing to try it out.

They sat in a row of chairs arranged in a large semicircle, joining eight men already settled there, who informed the newcomers that the teacher was making copies of handouts in the office and would return shortly. When the man walked in clutching a handful of pages, the guys looked at each other in surprise. The men's Sunday School class leader at Grace Fellowship Church was their mailman, Will.

"Welcome to the men's class!" Will greeted them, equally surprised to see these men in his class. He reached to shake Marcus', Cal, and Grant's hands in turn. "Guys," he continued, addressing the rest of the class, "these gentlemen are newcomers to our community. This is Marcus Van Zant, Calvert Sherman, and Grant Renniger. Did I get that right?"

"Spot on!" answered Grant, impressed.

Will handed out the sheets he'd made for the lesson, which included three Wuest's Word Studies from the Greek text, a definition from Lexham's Bible Dictionary, two notes from Metzger's Textual Criticism, and three recommended commentaries for further study. Marcus took one look and was giddy. The mailman didn't come to Sunday School to play; he came to teach.

Unsurprisingly, Marcus, the former pastor and lifelong theology nerd, loved the lesson. But so did Cal and Grant, who were amazed that Will's scholarly approach was also accessible and thought-provoking. Both assumed scholarly and accessible didn't coexist.

When the other men left the classroom to make their way to the sanctuary for the worship service, Marcus hung back.

"You teach a mean Sunday School lesson, and by 'mean,' I mean excellent," Marcus congratulated Will sincerely. "Did you go to seminary?" he jested.

"Trinity for my M. Div," responded Will in all seriousness, "and Southern for my Ph.D.

Marcus was stunned. "Can I ask?" he requested inquisitively.

"What's a nice guy like me doing on a mail route?" Will guessed.

"Yeah."

"Spent too much time in the classroom and not enough time with my family. My wife left me for someone she met online, and my career in ministry ended before it began. She lives with her new husband across town, and we share custody of our two boys. The post office pays most of the bills and has decent medical benefits. I do some online tutoring and research assisting to fill the gaps. God's been good."

"You know," Marcus responded, tapping an index finger on Will's chest, "all da while you were teaching, I kept trying to put my finger on what made your teaching so engaging to not only me but, as I observed, to da whole class. And now I know what it was: autentic humility. Nobody learns dat in a seminary classroom. You learned it by da severe mercy of your trial." Marcus then put a paternal hand on Will's shoulder, "Son, today I saw the fruit of your heartbreak. Know dat it wasn't wasted. I saw some refined gold gleaming dis morning."

"Soli Deo Gloria," Will croaked through a throat constricted with emotion over all he'd lost and what Marcus acknowledged he'd gained.

"Soli Deo Gloria," Marcus repeated, clapping Will on the back. They walked to the sanctuary together.

Marcus slid into the pew his friends occupied and didn't see his wife. He supposed she'd stopped in the ladies' room. When she didn't join them after the opening hymn started, he reached around Grant's shoulder and tapped Elodie on hers.

"Where's Ava?" he whispered across Grant.

"She went home. I thought she texted you. Sunday School class upset her. It was on motherhood. She was cryin'." Elodie whispered back.

Marcus hurried out of the church and down the three blocks to their home. Coming through the front door, he called, "Ava!" and heard no reply. He walked through the central hall, poking his head into the study, the living room, and the kitchen. He didn't find her. Finally, he climbed the stairs calling, "Ava!"

He opened their bedroom door and saw her sitting on the floor in front of the chifforobe, looking at herself in the mirrored door. In her hand, she held a pair of scissors. Her dress, shoes, and substantial chunks of red hair were scattered on the floor beside her.

"I did something," she said in a low voice.

"I can see dat," Marcus responded, walking over and sitting beside her.

"It felt good," Ava stated matter-of-factly. Her eyes were dry, but previous tears had drawn mascara streaks down her cheeks.

"Tell me about it."

"I might look a wreck, but I was in control. Nobody was doing this to me. I did this. Maybe it seems crazy, but it felt so satisfying, so empowering. Please don't be mad."

"I'm not mad. Since when have you ever asked my opinion about what you did wit your hair?" he asked with a playful smile.

She responded to him with a smile of her own - a spontaneous, genuine smile.

"I tink I can understand what you said about feeling good to have some control," he said as he shifted behind her to look over her shoulder into the mirror. Then, he wrapped his arms around her and asked, "How do you want to explain your sudden new look to da oders?"

"Marcus, I know they know."

"Now I'll ask you not to be mad at me. I had a tough patch too," he admitted.

"Tell me about it," Ava parroted his previous words with warmth.

"I got scared. You scare me sometimes. I know da grief is over your head. I've seen dis before – wit oder people in my ministry – but you're my wife. I have so much more at risk wit you. I freaked out a little, and our friends saw it. It's ok; Ava, dey love you."

"I'm sorry." Ava lowered her head and looked at him through her eyelashes. "I want to tell you not to be scared, but I can't when I'm scared too. I feel like I'm in the grip of something, Marcus. It has a hold of me and not the other way around. I've never experienced this before, and I feel powerless, and that's scary. But I do know this: both it – whatever it is – and I are in God's hands. He has us both. Unfortunately, that doesn't translate into feeling better. But I know it the same way I know two plus two equals four. It's a fact. Just a cold fact..." her voice trailed off.

"Okay," Marcus began talking before thinking about what to say. "It's okay. Our faith isn't based on our feelings. We have da unmovable bedrock of Scriptural truth beneat our feelings. You have dat to stand on – or be dragged across, as da case may be. We bot have dat."

Ava raised her head and looked in the mirror. She saw that Marcus' eyes had filled, and she felt for him. Ava was grateful to the God she knew was there but couldn't feel, that He'd given Marcus to her—such a good man. She picked at a few short locks on her head.

"Guess I'm not much of a hairdresser. This has absolutely no style to it. Do you think you could help me?" she asked.

Marcus retrieved his phone from his back pocket and spent 15 minutes watching how-to-cut-hair videos with his wife. He spent the next 10 minutes trimming her short locks into a decent pixie cut. Afterward, they vacuumed up the hair from the carpet and changed into casual clothes. They would go down to the kitchen to warm canned soup and make grilled ham and cheese sandwiches for their friends, who would be returning from church shortly.

Before they left the room, Marcus took Ava's hand and led her back to the chifforobe mirror to face it. He stood behind her right shoulder, wrapped his arms around her, and whispered a word: "Beautiful."

# CHAPTER TWENTY-FOUR

There were only two law offices in Faircourt. A village just shy of 4,500 didn't need more than that. Since the letter addressed to the Faircourt Friends Trust came from Luther Hall, Esq., Grant and Marcus called the other one: Joseph Robert Jacobs.

"He answered the phone himself," Grant complained to Marcus as they walked to Grant's Camry parked in the Tamarack St. garage. "Just don't have a good feeling about a lawyer who answers his own phone and says we can come right down to his office. Not much choice, though, unless we want a big-city Louisville lawyer. Joseph. Robert. Jacobs." Grant said the name slowly. "I'll tell you one thing: if he says we can call him 'Joe Bob,' we need to get out of there."

"Sometimes, you are too much, Grant," said Marcus, shaking his head. "Got your mind made up before we step foot in his office."

"They're all clues. I prepare by reading the clues, and I like to be comfortable with the clues' directions. How do you prepare?"

"I reserve my judgment until all da available facts are presented."

"In other words, you're not prepared. That's how people die, Marcus."

"What? We're going to a lawyer's office, not a drug den! Nobody's going to die."

"Says the man who God consulted about who would die today."

Marcus put his hands up in surrender. "Okay, Grant, you win. You get da last word on judging me for judging you for judging Joe Bob."

They chuckled at themselves and drove to the attorney's Main Street office with one of Grant's many Gaither CDs playing on low volume in the background. Their verbal sparring released some of the tension they both felt about the purpose of their errand. If there were any possibility they'd have to leave the home, neighbors, and church they were beginning to love, it would be a devastating blow for all of them. Promptly, they pulled up in front of the address where Grant's phone GPS directed them.

"You have arrived at your destination. The automatic guidance system will now turn off," said the friendly female bot.

"I can't believe you used GPS to go seven blocks," Marcus resumed the sparring.

"I believe what you meant to say was, 'I can't believe you got us to the right Main Street building without passing it twice because the numbers above the doors are too small to read.' You probably didn't realize you said it wrong," retorted Grant.

He turned off the ignition button and unbuckled his seatbelt. And then he said with seriousness, "We should probably pray, don't you think?"

"Agreed," replied Marcus.

They bowed their heads, and Marcus asked God to give them grace to faithfully represent Christ in their endeavor, for favor and justice in their domestic situation, and for faith to accept His will if it should conflict with theirs.

They walked up a flight of stairs to an office above Flour and Flake Bakery, a new Main Street establishment that recently replaced La Petite Champignon – a fine dining restaurant that would have done better in Louisville. They opened a half-lite wooden door at the top of the stairs with a semi-circle stencil of "Joseph Robert Jacobs" and underneath, "Attorney At Law" on the frosted glass.

"Hello, Grant Renniger?" the attorney greeted them, unsure which one was Grant.

"I'm Grant," he said, extending his hand. "And this is my friend, Marcus Van Zant."

"Pleased to meet you both; I'm Joe. Let's go back to my office and talk."

He was a young man, just about 40, judging from the few flecks of gray in his dark hair and trim beard. He was dressed business casual in a light blue golf shirt, navy Dockers, and polished cordovan loafers. Joe wore a fancy gold watch and a plain gold wedding band. And to Grant's dismay, he offered neither explanation nor apology for the absence of office personnel.

He led them across the reception area, which had two large black-framed windows that overlooked Main Street at the second-story level, where a hanging planter, filled with a colorful assortment of pansies, hung on the light pole outside. Below the windows sat four modern, black, and chrome chairs. Across from these was a black reception desk for the apparently, non-existent receptionist. All these sat on a large area rug of black and white speckled industrial carpet, which covered all but a two-foot border of a walnut-stained wood floor. A row of white metal filing cabinets on the far wall blended in with the room's clean white paint. The walls were adorned with a half-dozen black-framed, graffiti-motif prints in a riot of vibrant colors. A six-foot artificial olive tree in a far corner gave the room some artificial life.

They passed a large conference room, and a glance in suggested the same decorating scheme as the reception area – lots of black and white with splashes of bright color that baited the eyes and reeled them in.

The first two rooms looked professional but cold to Grant, who was continuing his assessment of clues. Joe's office was pleasantly calm. The walls were still white but a noticeably softer shade. The wall opposite the door was fitted with floor-to-ceiling black-painted bookcases filled with law books, family pictures including a pretty blonde woman with two young children, and a smattering of bric-a-brac: a small collection of smoking pipes, a random fishing reel next to an arrangement of lures on a plaque, a commemorative bottle of bourbon, and a harmonica. Joe's desk was a large antique, which Grant figured weighed a ton even before the lawyer covered it with stacks of papers and books. Behind the desk was a black credenza with piles of files, a coffee pot, and several mismatched coffee mugs, one of which said "World's Greatest Dad." Above the credenza hung two framed diplomas from Syracuse University.

"Have a seat, guys," Joe gestured to two red leather wingback chairs across from his desk.

"Here's the letter I told you about on the phone," said Grant, handing Joe the envelope that contained it.

"Ah, from my friend Luther Hall," said Joe in a tone meant to convey they were not exactly friends. He took the letter out, read it, and dropped it on his desk. "Just to be clear, you all are friends who went in on the house together for your retirement years, right?"

"Right," Grant and Marcus answered at once.

"And you're not providing health care services on the premises, running a gambling operation, or cooking meth, right?"

"Right," again came the synchronized answer.

"Do you suppose you'd have gotten this letter if you all were in your 30s instead of your 70s? No, you wouldn't," Joe, assuming their age, answered for them and continued. "Because people can go in together and buy real estate or other property, and your age doesn't matter. If someone wants to fling accusations that you're doing something you shouldn't, they have to prove it. Luther knows that. This letter is just bluster and meanness. So, who's mad at you?"

"We're not 100 percent sure, but we tink it's our neighbor across da street, Christine Williams. She didn't like us parking a truck in front of da house," Marcus replied.

Joe sat back in his chair and laughed. "Well, if Christine Williams is your neighbor, I'm 100 percent sure that's who's behind this. Luther is her brother, and this isn't the first time she's had him send a nasty-gram. Let's see; she's threatened the local grocery manager that the health department would close his store because her ice cream melted in the trunk of her car - *in July*. She threatened her podiatrist with a malpractice suit for missing a hangnail her pedicurist noticed. She even threatened her mailman with a trespass charge for walking across her lawn instead of staying on the sidewalk. You're the fourth or fifth victim she's sent seeking my services."

Marcus and Grant looked at each other in disbelief. "Will? Trespassing?" Marcus shook his head.

"Like the others, nothing will come of it," Joe reassured them. "She just wants to send the message not to cross her. It works for her because people steer a wide path around her after they get a letter from her brother. I'll respond to Luther with all the legal vernacular, and ole' Christine will be happy that she pushed you to see me. That's all there is to it. Consider the response letter my contribution to the community's well-being. Christine Williams is an unhappy menace."

"Tank you so much," Marcus breathed out with a heavy sigh as he rose to shake Joe's hand again. Then, he added thoughtfully, "Dey say 'hurting people hurt people.' I wonder what's causing her to be so malicious."

"From my experience, she won't thank you for trying to poke around that question. She's a biter!" Joe answered.

"We'll take that under advisement," said Grant, who also stood and offered his hand to Joe, delighted with the outcome of Joseph Robert Jacobs' services and his own vigilance.

"Welcome to Faircourt, gentlemen. I'm sure you'll like most of the rest of us. Bad luck about your neighbor, though," Joe said as he escorted them to the door. "Now, if you ever have any other legal needs, please keep me in mind."

"We certainly will," said Grant.

"I do have a question," Marcus paused with his hand on the door-knob.

Joe raised his eyebrows as the invitation to ask it.

"Does anyone call you 'Joe Bob'?"

"Not unless they want an elbow to the ribs or they're my Granny," Joe laughed.

# Chapter Twenty-Five

June was playing *Tis So Sweet To Trust In Jesus* in the living room while the others, save for Ava, who was sleeping in, and Marie, who was still in Atlanta, ate a late and leisurely breakfast of toasted bagel, fried egg, and cream cheese sandwiches prepared by Cal. Her song choice reflected the collective relief they all felt with the outcome of Grant and Marcus' meeting with Joe Jacobs. They were happy to put the threat behind them and give God thanks.

"It's a challenge to eat while she's playing that song," Grant remarked after swallowing a large bite of breakfast sandwich. "I just want to sing along."

"You should be careful about talking while you're eating. Dat's how people die, Grant," Marcus teased, using Grant's line. Grant frowned at him, forming creases in the corners of his dark eyes and across his forehead.

Elodie dabbed her mouth with a napkin and turned her attention away from the bickering boys. "These breakfast sandwiches are delicious, California!" she praised sincerely.

"It'll make a turd," Cal responded bluntly to the compliment, unthinking, as if she were one of the guys.

Elodie reminded him she was not one of the guys with a withering glare over the rim of her glasses. Cal grimaced at his lack of verbal decorum and the heat from Elodie's stare. He never got used to his mouth blurting the wrong thing, though it happened often enough.

"Don't you boys have somewhere to go or somethin' to do in your garage cave?" she asked.

"Ha! Garage cave! It's called a man cave," Grant corrected.

"Actually, I kind of like da term 'garage cave.' Lots of men have man caves, but who else has a garage cave? It's unique, like we are!" Marcus enthused.

"Whatever we call it, let's take the hint and give El her space," Grant said as he rose and put his plate and tea mug in the dishwasher he'd emptied earlier.

Marcus and Cal followed suit, and they all headed out the back door, trudging past the vegetable gardens and noting the corn seeds had sprouted as well as several weeds.

"We have our broder, Adam, to tank for dose weeds," lamented Marcus, waxing theological. He made a mental note to tell his wife the garden was calling for her attention, knowing the exercise and fresh air would help her sleep.

"But the bricks still look good!" said Grant, highlighting his single contribution to the garden project.

Marcus took his turn to frown at Grant. They reached the garage, and Cal punched in the code to open the overhead doors of the garage. He promptly went to work on June's jewelry box.

"Hey, Cal, do you have any wood scraps I might use? I just need one piece, maybe 4 inches by 16 inches," Marcus inquired, holding up index fingers indicating the required size.

"Look under the worktable on the left. There's a box with my small scraps in it."

"Tanks, man."

Marcus searched and found just what he wanted from the box. He then took a permanent marker from the tin can that served as a pencil holder on the worktable and hovered over his project for the next five minutes. Finally, when he was done, he held it up proudly. It read: "GARAGE CAVE" in thick lettering detailed with serifs.

"All it needs is a picture hanger and da perfect spot to hang it," he said.

"You could hang it over your fancy fishing rod holder," Grant suggested.

"I left dat rod holder on da wall in da parsonage garage back in Bloomington."

Grant flashed him a smile, showing all his teeth, and Marcus realized he'd walked into his joke.

"You guys do like each other, right?" Cal asked with laughter in the question he'd intended to be rhetorical. He'd been around long enough to observe their playfully hostile dynamic.

"Of course not!" Marcus answered emphatically.

"Don't be ridiculous. Only our wives like each other!" Grant insisted.

"We stay togeder for da sake of da women," Marcus added somberly in a quieter voice.

Then he and Grant looked at each other and burst out laughing.

"Cal, you and I've been friends for what, 15 years? Marcus and I have known each other for more than double that. So, see what you have to look forward to?" Grant explained.

"I've invested a lot in dis man over da years. Unfortunately, I've not gotten a big return on dat investment," Marcus said, taking up the explanation, "but we're broders at dis point despite my losses. I know if I kill someone in an unsanctified fit of rage, Grant is obligated to help me bury da body and take da secret to his grave."

"And vice versa," Grant said matter-of-factly.

Marcus walked over to Grant, and they spat in their hands and shook on it as a renewal ceremony of their macabre commitment.

"That's kind of disturbing, but I understand," Cal acknowledged before returning to his task.

"Oh, I meant to say something at breakfast," Grant said, "but Pastor

Jefferson texted me yesterday and asked if this evening would be a good time for him to stop by the house for a visit. So I told him to come on."

"Sorry, that doesn't work for me. I was planning to shampoo my hair this evening," short-shorn Cal complained without looking up from his project.

It didn't take long for Cal to figure out how to be playfully hostile.

# Chapter Twenty-Six

It was shaping up to be a perfect mid-Spring day outside. The temperature was on the verge of 70 degrees, with a smattering of bloated clouds lolling in the sky and an intermittent gentle breeze to carry the scent of blooming hyacinth and lily-of-the-valley through the neighborhood. Elodie, Ava, and June joined forces to open every window of the house to let the outside air refresh the inside.

"My momma always used to say, 'A day of airin' out the house was as good as a day of cleanin' out the house,'" remarked Elodie when they reconvened around the kitchen island.

"My momma always said, 'Spring airs a house's cares,'" said June.

"My mother was afraid of open windows," Ava recalled as she reached back into her childhood memory bank. "She made my dad screw them shut so they couldn't open," she added matter-of-factly.

June looked over at her from the junk drawer she'd been searching, trying to find a rubber band. Though she didn't give voice to it, June's expression of disbelief conveyed to Ava: "Wow. That's weird."

"My mother was afraid of a lot of things, June. She was committed to a mental hospital when I was eight. I didn't see her again until I was 14 and was allowed to visit. She came back home when I was 15. She was better then, I guess, but the screws never came out of the windows."

"Aww, Ava," June responded. "I had no idea. What a difficult thing for a child to go through. I'm so sorry."

Elodie, of course, knew Ava's childhood history. She met Ava and Marie at summer camp while Ava's mother was hospitalized. However, she did not know the detail about the windows of her house being screwed shut, and it saddened her to hear it as much as it had June.

"I'm sorry about the windows," Elodie said to Ava as she embraced her in a motherly hug.

"To tell you the truth," Ava responded after Elodie finally released her. "I'd forgotten all about the window thing until you both mentioned your mother's sayings. When you're a little kid, not having open windows really isn't on your radar as something to be concerned about. But I got concerned when I came home from school one day, and she was gone. And as far as my father knew, she wasn't coming back. I didn't know she was being committed and had no time to prepare for it." Ava took a slow, deep breath and continued. "I remember she had lines on her forearms, and when I asked her about them, she said they were her "zebra stripes." My father told me years later, when I was in college, I think, that the zebra stripes were scars from her cutting herself with razor blades and knives. But I hadn't known or understood her problems at the time. I only knew that her absence was an awful surprise. It was hard..." Ava's voice trailed off.

June and Elodie searched for words to soothe the child in Ava's heart, but before they could find them, Ava had connected her losses – the old and the new. She lifted a few of her new short locks, acknowledged them with a small laugh, and said, "Maybe I'm ready for a trip to the mental hospital, too."

June reached for her new friend's hand and led Ava to sit at the kitchen table. She nodded to Elodie to join them.

"Here's what I'm thinking," June began after they'd settled in chairs. "I think I'm incredibly blessed to be part of God's big family and part of His smaller family under this roof. Life is so hard. The past has been hard on all of us, and there will be hard days yet to come. But I can't imagine trying to get through it without God's help or God's family. Ava, this isn't the time to talk about me, but someday I'm going to share with you about a season in my life I could have gone to a mental hospital for help. Just know it's okay to be broken – over old or new hurts. I'd suspect anyone who claims they've never been devastated. I know you were a Pastor's wife for many years, and that came with an enormous burden of keeping your sorrows to yourself. My momma was a Pastor's wife."

With those words, Ava's face visibly softened. She did not know June would understand what her life had been like living in a storefront window display. She'd been such a focus of attention in their Bloomington church that she'd tried to keep as much of her life private and shielded from scrutiny as she could. But several church women sensed her reserve and judged her harshly for it. They said she was cold. Marie and Elodie had been her safe place through the years. They'd loved her loyally, just as she loved them. However, lacking a history with June, Ava had been guarded. She now felt safer being vulnerable and freer to be herself. It was a relief.

June continued as Ava processed her words. "I just hope that you'll understand that God has placed you in this house, with all of us, exactly for this season in your life. You didn't know a hard time was coming, but He did, and this is His loving provision for you in your storm. Look," she said as she waved her arms around, "what He made happen for you. And for me."

"And for me," Elodie chimed in. "We all needed this house and each other."

# Chapter Twenty-Seven

"Thursday Meeting in da living room in 30 minutes," Marcus reminded everyone as he and Cal put the last supper dishes in the dishwasher.

"I'll be back," shouted Grant as he headed out the back door for an after-dinner stroll around the neighborhood.

The ladies headed for the front porch to enjoy the spring air perfumed by honeysuckle vines scattered up and down Cedar Street.

"He sure will," Elodie muttered in response to Grant's departure. "He's gonna get three blocks away and find out he's gotta get back here real quick."

Ava and June looked at each other and giggled. They'd all seen Grant leave on a well-intentioned walk after a meal only to come bolting in the door not ten minutes later, shoot up the stairway, and slam the bathroom door in his haste. It had happened more than a few times.

"I don't know if it's gratifying or horrifying that we should know one another's habits so intimately," Ava wondered aloud.

"We should all be so blessed to be predictable and regular," June lamented.

They situated themselves on their favorite porch seats. Elodie and June favored the green-painted metal, 60s-style chairs that bobbed if you leaned back in them. Ava took the wooden glider, which she had all to herself since Marie was away. From their positions, they observed the neighborhood's early evening activity.

Micah was just pulling his minivan into his driveway to the rush of an enthusiastic greeting from Lovie and Chase. The ladies waved their hellos to the family. Bobby, dressed in a ratty t-shirt and dungarees, gave his sidewalks, walkways, and driveway a manicure treatment with an edger. Christine Williams was spreading bags of fresh mulch in her side-yard rose garden. A couple of pony-tailed teenage girls eating ice cream sandwiches walked down the street. One of them dropped a wrapper as she returned the wave of the ladies on the porch.

"Do you notice Christine Williams keeps looking over at us?" June observed. "Just quick little darting glances now and then."

"Yeah, glancing down her nose at us," replied Elodie.

"Do you think she's lonely in that big house all by herself? Have we ever seen anyone visit her? Maybe she just wants some company. She's got to have some nurturing instinct in her heart with how she babies those flowers. I'm going to go find out," said Ava as she rose from her seat and walked toward the street.

"Here we go!" Elodie muttered under her breath as she and June sank a little lower in their chairs, wanting to observe without being observed.

Ava had just reached the curb in front of their house when Christine Williams, anticipating her approach, pointed a dirty, gloved finger at Ava and spat in a surly tone: "Just stay on your side of the street!"

Without taking her eyes off Christine Williams, Ava bent down and picked up the ice cream wrapper on the road next to the curb. She held it up to ensure her neighbor saw it and turned on her heel in one smooth motion that wordlessly communicated: "It wasn't you I was coming for."

Ava wadded the wrapper and reclaimed her seat on the glider.

"I don't believe she's lonely and in need of company," chuckled Elodie.

"That's the rudest thing I've ever witnessed!" June gasped.

"I've never been so glad to have a piece of trash in the yard. Thank You, Lord! Maybe I was wrong about her tending those flowers with a nurturing instinct. She probably just threatens them to flower or else!" Ava said with an extended exhale.

"Maybe it's not a good idea to send Marie over there for gardening advice," June wondered aloud. "It'd be safer to send her to a tribe of cannibals."

Ava caught a flash of movement out of the corner of her eye. "Grant's back, right on schedule," she laughed, drawing June and Elodie's attention to him.

Grant was approaching the front walkway to the porch at a fast clip.

"What's the hurry, Grant?" Elodie asked mischievously as he reached for the front doorknob.

He ignored her and went into the house.

The ladies resettled themselves in the living room for Thursday Meeting. Marcus, Cal, and Grant joined them in turn. After nearly two months of these regular weekly gatherings, there wasn't much left to work out regarding responsibilities and schedules. But they all felt it was essential to maintain intentional conversation about the people and the happenings under their roof, so they continued the meetings. They shared plans, news, prayer requests, and even the odd reminiscence, as old friends do. Some of this happened organically during mealtime conversations, but they saved the difficulties and tricky bits of life for Thursday Meeting when they could give issues their undivided attention.

Marcus began the meeting by requesting confirmation of who intended to seek membership at Grace Fellowship Church. Pastor Jefferson had visited the household that week and answered questions about his background and theology, the church's history and membership requirements, and discussed the opportunities for senior members to participate in ministry. Each of the friends was able to share with him a bit about themselves and the spiritual gifts they possessed for service to the church. They all liked the young Pastor and believed he reciprocated their genuine affection and respect.

At Marcus' query, all present raised their hands, indicating they'd pursue membership. Marcus was pleased. It had never been a condition or requirement that they all attend the same church. They could have gone their separate ways – dividing and conquering in their community influence. However, staying together seemed to Marcus best for household cohesion and community influence. They'd hear the same lessons and sermons, participate in the same church family life, and concentrate their ministry efforts as a household family.

"Now that that's decided, I have some things to share," Ava began.

Marcus' head swiveled sharply to look at his wife sitting beside him. He hadn't expected she was ready to share anything, and he mentally braced himself for an emotional flood.

"First of all, for the record, Christine Williams is not lonely," she began.

"That's a true fact!" June interjected while Elodie nodded in agreement.

"Either that or I'm a magnet for rejection," Ava admitted with steady calm. "Don't feel bad, Cal. She doesn't like me either, and I didn't even have to say anything to her."

She took a deep breath and continued. "It's also time for me to say what's pretty obvious. I'm a bit wrecked. I know it. You all know it. My hair knows it," she said, acknowledging her drastic haircut and tugging a short red lock.

"I've never been through something so emotionally devastating in my life. I thought I had as a child. Maybe I've lost my resilience. But the first time Marcus and I made a decision solely in our best interest and not our daughters' – because they're adults – they threw us out of their lives like disposable waste. It's been seven months now, and I'm trying to wrap my head around the realization that every day that goes by is another day they make the choice anew. We're still garbage.

I had no idea my girls were capable of such selfish spite. Their actions are so hateful, it makes me wonder, when did they stop loving their dad and me, and how come we didn't see it? It had to be a long time coming because they didn't go from love to hate with the flip of a switch. It tangles my mind. And that's the maddening part. I'm compulsive about unraveling it – trying to make sense of it. I don't want to be because it's exhausting and unpleasant. So I try to escape from it with sleep or distraction, but it's always lurking in every unguarded moment, and I'm caught up in it again. The only thing I know for sure is that I don't have a problem. The problem has me."

She finished speaking with teary eyes but was not sobbing, as Marcus had seen her at some point every day for these many months.

He relaxed, took her hand, and said to their friends, "Ava's not wrong to feel so hurt. Sometimes I wonder if it's to my benefit or shame dat I can see da situation more clinically and unemotionally. I don't know if dat's a pastor ting or a man ting. It would scare me to feel it as deeply as she does. Honestly, I hope I never do. Right now, I'm focused on helping her find a solid footing and praying God grants repentance to our daughters."

A heavy quiet settled over the living room. June had tears in her eyes to match Ava's. Grant looked at his feet and made a mental note to replace, or at least wash, the laces in his gym shoes. Cal combed his fingers through his thin, silver hair with both hands in a subconscious hope that stimulating his head might inspire a soothing response. Elodie had her mad face on. It didn't take long for her mad words to fly.

"I'd like five minutes in a room with the both of em. I would tear them up! They were not raised to be selfish brats, and I know because I helped raise em. Puttin' their momma through such misery – who do they think they are? I'd remind them quick, fast, and in a hurry!"

"If that would work, El, I'd drive you to Bloomington myself," Ava smiled at her dear friend's feisty defense. "Marley's tried her best with them, but their hearts are ice cold. Marcus has reminded me a dozen times that God can warm their hearts again and make reconciliation possible anytime He wants. He's all the help we need. The fact that God hasn't done it already means He's still working something in us, them, or likely in all of us. It's just so hard to watch the weeks, and now the months, pass. What if it goes on for years? We've already missed Jordan and Luke's birthdays this year, and little Emily's is coming next month. You'd think it would be easier to wait on God at this age. But, I can't get a grip or resign myself to the loss."

"It doesn't make any sense to me," Grant blurted. "If you have a problem with your parents, you sit down and talk about it. You don't cut them out of your life! What is wrong with those girls?"

"Sin," was June's succinct reply. After a few seconds, she elaborated.

"Sin makes no sense. Think about it. What sin has any of us committed that has done us any favor? When have we ever sat back and evaluated an action that violated God's word and thought: 'Yeah, that was a good move.' Never, right?

We've all learned that, but maybe Mia and Marit haven't. But I guess they're about to learn...how does that saying go?...'Sin will take you farther than you want to go, keep you longer than you want to stay, and cost you more than you want to pay.' And I wonder if, like you, Ava, they don't have a grip on this problem; it has a grip on them. Could be."

June's words were not exactly comforting, but they were true. Ava considered the possibility that her girls, having committed to a sinfully anti-Biblical path, now had no more grip on themselves than Ava had on herself. She nodded an acknowledgment as she dabbed the tears that now spilled.

June got up from her chair and walked over to the piano. She sat down at the bench and closed her eyes for just a few seconds, remembering an old sorrow of her own. Then, she opened them and said, "Sometimes you can pray over a hurt for so long there's nothing to say to God that you haven't said 100 times already. The words run out long, long before the pain runs out. So I sing hymns as an offering of faith, and they also medicate my heart."

She played a few introduction bars to a hymn they'd all known since childhood. And then she sang in a sweet alto voice:

> How firm a foundation, You
> saints of the Lord, is laid for your
> faith in His excellent Word. What
> more can He say than to you He
> has said? To you, who for refuge,
> to Jesus have fled.

The others joined her for the following familiar verses.

> Fear not, I am with you. Oh,
> be not dismayed. For I am your
> God and will still give you aid.
> I'll strengthen you, help you, and
> cause you to stand – upheld by
> My righteous, omnipotent hand.

> When through the deep waters, I
> call you to go,the rivers of sorrow

shall not overflow. For I will be with you, your troubles to bless, and sanctify to you your deepest distress.

When through fiery trials your pathway shall lie, My grace all-sufficient shall be your supply. The flame shall not hurt you, I only design your dross to consume and your gold to refine.

The soul that on Jesus has leaned for repose,I will not, I will not, desert to his foes. That soul though all hell should endeavor to shake, I'll never, no never, no never forsake.[1]

June glanced at Ava when they'd finished the hymn. Their eyes met, and Ava silently mouthed, "Thank you."

---

1. Attributed to "K", 1787, How Firm A Foundation (Public Domain)

# CHAPTER TWENTY-EIGHT

"What's the game tonight, fellas?" Bobby asked over the Beach Boys' music playing in the Garage Cave as he walked through an open overhead door. He'd brought two six-packs of green-bottled beer and set one on either of the two makeshift cinderblock and scrap wood tables positioned at opposite corners of a card table.

Marcus, Grant, and Cal glanced at the beer and then at each other. They hadn't anticipated their guest might bring alcohol, and they were all teetotalers – Marcus from years of being a pastor and avoiding gossip, Grant because the last thing his bladder needed was a diuretic, and Cal because he took meds that would interact with alcohol. Yet, they didn't want to hurt their neighbor's feelings by refusing his contribution to their gathering.

"Was tinking about Rook tonight," Marcus answered as he retrieved the cards from a small pile of games on the workbench. Grant and Cal looked at each other in confusion because at dinner, they'd discussed what they should play tonight and had settled on Mexican Train dominoes. Mexican Train didn't require concentration, enabling them to focus on their conversation with Bobby.

"But we'll need our wits about us for dat one, so we probably shouldn't indulge," Marcus continued and nodded toward the beer.

Now Bobby was confused.

"Is sugar a problem for y'all?" he asked puzzled.

"When did they start adding sugar to beer?" Cal wondered with a grimace.

"What?" Bobby made a face of revulsion at the thought of sugared beer. And then he laughed and picked up one of the six-packs, holding it aloft for inspection. "Oh! You think this is beer. It's not. It's Ale-8-1 which is local pop. I guess it is packaged a lot like beer. And it does say 'Ale,' but it's soda pop. It's a Kentucky thing."

"Never heard of it," Grant said with a laugh, "but I'll try it! Pass one over."

Marcus and Cal held out their hands as well. Then, eagerly, they twisted off the caps, took their gulps, and gave it a verbal stamp of approval.

"Not bad. Sort of like Mountain Dew," Cal spoke for all of them.

"So maybe not Rook tonight. Let's play Mexican Train instead." Marcus pivoted.

He returned the card game and grabbed the dominoes from the workbench. As he dumped the dominoes on the table and turned them face down, Cal and Grant opened two family-sized boxes of Cheeze-Its, poured them into large plastic bowls, and set them next to the six-packs of Ale.

"Next time, I'm going to bring Cheer Wine," Bobby laughed. "That's soda pop too!"

"There seems to be a theme with the Southern sodas," Grant remarked. "Tell me you got something called 'Moonshine' with no alcohol."

"Not that I know of," Bobby answered as he helped turn dominoes over. "I do enjoy a cold beer after working outside on a hot summer afternoon, though. But I can't do it in the evenings. I'd be up three times at night."

"Me too!" exclaimed Grant. "Ruins a good night's sleep."

"I need my sleep, especially when I have to go to work in the morning,"

Bobby said.

"You work on Saturdays?" quizzed Cal.

"Just half a day to keep an eye on things. My sister and I took over our daddy's used car dealership and auto detailing businesses when he passed. She runs them when I go to Florida, and I run them the rest of the time. It's enough for both of us to do."

"I used to love tinkering on cars when I had good knees," lamented Cal.

"When you had good knees, June was still in high school," Grant teased.

"Ok, let's get down to business," Marcus directed. He briefly reviewed the game's rules and instructed everyone to choose 15 dominoes. "Hey, Grant, can you turn da volume down on da music a bit?" he asked.

Grant scowled slightly but did as he was asked. He turned to Bobby and explained, "Marcus never misses an opportunity to flaunt his superior sense of hearing."

"What's that you say?" Bobby asked, cupping a hand to his ear with a smirk.

"Exactly. Marcus can hear better than us because he doesn't use his ears to listen to anyone else. He's always doing the talking," Grant mocked.

"Well, someone has to be da voice of maturity and reason around here." Marcus brushed him off with a laugh and continued, "Alright! Double twelves to start. We'll begin wit Cal since he's..." Marcus hesitated.

"The best-looking man at this table!" Cal took advantage of the pause and finished the sentence for him.

"I was going to say since you were da old man among old men," Marcus clarified.

"Well, I don't mind that either," Cal replied. "Though 'Senior Statesman' has a finer ring to it."

"Sure, we can call you 'Senior–rita' if that's what you'd prefer," offered Grant, deliberately mishearing what Cal had said.

"As if I didn't get enough name-calling from Elodie. No thanks, buddy."

Bobby raised an eyebrow at the mention of Elodie's name and derailed the man-banter with a serious inquiry. "So what's Ms. Elodie's story? Is she mean?"

Grant and Marcus, who had known Elodie as long as they'd known their own wives, looked at each other, amused.

"What do you say, Marcus? Is Elodie mean?" Grant asked.

"Oh yeah, she's mean, all right. No doubt about it," Marcus answered thoughtfully and took his turn placing a domino tile.

"I have to agree. Yup. One hundred percent," Grant joined in nodding affirmation.

"She's refused to call me by my correct name since day one," Cal submitted his comment as evidence.

"But here's what else Elodie is," Grant continued with sincerity. "You can count on her to tell you the truth when no one else will because they want to spare your feelings. She's as loyal a friend as ever was. If you need her, she's there for you. And she's responsible and works hard. She loves God. Excellent cook. And she's man-conversant. She can talk about any sport and will know more about it than you do, except NASCAR. She doesn't like NASCAR. Her eyes aren't too good, but she can hear a fly in the next room – something even Marcus can't do."

"She's all dat and mean, too," Marcus confirmed with a laugh.

"She brought me the cake with Miss June and then stomped out of my house. " I didn't know what to make of it, so I thought I'd ask," said Bobby, shifting his attention to the game and frowning. "Gotta put my train up already."

"I wouldn't say that behavior is out of character for her," Grant chuckled and followed with a large swig of his Ale. "But I'd still trust her with my life."

"So would I," Marcus agreed.

"I've only known her a couple of months now, but I'll admit she's grown on me. However, I do have one helpful hint for you, Bobby. She likes to be called 'El Camino.' It takes her back to her college days and good memories. I think her mother had one at that time. So call her that next time you see her, and she'll soften right up." Cal suggested with a straight face.

When Bobby turned to grab a handful of Cheeze-Its, Marcus and Grant saw Cal mutter under his breath, "Forgive me, Lord."

# CHAPTER TWENTY-NINE

"Mornin' Calzone! Guess my assassins have failed again," Elodie greeted her usual breakfast companion as she spotted him at the kitchen table.

Cal smiled, tickled by her odd humor.

"Watch out for Grant, or you'll get run over," she warned. He's flying around here doing Marie's cleaning chores before she gets home." She took a peek inside the dishwasher. "I see he's already done his chore, too."

She filled a coffee mug from the pot Cal made and sat at the kitchen table.

"He's a man on a mission, alright," Cal agreed. "Reminded me twice in our conversation this morning that Marie was coming home today. Saw him put bedsheets in the washing machine and check that we had honey in the pantry for her coffee tomorrow."

"He looks after her like she's the last woman on Earth and has a threatening illness, too," Elodie groaned.

Cal opened his mouth to say something but thought better of it. He just grinned instead. They could hear June play *Take My Life And Let It Be* behind the living room doors.

"There's my girl!" Cal said in acknowledgment of the music.

"I'm not your girl, Cal, sorry," said Ava with a little smile as she walked into the kitchen.

Cal was flustered into silence. He was glad to see Ava being playful, but he felt nervous and unsure how to respond to her with all she was going through. In his own way, he was bearing her burden along with her. He earnestly prayed for her and Marcus and their situation; he just didn't know how to talk to either of them about it.

"Ava, go get Marcus out of the library and tell him to come help me make pancakes for all of us," Elodie instructed.

"You're a mind-reader, El Camino! I was just telling June yesterday I was thinking about pancakes. Haven't had them since we've been here." Cal was enthusiastic about the imminent prospect. "Should someone go find Grant?" he asked.

"Trust me. He'll be here," she answered.

Ava went to retrieve her husband, and Cal poked his head in the living room to let June know pancakes were about to happen. In a matter of minutes, the smell of cakes on the griddle wafting through the house vents drew Grant into the kitchen to join his friends, as Elodie predicted.

They said little as they distributed the second batch of hot cakes Elodie produced. They sat nearly shoulder to shoulder at the small kitchen table, passing butter and syrup.

Elodie stood and pointed to the pantry, asking, "Does anyone want honey for their pancakes?"

Grant lept out of his seat.

"No!" he shouted. "There's only a little left, and I'm saving it for Marie!"

Elodie sat down and surveyed the grins of everyone seated at the table. They knew she'd deliberately provoked his anxious outburst.

"Woman, you are going to give me a heart attack one of these days, and you won't think it's funny," Grant barked as he sat down and grabbed the syrup from Elodie's hand. "You *are* mean," he added, recalling last night's conversation about her in the Garage Cave.

Marcus and Cal immediately looked down at their plates with an unnatural interest in their remnants. They hoped Grant would not bring that conversation up and drag them into this tiff with El.

"I'm sorry, Grant," Elodie responded, trying not to laugh.

"Well, tell your face because your face is saying 'sorry, not sorry,'" he replied, but with a tinge of softness.

"That's right. Marie is coming home today," Ava chimed in, sweeping away the residual trace of tension. "I've missed her too, Grant."

"Me too," June added calmly. "It's not the same when someone's missing."

"Got that right," Ava said softly.

Cal gave his wife a gentle kick under the table for saying the exact thing he dreaded accidentally saying himself – something that would make Ava sad or emotional. June shot him a perturbed look and reached over to give Ava's hand a gentle pat. June would not walk on eggshells with her. She met Ava's grief head-on, knowing it was what she had appreciated when mired in her own grief many years ago.

Later that afternoon, while Grant mowed lines across the yard, June sat on the porch with Ava, and they talked about children and grief. June shared with Ava her 20-year season of begging God for children that never came. She shared her bitter jealousy of Cal's ungrateful sister, who had five children and called them all "mistakes." She revealed she'd never go to a baby shower for fear of crying through it. June also admitted she felt less than a woman, and Satan used it against her by tempting her to level the field and make Cal feel less of a man. She confessed a years-long cycle of pleading with God for compassion, accusing Him of indifference, then ignoring Him in exhaustion and petulance. Eventually, she credited

God with getting her through her sorrow until she could appreciate all God had given her instead of focusing on the one thing He'd withheld from her.

"How did you know it was God who helped you? Did you ever think time healed your wound? How did you know He helped you and that you weren't simply numbed by the passage of years?" Ava needed this answer to a critical piece of her struggle. She needed assurance God was at work, and He hadn't left her to drift and grow numb to her sorrow.

"Here's how I know: God's word is true. In the end, it came down to that. I had let my longing and dissatisfaction become my clearest reality, my most reliable measurement of truth. I didn't want to believe that my desire wasn't paramount to God as it was to me. That was the risk of letting Him speak louder than I was. He might want holiness for me when I merely wanted happiness.

Sometimes I told God that if He wouldn't give me a baby, I'd be satisfied if He'd just take away the painful yearning for one and replace it with contentment. I believed that would be confirmation He cared about me and that it might be enough. I hoped it would be. But the subjective confirmation I thought I needed to feel in my heart, He spelled out objectively in black and white in a book. He loved me and gave His only Son to suffer and die for me. He never promised I'd get everything I wanted. On the contrary, He said this life would be hard and full of troubles. But He did promise He'd take me home to Himself for eternity and be close by me until that day.

I knew His Word said these things before I got married. But I learned there could be a great distance between knowing and truly believing. Ava, I know God helped me because He used my deep sorrow to close the gap between them. Time alone can't do that. Time, by itself, works against us. But time, as a tool in God's hands, is a drip feeder for our sanctification. He used it to turn my knowing into believing."

Ava looked away, searching the branches of the yard's large magnolia as she processed June's answer.

The two sat silently in their porch chairs, watching Grant make lines with the mower until the Norman's van pulled into the driveway next door. Lovie spied them and walked through the lilac hedge onto their porch. It was clear from her sweaty hair and rumpled clothes that she'd had a hard afternoon playing outdoors. Wordlessly, she climbed onto June's lap, throwing her little dungareed legs over the metal arms of the chair and resting her head against June's chest. June gently rocked her in the bobbing chair and stroked her tangled blond tresses. She looked over and met Ava's gaze – and matched her delighted smile at this timely gift of a child's love.

# Chapter Thirty

Marie was supposed to arrive at the Louisville airport at 6:30 pm, but mechanical issues with the plane delayed her flight by two and a half hours. By the time Grant picked her up and got her home, it was after 10 pm, and everyone had already gone to bed. They left the porch light and a table lamp in the center hall on in anticipation of their late arrival.

Marie led the way upstairs, and Grant followed closely behind, carrying her suitcase. A nightlight in a wall outlet in the upstairs hall provided sufficient light for residents to find their room at night without flooding the transom windows above each door.

The Renniger's bedroom was the first room on the left at the top of the stairs. Marie opened the door, let Grant pass through, and closed it behind him. Then she collapsed across the bed.

"I'm glad to be home," she said, keeping her voice volume low in consideration of her sleeping roommates.

"And I'm glad to have you home," Grant replied. "This bed has been cold and lonely while you were away."

"It's nice to be missed."

"Did you miss me?"

"Maybe a little, I did," Marie responded coyly.

"I did your chores this morning so the house would be clean for Sunday just like you like it."

"You did? Well, thank you very much; I appreciate that. But a girl might think you were angling for favors," Marie whispered, knowing that was precisely Grant's motive.

"If I were, would I have a chance of your favors?" he asked hopefully while switching on the Bluetooth feature of the modern Victrola in their room. It instantly paired with a playlist on his phone.

The truth was, Marie was exhausted after preparing a month of freezer meals for David and Liza before starting her trip home. Then she had to deal with the long delay, which got her home much later than expected. But Marie reminded herself of two things. First, if it was a problem that her husband still found her desirable at 62, she needed some genuine issues. Second, as she'd told several young brides-to-be over the years, including Ava's daughters: There are legitimate times to decline your husband's advances. But why say no when you can say yes? You'll never regret saying yes.

"I'd say your chances are better than average," she answered with a smile while patting a place on the bed beside her.

Elodie drank too much sweet tea after dinner and was up for her first trip to the bathroom for the night. She was exiting the hall bathroom when Ava stepped out from her room.

"Still having trouble falling asleep?" El asked her.

"Yes. I took a sleeping pill and two melatonin gummies, but they're not working, and Marcus is snoring like a mill saw. So I thought I'd go to the kitchen and have a little piece of leftover cake. Want to join me?

"Sure. Why not?" Elodie was game.

Elodie was about to take her first step down the staircase when she stopped short.

"I hear music," she whispered.

Ava stood still and listened. "Yup. It's coming from Grant and Marie's room."

Elodie backed away from the stairs, taking two steps closer to the Renniger's bedroom door. Without knowing why, Ava followed.

"It's Barry Abbott!" Elodie whispered a little too loudly in her shock.

"Shhhhh!" Ava admonished, eyes bulging in emphasis.

"Who knew Grant liked 80's soul music? Never would have guessed *Lover Of My Dreams* was his jam," Elodie whispered more quietly.

Then she cupped her hand over her mouth to silence screams of hysteria she thought might overwhelm her. The women clearly understood what was happening on the other side of the door.

"We should *not* be listening to this," Ava mouthed. They stood listening for a moment.

*When I taste your kisses, I can't make up my mind*
*if they're sweet like sugar or smooth like cream,*
*but this I know, they're one of a kind.*
*Yeah, baby, you're the lover of my dreams.*

"Okay, we need to go!" Ava said, pulling Elodie by her arm, to the staircase and down it.

They settled themselves with pieces of cake and glasses of milk at the kitchen table, still grinning about what they'd discovered going on upstairs.

"We couldn't help hearing their music, but we didn't have to listen outside their door to it," Ava scolded them both.

"You're right. That was wrong," El agreed unconvincingly. She dug into the cake she had skipped after dinner. "Hey, this is pretty good. I like the pineapple in the pudding and the toasted coconut and cherries. Very tropical. June has some good recipes. What's this called?"

Ava swallowed the bite in her mouth and washed it down with a gulp of milk before responding. "It's called Better-Than-Sex Cake," she answered flatly.

They both lost their composure and convulsed themselves, trying to stifle their laughter so they wouldn't wake the Shermans, whose bedroom was just 15 feet away.

"I don't know how I'm going to look them in the eye tomorrow at breakfast," Elodie confessed when she finally spoke.

"We are going to behave!" Ava commanded sternly.

It was a full house in the kitchen for breakfast the next morning before church. Ava and Elodie were the last to arrive and heard the tail end of Marie's recounting of her time spent with David and Liza the previous week.

"Sorry about da snoring," Marcus apologized to Ava because he'd noticed her missing during the night.

"It's ok, and I got to sleep eventually after some medicinal cake."

"Oh, night nibbling, were we?" asked Cal, who was sorry he hadn't thought of it himself.

"June, would you mind passing me a box of cereal?" Elodie asked as she took a seat.

"Which one do you want?"

"I don't know. I can't make up my mind," Elodie said slowly before pointing to the granola and giving Ava a side-eyed glance.

"Don't!" Ava pleaded with her eyes.

"I need the milk too. Would you pass that, Marcus?"

"Ooh, it's smooth like cream," she said, taking the carton of skim milk from his hand.

Marie looked quizzically at Elodie, who pretended not to notice. Ava noticed and knew in her heart Elodie had no intention of behaving. She watched as Elodie nonchalantly flipped the tag from the tea bag hanging from Grant's mug.

"Honey is good in tea. Sweet like sugar!" she commented to no one in particular.

Ava cringed, knowing Elodie would continue until she got a reaction.

"There's not much left in this box," Elodie seemed to complain as she shook the granola. "Maybe I should mix it with the oat cereal and make one of a kind? Yeah, baby."

That did it. Marie's eyebrows flew upward and her jaw downward as it dawned on her that Elodie was clumsily inserting phrases from Grant's mood music into her banter. Ava got up from the table, ostensibly to retrieve a cup of coffee but actually to hide her mirth. She had never mastered the poker face.

Marie looked around the room to see who else was in on the joke. No one seated at the table except Elodie seemed amused. She glanced over to Ava, standing at the kitchen island with her back to the table, and saw her shoulders bouncing lightly up and down – laughing. Next, she looked at Grant, who was talking with Marcus about the upcoming Sunday School lesson. He'd been oblivious to it all. Just as well, she thought. Finally, she turned her attention back to Elodie, who was eating her granola but looking over the rim of her glasses back at her.

"Jealous?" Marie mouthed to her before flashing her a stuck-out tongue. She did this quickly, but not quickly enough for Grant to miss it.

"What are you making faces at El for?" he wanted to know as the entire group suddenly looked to Marie for a response.

Marie was evasive. "How many people in this room think Elodie Ford should have a tongue stuck out at her without any reason required?" she asked.

Everyone raised a hand, including Ava, who had turned around to face Marie. Grant raised both his hands and waved them around for added measure.

"Can't say you're wrong," Elodie chuckled and set upon her cereal again.

# Chapter Thirty-One

"Hey there, Micah! Good to see you!" Grant fairly shouted as he opened the front door and greeted his neighbor standing on the other side.

"Good to see you, too," Micah responded sincerely but significantly less enthusiastically. "Would Miss June happen to be at home?" he asked.

"She sure is. I'll get her. Won't you come in?" Grant ushered Micah inside with a sweep of his hand.

Micah waited in the entrance hall and caught a glimpse of the television broadcasting a re-run of Gilligan's Island through the partially open pocket doors of the living room. Whatever he imagined his neighbors watched on their television wasn't Gilligan's Island, but it made him smile, nonetheless. Seven castaways figuring out life on an island playing in the home of seven senior citizens figuring out life in the house next to his. Of course, they would watch this show.

Grant came back from the kitchen with June following behind, bringing with her the clinging scent of fried onions and garlic.

"Here she is!" Grant presented June like a promise kept to Micah and then reclaimed his seat in the living room with Marcus and Gilligan.

"Hey, Miss June," Micah began before he was distracted by the scent she carried from the kitchen. "Wow! Whatever you're cooking should be made into perfume!" he gushed.

"I was just starting this evening's dinner. That's fried celery, onions, and garlic for Shrimp Creole," June answered, smiling. She appreciated the compliment, even if it was indirect.

A longing washed over Micah that couldn't escape expression on his face. The smell of onions and garlic was the same whether June or Dahlia cooked them in this house or his house. He didn't make these connections with cognizant logic. Micah knew only that he felt gut-punched at the moment. And that he missed his wife and her cooking. He sighed deeply.

"Is everything alright, Micah?" he heard June ask.

"Fine," he answered mechanically and then more accurately, "Well, not fine exactly." He brushed away the spontaneous sentiments from his mind and remembered why he'd come to see her.

"My sister, Shelby, told me today that she's accepted a position with a company in Nashville and will be moving in two weeks. It's a big promotion from her current work-from-home job. But before this opportunity came up, the plan was for her to work from my home and watch Chase and Lovie while they were off from school this summer. Of course, I'm happy for my sister, but I'm scrambling for childcare now. So I was wondering, since Lovie is so attached to you, would you be interested in a summer job?"

"Aww, Micah, I'm sorry to hear that. I know you and the kids will miss her very much. But I can't take the job." June saw no sense in offering false hope by saying she'd think about it. She also knew time was of the essence for Micah to find someone because the last day of school was this week. Though she didn't owe Micah an explanation, she gave him one.

"My husband's health is precarious. We're on a treadmill of symptoms, treatments, side effects, and aging issues. I have to be focused on his needs and care. That's my season of life right now."

"I completely understand, June," Micah responded. "I didn't realize Cal was dealing with so much. And you, too. You were just the first one I thought..."

"I'll do it!" Elodie cut him off mid-sentence as she hurried down the staircase. "I was thinkin' about lookin' for a summer job, and here you are – the answer to prayers I didn't even pray yet. Isn't it amazin' how God works?"

"Well, I guess so," Micah responded with a startled expression that quickly melted into relief.

Elodie launched into her sales pitch. "I'll come over in the mornin's when you leave for work. I'll see they get breakfast and lunch, play outside, and read a book. I'm all for kids readin' in the summer. They don't need to be lettin' their brains go to mush while school's out. And we'll go for explorin' walks, and they'll learn how to play gin rummy and bake a decent cookie – you know, life skills. I'll work with them in the garden and show them the difference between a vegetable plant and a weed. They'll make their beds or die tryin'. Kids don't learn a work ethic without responsibilities. Does that sound like a plan to you? Good!" Elodie supplied her own response. "When do I start?"

Micah was overwhelmed and delighted with Elodie's enthusiasm. "You start this Friday. The kids' last day of school is Thursday. But I don't know if I can afford Mary Poppins!"

"You just pay what you can. So you leave for work at 7 am?"

"7:30," Micah responded.

"Perfect!" said Elodie. "I'll be at your door Friday at 7:25."

"Thank you so much!" Micah enveloped both Elodie and June in a grateful hug. He turned to open the front door to let himself out and spun around again.

"When the Scotts sold this house, the kids and I hoped another family with kids would buy it and move in. You all are not what we hoped for, but you're much better. We didn't know to wish for a family of senior citizens to move in. Is this coming out right? I'm not offending you, am I? What I mean to say is, we love that you're our neighbors, and we wouldn't trade you for any amount of kids."

June and Elodie looked at each other and grinned.

"Youth is overrated," June responded with a laugh.

"This was no accident, Micah. God put us in this house to be your neighbors. We love you, Chase, and little Miss Lovie. So just know we're pretty happy about it, too," Elodie answered with uncharacteristic but sincere affection. She patted Micah on the shoulder as he turned to go.

When the door closed behind him, June asked, "Have you really been thinking about getting a summer job? I didn't know that."

"Absolutely, I was! It just started when I was upstairs in the hall and heard him ask you if you wanted to watch his kids. I knew you couldn't do it, and the man was in a fix. I don't know what happened. Think I got the Holy Spirit boot to my backside, and next thing I know, I'm comin' down those stairs offerin' to take the job - no time to think it over. But I know that's my callin' for the summer. Those kids are my summer callin'."

She rearranged the phrase as if she were rearranging the cushions of a chair she intended to sit in for a while. She was determined to get comfortable with it.

# Chapter Thirty-Two

Jonathan Jefferson looked wistfully at Bobby McBride's house as he stood on the front porch of his new church members' home, waiting for Marcus to answer the door. It had been a long time since he'd been welcomed under the McBride roof. Soon enough, Marcus came to the door and interrupted his reverie. He ushered Jonathan into the study while he ran upstairs to retrieve a book from his nightstand that he intended to recommend to his Pastor.

Jonathan could tell, as he pushed his hands into the pockets of his khaki chinos and perused the authors of the books on the shelves, that he and Marcus were well-aligned theologically. They read the same dead guys: Edwards, Spurgeon, Baxter, Ryle, Tozer, and Lewis. Jonathan was glad Marcus had joined Grace Fellowship. He was grateful to have a seasoned, retired pastor adding spiritual weight to his church. Jonathan hoped he'd be a welcome influence not just to the congregation, but also to himself. His enemies - the world, the flesh, and the devil – were the same as everyone else's, and he'd lose a skirmish with them too frequently for his liking. Jonathan feared losing a significant battle. Instead of being intimidated or threatened by someone more experienced or learned, as other young pastors might be, Jonathan saw Marcus as a sponge to draw from and a buffer from pride. He respected him and welcomed his mentorship. He nurtured the idea that he could be a Timothy to Marcus' Paul. Jonathan was a sinful man, but he was not a spiritually arrogant man.

Marcus, with Luther's biography in hand, closed the study door and invited Jonathan to have a seat and a discussion. They'd just settled themselves in their chairs when they heard shouts:

"He's dead! He's dead! He's dead!"

Marcus bolted toward the kitchen, where the shouts came from, with Jonathan on his heels. There they saw Grant dancing around the island, oblivious to anyone else and shouting in a sing-song voice on repeat, "He's dead! He's dead! Oh, yes, he's dead!"

"Who's dead? And why is Grant delighted about it?" Marcus, recovering his nerves and wind, directed his question to Marie, who was sitting at the kitchen table with Ava, cookbooks spread out before them.

"One of the golf starters at Grassy Fields Country Club passed away, and Grant just got the call to replace him. This is how we celebrate free golf," Marie answered with a sigh and an exaggerated eye roll.

"Congratulations, Grant," Jonathan said, stepping in from the kitchen entrance where he'd not been seen. The voice of his Pastor snapped Grant out of his revelry, and when they made eye contact, Grant drew a deep breath.

"Oh, tell me I'm not going to hell for this!" Grant moaned, embarrassed.

"I believe an infraction such as this is a one-way, non-stop ticket to perdition, my friend," Jonathan answered with seriousness. "Unless," he continued, "you can secure your Pastor a primo starting time on a Saturday morning. And, just something to keep in mind, free rounds of golf will get you first-class seating in heaven."

"Who is this heretic in our kitchen selling indulgences for golf favors?" Ava chimed in with a smile for the young Pastor.

"Baby, I love it when you talk Reformation," Marcus gave her a wink. He'd been reading the Martin Luther biography to her in bed each night to loosen her mind's grip on her own troubles and sorrows before she slept.

Marie leaned over to whisper a swipe at her friend for laughing about her romantic encounter with Grant the previous weekend. "So it's church history that spices things up for you two, huh? Never would have guessed that."

"Church history or sometimes art history. We mix it up," Ava clapped back with a little laugh.

"Helloooo. Pastor standing here," Jonathan said with feigned shock. He had excellent hearing.

"I'm afraid dat's not da deterrent with dese two dat it might be wit oders," Marcus apologized. "They're brutally fortright and intimidated by no one. Dere's nuting dat can be done about it. Grant and I have tried to refine dere manners, but da best we've managed is to make dem tolerably acceptable so dat we can take dem out in public."

"And they don't drool anymore. Don't forget we stopped that," Grant added cheerfully, glad to have the focus of attention off himself.

"Much, anyway," added Marie as she pretended to wipe something away at the corner of her mouth, her gold chain bracelet slipping down her arm and catching the light.

"Would you care for a cup of coffee, Pastor?" Ava stood to start a pot.

Marcus answered for him. "We're going into da library to continue a more cerebral conversation den what's available in dis kitchen. But if you'd like to bring us two cups when it's ready, dat would be appreciated."

"Alternate suggestion," Marie offered. "How about you stay in the kitchen and make Pastor Jefferson one of your delicious pour-over coffees? Ava and I need to go to the Mexican grocery store for a special adobo, and we'll take Grant with us so he can make sure we stay in the social range of 'tolerably acceptable.' Then we'll all be out of your hair and your cerebral conversation."

"I'd love to try a pour-over! Never had one before," Jonathan spoke up quickly.

"We're off then!" Ava settled the matter.

She and Marie closed their books and left them in a stack on the table. Grant opened the back door and held it for the ladies to pass through.

"Let there be no more heresies in this kitchen while I'm gone," Grant said over his shoulder and closed the door behind him.

Marcus gathered the implements he needed for their coffees. "Never had a pour-over, huh? Prepare your tastebuds for shock and awe," he said confidently.

Jonathan's thoughts were elsewhere. "I stood in your kitchen for only five minutes and got a totally different take on your household than when I came for my official pastoral visit two weeks ago," he confessed. He was still processing the interaction he'd witnessed.

"Was da curtain in front of da Wizard drawn back?" Marcus inquired.

"A bit," Jonathan chuckled. "I realize you're not intimidated by me, but I'm a little intimidated by you all."

"Tell me about it," Marcus probed as he roasted the coffee beans.

"I'll have to think about it some more. Right now, all I have is a mental picture contrasting the relationships Kesha and I have with our close friends with what I've seen here. We're like rough stones on the side of a road, and you all are like smooth stones next to a beach. We're insecure and uptight, where you all are self-deprecating and chill. You don't take yourselves seriously. So, is that age, sanctification, personality, or what?"

Marcus considered his answer as the coffee beans swirled in his converted popcorn popper and filled the kitchen with a rich aroma.

"It's love," he eventually responded.

# CHAPTER THIRTY-THREE

Cal lay in his bed in the Sherman's first-floor bedroom next to the kitchen, listening to the sounds of his friends as they chattered and clattered, assembling plates of hot dogs and chips for their lunch. He knew they were having hot dogs because he heard Marie talking about making zucchini relish once they were ready to harvest from the garden, and because he could smell the peanut oil they always fried hot dogs in.

After their group effort to weed the gardens before lunch, they were all hungry. All except Grant, who was on his first day at the new job at the golf course, gleeful to escape the weeding at home. Cal was not gleeful to have escaped it. He'd much rather have been outside helping his friends and having lunch with them now than be sidelined with a flare-up of diverticulitis.

In the last ten years, Cal's body had become his enemy. He'd suffered through two types of cancer and their awful treatments, one hip and two knee replacements, low levels of minerals and hormones which zapped his energy, degenerative spinal stenosis, diabetes, and lately, this diverticulitis misery. June said it all would make a lesser man cry. She didn't know that occasionally Cal did.

From an emotional standpoint, each malady and side effect was like having a heavy rock added to the load he had to carry. Although symptoms, pains, and lethargy could be temporarily alleviated, they were never banished. The emotional rocks could settle and compact as a load, but they didn't get lighter.

There was one rock that far outweighed the others. Little by little, with each new diagnosis, Cal had become less of June's protector and she more of his. She was eight years younger, but the gap seemed like twenty and ever-widening. He imagined June's life was like his truck, and he was making her drive with the parking brake on. His health issues were a constant drag that kept June from doing things she loved, and Cal hated it for both of them. Some days, like today, he'd just as soon be unalive.

But Cal did not have the choice of setting his load down and walking away. He knew Jesus said, "He who endures to the end will be saved." Moreover, he feared God enough to believe He meant it and, unfashionably but unashamedly, called himself a God-fearing man. So with the automatic door to the exit permanently disabled, Cal was training himself to turn his focus from all the things he couldn't do with June to the one thing he could usefully do: pray.

June had always been the better prayer warrior. She was more spontaneous and also more disciplined at it. She almost had a monopoly on Sherman family prayers. But unbeknownst to everyone but God Himself, that was changing.

Cal sat up in bed. Weak and physically distressed, he wiped away the self-pity that had leaked from his eyes and began to pray.

*Gracious God, You are King over all creation and all times. What a comfort it is to know You sit on a sovereign throne, and all things happen at Your command to serve Your purposes. I know this is true of my discomforts which are only temporary and light afflictions in the grand scheme of eternity. Yet, You know I am a man made of dust, and my burdens seem heavy to me. Sometimes, it seems too heavy, and I confess my heart has grumbled against You and accused You of unkindness. I know You are only and always good, and I have slandered You with unworthy thoughts. I ask Your forgiveness for this sin, and I'm grateful to know I have it because You have adopted me as Your child. You may appoint additional burdens for me, but You will never make me suffer the burden of condemnation which I justly deserve but which Jesus took upon Himself in my place. If my knees would let me skip around this room for joy, I would. You would laugh.*

*Lord, I long for you to delight in me. I know I can do nothing to make You love me more than You do. But I want to hear "Well done, good and faithful servant" when we meet. I've proven to my satisfaction that I'll never be able to do that without Your help. I'm selfish, prideful, and sometimes lazy. I don't give You much to work with, dear Lord. But I ask that Your strength would overcome my weaknesses and that Your name would be glorified in Heaven by any service You would accomplish through my pitiful self – whether that service is known or unknown on Earth. This is my heart's desire, and I boldly ask it for myself.*

*Father, I also want to ask something for my sister, Ava. You know, much better than I, all she's going through and what You're accomplishing through her suffering. So if I ask wrongly, consider my ignorance and fix my prayer. I ask for a bit of relief in her spiritual battle and encouragement to strengthen her faith and fight. Is it crazy to hope these might grow with her hair like Samson's did? I ask that for her because I'd want someone to ask that for me in the same situation. Jesus was abandoned and heartlessly scorned by those He loved. It must have grieved You to see Your Son treated that way. I ask You to look on Ava with a Father's pity and give her everything she needs to walk this hard road. Bring her to the end with more resemblance to our Savior who walked that road, too.*

*Gracious God, I also remember to You our neighbor across the street, Christine Williams. She is not my sister because, for all I can tell, she is full of hate and spiritually dead. This enemy of Yours is also my enemy. But I was once Your enemy and spiritually dead until You gave me life. So I ask You to do another great work: draw Christine Williams to Yourself and give her life. She will not be saved unless You save her. Find her on her Damascus Road and bring her to her knees in repentance. Help our household to be a conduit of your grace and show her the love of Christ. We surely do need your help with that.*

*Father, I thank You for doing this strange thing and bringing June and me under this roof in this household of believing friends. I'm so grateful that June won't be alone when I'm gone. Most people have children to look after them in old age, but You gave us old brothers and sisters in Christ, and that's good too. And you brought June and Lovie to each other. Lord, if You never gave me another blessing on this Earth, that would be enough. Thank You for a little girl for my wife to love and who loves her. Thank You for Grace Fellowship Church and Pastor Jefferson. Thank you for new friends, Bobby McBride and Will. Lord, all these are riches upon riches from Your hand. May I be the blessing to them that they are to me.*

*God, thank You that You hear the prayers of sinful men like me – saved by grace through faith in Jesus our Savior and in whose name I pray. Amen.*

Though he couldn't see it now, the rocks piled on Cal's load had created spiritual muscle.

# CHAPTER THIRTY-FOUR

"Is Epsom salt the same thing as ocean water salt?" Chase asked as he measured three cups from a bag and transferred them into the large mixing bowl Elodie found in the Norman's cupboards.

"You mean, is it sea salt? No," Elodie answered before adding too much additional information. "It's actually not salt at all. It's magnesium sulfate, and if you eat it, it'll make you poop. But it's also good for soaking tired muscles and stiff joints, and that's how Miss June will use it. Okay, now, Lovie, pour in this bakin' soda and mix it up a little."

Lovie concentrated on her task, stirring carefully while Elodie added lavender colorant and essential oil. They were crafting scented soaking salts to put in a glass jar decorated with glued-on pink and purple ribbon and artificial lavender flowers.

Elodie bought the components from the local Dollar Town with some of the money the children earned by helping Marie weed the side yard flower bed and helping Marcus clean up the Garage Cave. This was the present, purchased by their hard work, that the children would bring to Miss June's surprise birthday cookout.

Elodie was a week into her summer stint of minding Chase and Lovie, and she was rather pleased with the progress she'd made on the organization of the household and the children. It appeared that since Dahlia's passing, no one had taken up the tasks of dusting furniture, getting clean laundry from baskets to bureaus, or watering plants. So on day one,

Elodie taught the children how to do each job correctly and assigned them future responsibility for these duties. She also taught them how to make their beds. They moaned and groaned but admitted things looked better.

After he picked up his room, Chase confessed, "It looks like Mom was here. This would make her proud of me."

Elodie sat on the floor in Chase's room and patted a spot next to her, indicating he should join her. Hesitantly, he did.

"I didn't get to meet your mom," Elodie began. "Can you tell me what she was like?" Elodie was channeling her inner Marcus by asking the probing question.

Chase stiffened, looked away, and was quiet. She thought he'd decided to refuse her request and let the silence be. The only noise was Lovie in her room instructing her dolls that they would also have to fold their clothes and put them away from now on.

Chase kept his gaze averted but slowly began, "She ate popcorn every night after I went to bed. I could hear it popping in the microwave, and just a little while later, I could smell it in my room. I always tried not to fall asleep before I smelled the popcorn." He paused. "She had ticklish feet like I do. It doesn't bother Dad or Lovie, but Mom and I can't handle it." He remembered more and smiled. "She could spit a pumpkin seed further than either Dad or me. Last Fall, we had a contest on the front porch, and she won." Now he was on a roll. "She had a pretty laugh. Her hair was blonde, and her eyes were green. Lovie looks like her. I don't know why, but it makes me mad."

Elodie flinched instantly, panic stricken. It was easy enough to channel her inner Marcus when it came to asking a question, but her inner Marcus was AWOL when it came to providing answers. Now that she'd drawn him out, she felt she owed a response to this vulnerable boy sitting next to her. She couldn't wreck the child after her first week. She'd have to wing it.

"Why do you think it makes you mad?" Elodie heard herself ask. *"Oh, Lord, here we go further down the rabbit hole. What am I doin'? I'm doin' stupid!"* she berated herself inwardly.

"Hmm. I think it makes me mad that Lovie's here and Mom isn't," Chase replied, unaware of Elodie's regret or turmoil.

"I understand that."

"You do?" Now Chase was asking the questions.

Elodie was desperate to regain her equilibrium but still consigned to winging it. "Yeah. A man-cub needs his mother more than he does a sister."

Chase looked stricken, and the color drained from his face. "Who told you?" he demanded angrily. He didn't wait for an answer but sprang to his feet and said, "Lovie told you! She has a big mouth, and I'm going to close it for her."

He made for the doorway, but Elodie lunged from her sitting position and caught his foot in one hand and his waistband in the other. She pulled him back, and he fell into her lap. He scrambled out and stood up, but her grip on his belt held him fast.

"Who told me what?" she asked firmly.

"She called me 'man-cub.' Mom called me her man-cub," Chase shouted at her as tears gathered in his eyes.

"Nobody told me. That's the truth," Elodie spoke soothingly.

Chase wasn't sure he believed her but stopped tugging against her grip.

"Did the two of you watch Jungle Book together? I love that movie, and if I had a boy of my own, I'd have called him my 'man-cub' too," Elodie said sincerely.

He gave her the benefit of the doubt and sank to the floor, lowering his head. "We watched Jungle Book together a lot when I was little. Even though we didn't watch it so much anymore when I started school, she still called me 'man-cub.'" The tears spilled down his cheeks, and none followed.

They sat there for a minute until Chase, still remembering, managed a smile and added, "I'm really glad it didn't become what everyone called me, like Lovie."

Elodie requested elaboration on that comment with a cock of her head.

"Lovie isn't her real name. Her real name is Meredith, like my grandma. But Mom started calling her Lovie when she was a baby, and then we all called her Lovie."

"Did not know that," Elodie responded as she rubbed the leg that had taken the brunt of Chase's crash landing. Now that she'd instigated a crisis and navigated through it, she promised herself she'd never channel her inner, outer, or anywhere Marcus. Probing questions were best left to the professionals.

It'd been a week since that inauspicious day, and it had gone better since Elodie kept her promise to herself. The house was tidier; the kids were well-fed and tired at the end of their days; and the ivy clinging to life before it was mercifully watered showed signs of recent growth. She felt she'd squashed the boy's aggressive outbursts toward his sister by shaming him out of them and felt no remorse about her method. She was sure it was how her blessed mother would have handled it. And if that wasn't enough, the worry lines on Micah's forehead were less pronounced when he greeted his children in the driveway each evening.

# Chapter Thirty-Five

Cal was recovering from a prolonged bout with diverticulitis and had no choice but to let Marcus borrow his beloved truck. He needed it to pick up the tables and chairs they'd arranged to borrow from the church for June's surprise party – an errand Cal had planned to do himself before he couldn't. He consoled himself that Marcus would only have to drive it three blocks and back, and he handed over the keys with encouragement to "Drive carefully!"

It was late afternoon, and there were only two hours to get the back-yard set up and decorated, and the buffet table spread  with platters of food before Grant arrived home with June. He'd driven her to a medical equipment store in Louisville to look at lift chairs for Cal. Before they left, Grant had mowed beautiful straight lines across the lawn so it looked pretty as a baseball outfield.

In just 20 minutes, Marcus was pulling into the driveway.

"That was quick!" remarked Ava.

"Yeah, well, don't tell Cal," he replied as he walked around the truck and opened the tailgate. "I don't tink he knows his truck goes faster dan 20 miles per hour."

Ava and Marie helped him arrange the three circular tables and chairs in the patch of lawn between the house and the garden. One long buffet table was set to the side. Then they put Marcus to work inflating teal balloons from a small helium tank while they unfolded disposable yellow and white checkered tablecloths and covered the tables. The circular tables were also set with teal napkins, plastic cups, and paper plates with a floral spray of yellows, teals, and a hint of baby pink. Mason jars with small bouquets of daisies and a raffia bow served as centerpieces. Next, they strung two jute ropes decorated with white, teal, and yellow fabric scraps over the tables and tied a helium balloon to each chair. The final touch was a HAPPY BIRTHDAY banner in an array of metallic cardboard letters, taped to the back wall of the house and framed with crepe paper streamers. The ladies hoped they wouldn't wilt in the heat and humidity.

"T-minus 30 minutes," warned Marcus.

"We're in good shape. Decorating is done, and now we can bring over the food from the Normans," confirmed Marie. "If you wouldn't mind, Marcus, be on the lookout for Will and direct him to park at the Garage Cave. We'll get Elodie and the kids to help us with the food."

Right on cue, Will and his boys pulled into Garage Cave driveway as Marcus had directed him to do earlier that day. He didn't need Marie to control every little detail for him, though 40 years of telling her that had not been convincing.

Marcus walked over to the Garage Cave driveway. "Glad to see you brought your muscles," Marcus addressed Will, indicating with a nod that he was speaking of his sons.

The boys beamed.

"This is Sam and Silas," Will introduced them as they each put out their hand to shake Marcus' in turn. They were teen versions of Will himself: dark-haired, fair-skinned, and athletically built.

"We have June's present stashed right behind da garage and could use your help to get it to da backyard," Marcus directed.

They followed Marcus and then surveyed the large object before them.

"It's a water bowl for chickens," Marcus said seriously.

The boys were too old to be taken in, and his joke fell flat. Marcus realized it and corrected his course.

"It's a stock tank. I'm told dis is to be a kiddie pool for old people," he corrected.

This actual explanation the boys found hilarious and guffawed until they caught their Dad's mean-mug look indicating they should stop.

The four of them grabbed a place on the rim of the tank and hurried it over to the area Marcus designated between the main garage and the gardens. When it was settled, he ran a hose from the house to fill it.

Will introduced his boys to the other guests assembling in the back-yard. Chase and Silas needed no introduction because they had been good friends since starting at Faircourt Middle School two years ago. In seventh grade, they shared the same homeroom and were locker neighbors.

It was to be a small neighbor-family party: the family of friends, the Norman family, Bobby McBride, and Will and his boys. As their post-man, Will was considered a fixture of the neighborhood. So when he initially declined the invitation because it was his weekend to have his boys, he was encouraged to bring them.

"T-minus ten minutes!" Marcus bellowed.

Elodie went inside the house to retrieve one last thing.

"Hey, Calamity, you ready to party?" she asked as she knocked on his bedroom door.

"I am. You can come in," he answered with a weakness in his voice Elodie was not expecting.

She opened the door and saw him standing by the bed with one hand touching it for balance. She thought he looked smaller than he was five days ago when he took to his bed. His overalls hung a little looser, and the arms that poked out of his tee shirt looked thinner. It had been an effort for him to get dressed and shaved. He looked ready to go back to bed instead of socializing. Elodie walked over to him and took his arm.

"You should escort me to this shindig like a gentleman would," she said tersely. And then, after several steps together, she asked quietly, "Did I ever tell you my little brother was named Calvin? I know that's not your name, but it's pretty close. He passed when I was in college."

"No, but that explains a lot," he chuckled and instantly hoped she wouldn't press him about what it explained. She didn't, and he was glad. He wouldn't have known exactly what to say and would have blabbered and probably said the wrong thing. He had a knack for that.

Cal allowed Elodie to pretend he was helping her. She settled him at a table with additional assistance from Bobby, who swooped to Cal's other side as soon as they stepped outside.

"Here they come!" Lovie shouted from her lookout position in the lilac hedge. She tried to make herself invisible there while everyone else hid around the corner of the house. Grant pulled into the driveway and pressed the buttons that opened their windows. Unsuspecting, June looked at him to question why he wanted to let the heat in, but before she could ask, they were at the garage, and people were shouting "Surprise!" and "Happy Birthday!" at her.

"Oh, my!" she laughed with genuine astonishment. And then she turned to Grant. "How many lies do you suppose you told me today to make this happen? June, we have to go today because it's my *only* day off. June, we have to take my car because Marie thinks it's making a noise. June, if we take our time, we won't have to help Ava weed the garden this afternoon.'"

Grant just smirked and got out of the car.

June exited as well and threw up her hands. "I live with liars in a den of lies!" she laughed. She stepped toward her husband and stood behind him, admiring the scene. "Oh, this is lovely! How beautifully decorated! Of course, teal – my favorite color. Thank you all so much."

She heard it before she saw it - running water in the stock tank pool. June was beside herself with delight.

"Oh, you all remembered! We all are going to love this on hot summer days! Like this one!" she added with a wry smile at Marie, who was always game for spontaneous fun.

Grant saw that look and headed them off. "Let's thank God for the food and eat!" he exclaimed.

The guests swarmed the buffet table loaded with Elodie's fried chicken, cole slaw, corn casserole, buttered rolls, cowboy baked beans, and pitchers of lemonade. Bobby turned on the boom box he'd been asked to bring, and out poured classic pop songs from the 1950s – the era June was born.

"This is some fine chicken, Miss Elodie," Bobby complimented her. "Neither the Colonel nor Popeye's can hold a candle to it!"

"My momma's recipe," Elodie demurred. And then she added, "That's a nice old-school system you've got there," with a nod to his boom box.

"I was a cool cat with it back in the day," he responded with his wide, toothy smile.

The smile Elodie despised jerked her back to her senses. Elodie knew his type, smooth and selfish. She turned her shoulders away from him and toward June, seated on her other side, ending her oh-so-brief foray into conversational civility with Bobby.

Lovie approached the table, wiping lemonade drips from her chin, "Miss June, would you like the kids to try out the Chicken Bowl Kiddie Pool for you?" She asked as if her lips were dripping honey instead of lemonade, and June could not deny her.

June placed her hands on either side of the girl's sweaty cheeks and responded, "You are a good girl to ask permission. But I want you to remember that you must always ask permission to go in the water. If it's okay with your dad, it's okay with me!"

And before you could say "Happy birthday," four barefoot kids splashed around in the tank to Chuck Berry. Marie and Ava watched indignantly for half a minute. This wouldn't do. These kids needed to know how to Twist and needed to know it now.

"Should we show 'em how it's done?" Ava asked.

"Immediately!" answered Marie.

They flung off their sandals and jumped with the laughing kids in the tank. There was a Twist dance party in the stock tank pool in no time.

June reached over and patted Cal's hand. She was glad he was outside in the fresh air, even if it was warm and humid.

"Told you a stock tank would be a wonderful addition. Nobody even cares it's only a third full," she observed.

"As long as your heart's full, my dear," Cal patted her hand in reply.

"It sure is," she whispered to Cal and God.

# CHAPTER THIRTY-SIX

"**G**ood afternoon, ladies," Will greeted Ava, Marie, and June as he walked up the sidewalk with their household mail in his hand.

He handed it to Ava, who held an outstretched arm to receive it. The ladies were relaxing on the front porch with glasses of iced tea, just passing the time. It was another hot day in two weeks of sweltering days – in the upper 80s - for the month of June. Elodie had taken Chase and Lovie for a stroll to Dollar Town in search of squirt guns. They were expected back shortly to watch a rerun of *I Dream Of Jeannie* with Marcus, who had absorbed the kids in his afternoon ritual of nostalgic programs.

"Wait just a second, Will," said Marie. "I'm going to get you a bottled water from the fridge. You look just about melted."

"Thank you, Marie. That would be greatly appreciated."

Ava fanned herself with the mail as June engaged Will.

"You're raising two perfect gentlemen, Will. Both of your boys greeted me in church last Sunday. Not many teenagers acknowledge the seniors at church, but Sam and Silas spoke with me for a few minutes and were completely charming. Although if I were a woman who speculated, I'd guess it made Mrs. Akin jealous from how she stared at us."

Will beamed, accepting the compliment. "Well, they had a wonderful time at your birthday party, Miss June. And as growing boys, they'll never forget anyone who feeds them."

Marie was back with Will's water.

"I bless you for this, Marie," he said as she handed it to him.

He held the cold bottle to his forehead for a few seconds, then turned down the stairs to continue his route. "See you on Sunday," he called back to them before the old magnolia obscured him from view.

"Hate to ask you to give up your make-do fan, Ava, but could you check if Grant and I have won the Grand Prize Sweepstakes?" Marie asked jokingly.

Ava rolled her eyes but obliged and looked through the small mail collection in her hand. She pulled out a square pink envelope and bruskly handed the rest to Marie.

"I don't think so, but you can double-check," she said with agitation as she turned and darted into the house.

Through the front-door window, Marie saw her bolt up the stairs. June and Marie looked at each other and wordlessly communicated their mutual concern at Ava's abrupt departure.

"This can't be good," Marie sighed.

"Ava," Marie quietly called as she knocked lightly on her bedroom door. There was no answer. She repeated the call and, with still no response, opened the door and stepped in. Ava lay face-down on her bed with the pink envelope still in her hand. She'd buried her face in her pillow to muffle her sobs, but Marie could see her shoulders heaving.

"Ava, sweetie," Marie said as she closed the door and walked over to Marcus' side of the bed, where she lay down next to her disconsolate friend. She said nothing more for a few minutes but rubbed Ava's back to let her know she was not alone. Then, when Ava's sobs subsided, she gently asked, "What was it, girl?"

Ava turned over and sat up against the pillows. Marie followed suit.

"Mia sent our birthday card for Emily back unopened," Ava lamented as she reached for a tissue on her nightstand and blew her nose.

Marie sighed deeply. "That sucks," she responded inelegantly but with heartfelt sympathy. "Sucks for both you and Emily." She scooched closer to Ava and wrapped her arms around her. Ava leaned into her friend's embrace – at ease with her emotional and physical support.

"She wasn't two and a half when I last saw her. Now she's three, and she probably doesn't remember me. If I saw her tomorrow, I'd be a stranger. My mind cannot make peace with the thought of being a stranger to that sweet little girl. But the thought is like a marble that keeps going around and around in an enormous funnel and never reaches the bottom. It's maddening!" She paused to blow her nose again. "Oh, Marie, I was doing better. I was! At June's party, I felt almost like a normal person. And now I feel like I've lost every bit of progress, and I'm back at the starting line."

"That's a lot of power for a small pink envelope," Marie was uncondemning but matter-of-fact as she processed Ava's words.

"Right?" Ava agreed, shaking her head. "But there it is."

"Sometimes grief is two steps forward, one step back, or five steps forward, 18 steps back. There's nothing I can do to change your situation, but I want you to know I'm here 18 steps back with you."

"If you want to be back at 18 with me, you're going to have to cut your hair like mine," Ava attempted to lighten her mood for Marie. She didn't enjoy being around herself, so why should her friend? She feared Marie, and Marcus, too, for that matter, would get compassion fatigue as her sorrow dragged on.

"Upon further reflection, maybe I'll just hang out at around 15 and wave at ya," Marie teased.

"Listen, I know the best thing for me right now is to call it a day and go to bed. Sleep helps me break the mental cycle. Would you mind telling Marcus and making my excuses at dinner?"

"I will," Marie squeezed Ava before she let her go. "Sleep tight," she said before she closed the door.

Ava changed into a sleeping t-shirt and shorts. She entered the Jack and Jill bathroom she and Marcus shared with Grant and Marie, washed her face, and filled her nightstand glass with water. Before she climbed into bed, she closed the windows' blinds, opened her nightstand drawer, and retrieved a bottle of over-the-counter sleeping pills. Ava downed four of them with the water. Sleep came right away between being emotionally spent and going a little heavy on the medication.

She woke up and heard Marcus' light snoring beside her. A quick look over his body to the clock on his nightstand informed her it was 1:30 am. There was still a lot of night left.

Ava's mind wandered where it usually did when it wasn't occupied – her sorrow over Marit and Mia's rejection and the painful separation from Jordan, Luke, and Emily. Robby was too new in the family to occupy much of Ava's emotional energy, and Mia's husband, Brad, had never earned her or Marcus' respect. He ran Mia like an appliance and complained she was clingy.

Ava felt her throat tightening and the tears forming in her eyes for her girls and the children. Then, she got mad at herself. *"Is this fun for you? How many hours have you already marinated your brain in this toxic soup? Is more of it going to help you?"* She berated herself silently. Maybe a change of scenery would help. She got out of bed, found her summer robe on the hope chest, and crept out of the room.

All was quiet and dark downstairs except for the illumination of the small lamp in the center hall. Ava walked back to the kitchen and opened the refrigerator door. She'd skipped dinner but saw nothing in the fridge that seemed worth the effort it would take to eat. She closed the door and stood in the dark kitchen, unsure of what to do next. Her eye was drawn through the window to the light over the garage door. Moths and assorted bugs were banging their bodies against the fixture in senseless oblivion.

"I feel ya, guys," Ava whispered to them.

She opened the kitchen door and stepped out to the driveway for a better look.

*"I guess this is where the party is tonight,"* Ava thought. She stood watching the insect chaos for a minute or two before she heard purring. Rover had crept across the yard and deposited something at her feet. He purred to draw her attention to it. Ava bent down to investigate.

"Eww! Thanks but no thanks," she yelped, recoiling from the proximity to the lifeless bird. She hurried away from it, walking past the brick-lined gardens to the expansive yard between the house and the Garage Cave. Enough light from a half-moon shone above a cloudless sky to illuminate her way. When she got to the middle of the yard, she took off her robe, spread it out on the grass, and sat down. She took several long, deliberate draughts of the cool night air.

"God," she called to Him out loud, "do You know about that little sparrow in my driveway? Did You care that the cat mauled her? Did You see it suffer when it was in the cat's jaws?"

After a thoughtful pause, she continued, "What about me? Do You see me?" And then louder as tears gathered and blurred her vision: "I don't think You do! What does a person have to do to be seen by You? To be pitied by You?"

Ava grew furious. She stood up, removed her t-shirt and shorts, and then laid down, naked and face-to-the-sky on the bathrobe. She sobbed and demanded, "Do you see me? Can you see me now?"

Crickets. Literally, crickets were all she heard in the neighborhood's night. She turned over on her stomach, rested her head on her folded arms above her shoulders, and wailed into the tiny cave of space they made.

Bobby was a night owl when he didn't have to go to work the next day, indulging in midnight movies on the classic movie channel. He'd just opened his back door and was about to call for Rover when he heard a woman's distraught sobs.

Bobby looked toward the sound and was stunned at the drama un-folding in the yard across the street. His mind raced to decide what action, if any, he should take. Should he pretend he never saw this, close his door, and leave Rover to figure it out for the night? Should he go over and help her – was it Ava? - back to her house? He was pretty sure she had no clothes on. That would be a new level of awkwardness for him. But she was clearly in a bad way.

He made his decision and darted into his house. Bobby grabbed his cell phone from the kitchen counter and dashed to the living room to retrieve a blanket off the back of the couch. He scrolled through his phone's contact list and pressed Marcus' name when he came to it.

"Hello," said a groggy voice.

"Marcus, it's Bobby. I apologize for the late hour. Is your wife with you?"

"What?" Marcus responded, though he'd heard the question clearly enough. He looked over his shoulder to the other side of his bed and saw that Ava was not there. "No, she's not!" his anxious voice answered.

"I've found her then, and I think she's had a breakdown. Come out to the Garage Cave."

Bobby put the phone down and held a corner of the blanket in each hand high enough to only see the ground where he was walking in the semi-darkness. He walked across the street and then across the yard, guided by Ava's cries, to where she lay and covered her body with the blanket. Ava seemed to have no idea he was there as he waited for Marcus, who was sprinting out the kitchen door.

Bobby spoke softly to her as he waited for Marcus to reach them. "It's okay, girl. You're going to be okay."

# CHAPTER THIRTY-SEVEN

Marley sat in one of the crewelwork rocking chairs in the study with her dad and drank a cup of ordinary, brewed coffee instead of the pour-over he would have made for her under happier circumstances. Marcus called her as soon as he'd brought Ava into the house and put her back to bed in the wee hours of this morning. He hoped his oldest daughter might help him decide what to do next.

Sensing her dad was near a breaking point himself, Marley threw some clothes in a suitcase and made the three-hour trip to Faircourt posthaste. Both Marcus and Marley were glad school was out for the summer. Adam, Marley's husband and a high school principal, could manage their seven-year-old son, Ethan, without calling his parents for reinforcement and providing explanations.

"Dad, how are you doing?" Marley asked as she set her coffee cup on the table and folded her legs up in the chair. She'd had just an hour of sleep in the guest room.

"Miss Marley, we'll have time to talk about me after I sort out what to do for Mom. It would ease my anxiety to focus on da priority here."

He was seated in his leather chair behind his desk and not in the matching chair closer to Marley – which she'd noted. Behind that desk was where he'd sought answers and often found them as he'd prepared sermons. It made sense as her dad's place of emotional refuge when Marley thought about it. And in her mind, she was not there to give him answers. Instead, she'd come to help him think through options and find his own answers.

Marley's relationship with her sisters was itself in a precarious position. Marit and Mia knew she maintained a close relationship with their parents, and it galled them that their older sister was oblivious to their parents' failures and unwilling to correct them by whatever means necessary. Mia hadn't invited Ethan over for Jordan, Luke, or Emily's birthdays as she always had.

Her sisters' disloyalty and vindictiveness, which extended to innocent Ethan, shocked and saddened Marley. She was trying her best to pacify their spiteful ostracism. Telling their dad outright what to do for their mom might somehow come back to bite her. She didn't want to risk that for Ethan's sake.

"So, what do you see as your options, Dad?" she inquired.

"I can only tink of tree," he answered. "One, and dis is my least favorite; she goes to a hospital for in-patient psychiatric care. Two, she stays home, and we keep doing what we've been doing. So dat is my next, least favorite option. Or tree, dis is a big ask, Miss Marley, you stay here for a while and be her medicine. I tink she needs to feel like a mother again. Maybe. I don't know," Marcus shook his head.

He swiveled his chair to look out the window and hide his face from his daughter. Then, subconsciously, he braced for a negative response.

Marley responded thoughtfully, balancing her reticence to advise with her father's need for objective support.

"Dad, I know it would cause you more anxiety to give Mom's mental health care over to the psychological philosophies and therapies-du jour of professionals you don't know. So, I agree it's not the preferred option. I know you think doing more of the same and expecting a different result might be foolish, but your influence might have an incremental benefit over time, with a setback now and then. But of course, I don't know that to be a fact. I do know that if I were in the same condition as a mom, both of you would move Heaven and Earth to be there for me. So I'll stay as long as possible, but you know it's not entirely up to me. I have to talk to Adam about it."

Marcus swiveled around slowly to face his daughter. "You don't tink it's wrong if I don't send her to a hospital?" he pleaded for reassurance.

"No, Dad, I don't," she responded. She saw the relief wash over his tired face.

"The big guns are here now. Let me have a crack at her!" she smiled at her father's brightening countenance.

"Come on. Feed me some breakfast if you're going to put me to work," she said as she unfolded herself from her chair and took her father's arm.

Cal, Elodie, and Marie were seated at the breakfast table when Marcus and Marley entered the kitchen. Elodie and Marie flew to Marley.

"Marley Marie!" Marie greeted her and wrapped her arms around her. Elodie enveloped her from the other side.

"Marley Sandwich!" they all said in unison as they had countless times, starting when Marley was a curly-haired toddler. Marie and Elodie saw no reason to end this custom, though they agreed to do it on the down-low for a time when she was a teenager.

"Cal, this is my oldest daughter, Marley," Marcus introduced.

"Correction! Her name is Marley Marie after yours truly," Marie gushed.

Cal stood up slowly and extended his hand. "Very nice to meet you. My condolences on your unfortunate paternal parentage," he added with a laugh - not yet privy to the reason for her visit.

"Cal, you are the first person who's ever offered sympathy for my plight, and I thank you," Marley returned the good-natured teasing of her dad.

"Does your mom know you're here? She wouldn't be sleeping in if..." Elodie tried working out her own answer.

Marley looked to her dad, who responded: "About dat," and motioned for them to sit back down at the table.

Marcus recounted the events of the early morning hours as they'd slept, including the embarrassing but pertinent detail that Bobby McBride had found Ava lying naked in the yard. Marie kept her eyes fixed on Marley Marie as Marcus explained the situation and noticed her head bent as if bearing her mother's shame. However, she lifted it when she heard the piano music and looked to Marie to inquire about the source.

"That's June playing. She's Cal's wife and, hands down, the sweetest woman in the house because your mom, Auntie El, and I give her zero competition for that title," Marie explained.

June was playing Rock of Ages in a slower time signature than the music was written. It sounded mournful to Marley's ear.

Marcus returned them to the subject of Ava. "I tought about hospitalization for her, but Marley and I agreed not to do dat. Yet, anyway. Marley's going to stay with us for a bit to see if she can help Ava remember she's a wonderful mother."

Heads nodded an agreement, though Marley detected a reservation in Aunt Marie's approval. Marie was biting her lip, and Marley understood she was mentally biting her tongue. She determined she'd find out what Aunt Marie was thinking. But first things first.

"Auntie El, how's your French toast game these days?" Marley hinted.

"In fightin' form!" Elodie answered, standing to gather the ingredients she needed to prove it.

Elodie began to sing the song June was playing, jumping in about the third verse with her contralto voice: *Nothing in my hands I bring, Simply to Thy cross I cling, Naked come to Thee for dress.*" She stopped mid-verse, mortified and hoping the others had been absorbed in their conversation and hadn't heard the lyric given the painfully recent event. She looked over to the table. All their eyes were looking back at hers. Finally, Marie addressed the situation directly.

"Well, if that isn't God's truth for all of us! We're all as good as buck naked before God and need the righteous robes of Christ to cover our shame. I know I do!"

"Yes, and amen!" declared Cal.

Marcus managed a wry smile while Marley let go of a full-faced grin. She loved her momma's friends, including this new one, Cal.

# Chapter Thirty-Eight

"Momma?" Marley called softly as she opened her parent's bedroom door and stepped in. Standing at the window dressed in a nightgown, Ava turned at the sound of her daughter's voice.

"Oh, Marley!" Ava rushed to her and hugged her tightly. "Marley, I've shamed myself and your father! I don't know how I can ever leave this room. I didn't mean to, but it's done. I'm so sorry, Marley!"

Marley wrapped her arms around her mother and said soothingly, "Mom, you don't owe me an apology." She embraced her mother for a while and said, "Come sit on the chest with me."

She walked over and sat down, patting the space beside her. Ava complied with her request and sat beside her daughter on the old chest at the foot of the bed. Marley looped her arm through her mom's and laid her head on Ava's shoulder.

"How many conversations do you think we've had sitting on this chest?" Marley mused.

"At least a hundred, maybe more," Ava reflected.

"At least. Do you remember the time I came home after the first date you and Dad let me go on?"

Ava didn't recall it and guiltily admitted, "I'm sorry, honey. The particulars escape me."

"I came home crying, and we sat right here," she lifted her head from her mom's shoulder and patted the side of the chest with her free hand.

"I told you I accidentally blew up Casey Rogers' car with an audible, rotten-egg-smelling fart that gagged us both and that I'd never get another date or go to senior prom."

Ava searched her memory for the matching details and came up empty. "I don't remember that, but I'm sorry that happened to you, my poor girl."

"I will never forget how humiliated I felt. I never wanted to return to school and face Casey or his buddies. I think I even asked if you and Dad could homeschool me. Anyway, you know there's a reason you don't remember it."

"Mental decay?" Ava sighed.

"No. You don't remember it because it didn't happen to you. That's ok. None of us remembers the embarrassing things that happen to other people. We only remember our own social traumas. Think about it. Do you remember anything embarrassing that's happened to Dad?"

"Not off the top of my head," Ava answered slowly, comprehending.

"Mom, this isn't going to be the thing that makes your friends stop being your friends." Marley paused and added: "By the way, I went to Senior Prom with Casey Rogers."

Ava smiled weakly.

"Mom, you haven't had breakfast or lunch. Why don't you come to the kitchen, and I'll make you a fried bologna and onion sandwich. You love those."

"Aw, Marley, that's sweet of you, but do you think I could have it in my room? I'm just not ready to face everyone yet. But I will tomorrow. I Promise."

"Sure, Mom. I'll bring you a sandwich now and some dinner later."

Marley returned 20 minutes later with the sandwich, three chocolate chip cookies, and a glass of skim milk, which Ava gratefully accepted.

"I want you to enjoy this, so I won't hover here and watch you eat. I'll be back a bit later, okay, Mom?"

"Okay, Marley. And thank you – for being here, for what you said, for the sandwich, for everything."

Marley left Ava's room, went to the guest room, and unpacked her suitcase. Adam had agreed to take it a day at a time and leave her return date open-ended. He loved his mother-in-law and hated that Marit and Mia's cruelty had taken such a toll on her and a creeping one on his own little family.

Marley had left the guest room door open and looked up to see Marie standing in the doorway.

"Would you be interested in taking a little stroll to see the sights of Faircourt before dinner?" Marie invited.

"Interested and delighted! I'm just finishing getting myself put away. Give me a minute to go potty, and I'll meet you on the porch," Marley answered.

When Marley headed for the front porch, she saw her dad sitting in the living room with Uncle Grant and Auntie El, watching an episode of Green Acres. She walked behind her father's chair, kissed the top of his head, and said, "I'm off for a walk with Aunt Marie. Be back soon."

Marie and Marley started down Cedar Street as rain clouds assembled in the late afternoon sky.

"I haven't seen the weather report, but I sure hope we get some rain from these clouds. It's still only June, and the lawns are starting to crisp," Marie said wistfully.

"Don't you have some bones that tell you if it's going to rain?" Marley teased.

"No. But I have a tooth that tells me when a sassy pants is within arm's length, and it feels like I've flossed it with barbed wire right now.

"Sorry about that," Marley laughed. "But speaking of feeling pained, I thought I detected a look of discomfort on your face this morning in the kitchen. Dad mentioned my staying for a while, and I thought maybe you weren't a fan of the idea."

"It's not that at all! You are always welcome – that's why we have a guest room," Marie said as she gave Marley a reassuring, circle-shaped rub in the middle of her back.

"Then what is it?"

Marie wondered how to express her concern to Marley most kindly.

"Imagine you're trying your best to soothe a crying, colic-y baby," Marie began. "You hold her close in your arms and gently bounce her up and down; you try rubbing her tummy – you're doing everything you know to calm her. But the child's non-stop wailing is on your last nerve, and you're desperate for quiet. Got the picture?"

"You just described my first four months of motherhood with Ethan. I've got the picture."

"Do you think you'll notice the birds singing outside with that baby wailing in your arms?" Marie challenged.

"It's not likely, no. I'm afraid I'm missing your point, though."

"My point is this: It's not likely you'll be able to distract your mom by reminding her she has a daughter who loves her. You know she loves you and is grateful for you, just like she is for your dad. But she's got her arms full of pain like a screaming baby. All her attention is focused on it. Before she can be comforted by the presence of anyone else, that baby needs to hush. So, I'm concerned your dad is putting an unreasonable expectation on you, or that you're putting one on yourself, or both are happening. I don't want you to be hurt if you're not the miracle "medicine" we wish any of us could be for her. That would be hurt upon hurt, sweet girl."

Marley sighed and walked the next block with Marie in silence. She didn't like what she heard, but she couldn't argue with it.

"I guess it's our egos that make us want to be the one to fix what no one else can. It made me feel big-league that Dad thought I could help. I fantasized about how proud he'd be of me when I made Mom better. If my sisters' stock was down, this was an opportunity for mine to shoot up. That's the transparent truth," Marley confessed. "All my righteousness... just a filthy rag."

"Marley Marie, you know how to wear your big-girl panties. You got 'em on all the time, don't you? I admire that about you. As Auntie El would say, 'You grown!' But listen, I'm not saying your being here won't do any good for your mom. You'd be a balm to any mother's heart, my girl."

"Ha!" Marley laughed. "Please tell Adam I always wear big-girl panties. I'm afraid he's seen me act like I'm in diapers more than once."

"I'll call him tonight!" Marie promised flippantly.

"You're right about one person being unable to replace another. I know if God forbid something would ever happen to Ethan; having another child wouldn't erase the pain of losing my boy. Nothing could. I'd just have to figure out over time how to go on. So, Mom needs time to figure out how to go on, too. Right?"

"I think that's right," agreed Marie. "God is at work. But He works through time."

# CHAPTER THIRTY-NINE

Ava kept her promise to rejoin the household society the next day, but she wasn't ready to go beyond the confines of its walls. So, while the others went to church, Marley stayed home with her, and together they planned and prepared Sunday lunch – baked Capre-si chicken, twice-baked potato casserole, and steamed sugar snap peas fresh-picked from the garden. June had made an ice cream cake on Saturday evening for Sunday dessert.

As they worked side-by-side in the kitchen, Marley commented, "Mom, your description of this house didn't do it justice. It's a beautiful old lady! I can't decide if my favorite thing is the woodwork in the entrance hall, the beautiful pocket doors in the living room and dining room, or the charming transom windows above the doorways upstairs. Maybe it's the combination of everything that makes me love this house. I can absolutely see why you, Aunt Marie, and Auntie El fell in love with it."

Ava nodded in agreement. "Funny, that's exactly how I describe this house: a beautiful old lady – as I aspire to be."

"Maybe I heard you say that," Marley conceded. "So tell me, has it worked out how you and Dad hoped it would? I know it's only been a few months, but do you still get along with your friends now that you live together 24/7? Does Dad have enough to do? What about the new couple, Cal and June?"

"Whoa, lots of questions. Let's see, yes, for the most part. We get along as well as we always have. Grant gets irritated with Elodie occasionally, but that's not new. She tries to irritate Cal, but he refuses to take the bait and gives it back to her. Your dad? I guess he's had his hands full with me and my issues. Does that count?" She punctuated that assessment with a tiny dismissive laugh and continued.

"He's been meeting regularly with the pastor of our church, Jonathan Jefferson, who's about your age, I think. It's not a formal mentorship, but Dad seems to see him as a younger version of himself and would like to help at the church however he can. Your dad would have to find something to do with his retirement no matter where we landed after living at the Delaware Street parsonage. I think he's content here.

What else did you ask me? Oh yeah, Cal and June. Lovely couple. I spend more time with her naturally. She's a godly woman, and we're all the better for her being here. She blesses this household with hymns on the piano when she has her morning quiet time. June's a wise woman, too, and not nearly as flighty and boisterous as El, Marie, or me, and I think we all wish we were a little more like her. Cal has more health issues than the rest of us combined, but he's pretty likable. Funny sometimes. He fits in well with your father and Uncle Grant.

"Sounds like a good start," Marley remarked.

She took a quick peek back at the recipe book so she wouldn't spoil the casserole. She believed the difference between a half cup of sour cream and a full cup of sour cream could be the difference between happy tastebuds and the trashcan.

"Have you made any new friends since you've been here, at church or with the neighbors?" Marley continued gathering information.

"I've met lots of lovely women at church. Your father and I go to separate men's and women's classes. But Marie, Elodie, and June are also in my class; we've become a unit there. We'll have to address and change that at some point. We want to broaden our social and ministry horizons.

As for neighbors, we have a doozy across the street – Christine Williams. Her name is all I know and will probably ever know about her. She's not the friendly sort. Next door are a newly widowed young father and his son and daughter. Auntie El is minding the kids while school's out. You'll see them here most late afternoons watching television with your dad. Across Tamarack Street is a widowed man named Bobby McBride. He comes to the Garage Cave on Friday evenings to participate in the men's game night."

Ava stopped trimming fat off the chicken breasts. She set her knife down and added regretfully, "I guess I'll have to spend the rest of my life avoiding him." She winced at remembering her shameful scene.

"Mom," Marley also stopped her task and took her mother's hands in hers. "That's not necessary. When Dad called me, he told me Mr. McBride saw you from his back door and held a blanket up as he approached you. So, he didn't exactly get the view you give to Dad if that's what you're worried about. And Dad gave him the summary version of what you've been going through with Mia and Marit. He said Bobby told him he has a son he hasn't seen in something like 19 years. It's okay, Mom. He understands. You don't have to avoid him, and when you see him, he won't throw it up in your face." She let go of her mother's hands.

"It's just soooooo embarrassing!" Ava whined, throwing her free hands up in the air.

"I know, Mom. But you'll get over it. Everyone else has." Then, to move the conversation forward from the quagmire of her mother's mortification, Marley asked: "So, I hear you saying this move has been good for you and Dad." She'd picked up her father's pastoral phrases.

"Yeah, I think so, Pastor Van Zant," Ava teased, recognizing the one who undoubtedly influenced her comment.

Marley laughed. "I'm glad to hear that, even though," she paused and then plowed ahead, "even though it cost you so much, you probably wouldn't do it again if you could go back."

"You're wrong about that," Ava responded quickly and noted the look of surprise on her daughter's face.

"Come sit with me," she beckoned toward the table, and when they were seated, she began earnestly.

"Marley, I've thought about it, and I would do it again. I'd try to be better prepared, but I would. How else would your father and I have truly known what's in your sisters' hearts if we hadn't gone against their wishes for us? We believed they loved us because that's what they told us and because that's what we wanted to believe. But love is more than words, and brutal truth is better than comfortable pretense.

So many times, I thought if I'd just paid attention to the warning signs – and there were signs with both of them – it wouldn't have been so far a fall from my idealized beliefs about who Mia and Marit are to the acceptance that they're broken sinners just like I am. But I ignored the signs of their selfishness because I wanted to believe they were better than I was. I wanted to think I'd done a better job with them than my mother – and all her crazy issues - had done with me. Because of that, I brought a lot of this on myself. I own that, though it's no comfort to me.

I have mourned your sisters' rejection hard - like a death with no bodies to bury, no rituals for structure, and no flood of condolences. It's been grief in isolation. Honestly, much of that was self-imposed because I was ashamed for others to know of their heartless disrespect for us.

So, my girl, learn from my mistake. Don't put Ethan on a pedestal. Remember, the best he will ever be as a man is a sinner saved by grace. If you remember that, you'll spare yourself what you see I did not spare myself."

"I tell Ethan all the time he's the best kid there ever was," Marley said quietly and deliberately, adding, "and I believe he is. I've never met a boy who's as bright, kind, and funny as he is. So it never occurred to me there might be a danger in telling him that – for both of us."

"I think it's natural for parents to believe only the best about their child because they love them and want it to be true. But we can fall into the trap of not seeing what needs to be seen and corrected. And then you get this," Ava made jazz hands, indicating herself. "I'm not saying don't encourage Ethan with compliments when warranted. He is a wonderful boy. Instead, I'm advocating for realistic expectations of him."

"I get what you're saying, Mom. I can see in my mothering that I don't want to have realistic expectations of him. I want my dreams and hopes for him, and I want to think he wants what I want. But it's one thing to realize that and another thing to turn that spigot off."

"You got that right!" Ava laughed. "In my case, the spigot was ripped right off the building with a backhoe. Hopefully, you can manipulate yours with more subtlety and finesse."

Marley got up from the table and hugged her mom. She did not know why Mia and Marit thought they no longer needed a mother.

# Chapter Forty

"Will those assembled for Thursday Meeting please come to order!" Marie voiced her command with authority to impress Lovie and Chase. They were in attendance because their father's van broke down on his way home from work, and no one minded them being there with Elodie. June and Lovie, Cal and Grant, and Marcus and Chase ceased their side conversations and gave Marie their full attention.

"As most of you know, except for Elodie, Lovie, and Chase," Marie saw no reason to exclude the children from benign household information, "Ava and Marley Marie are on their way to South Carolina to luxuriate in the seaside beach house of Marley Marie's college roommate. My college roommate lives on 60 acres in frigid Montana and sells taxidermy from a trailer with her husband, but I'm not bitter."

Marie was hamming the spotlight now.

What did not need to be brought to the small visitors' attention was that after several days of her refusing to leave the house, Marcus and Marley hatched a plan to give Ava a change of scenery. Marley called her good friend, explained the situation, and secured the use of the beach house for a week for a mother/daughter getaway. A free week of ocean waves was too good an offer for Ava to refuse, and she was easily persuaded to pack and hit the road immediately.

"My college roommate runs a sweat lodge in New Mexico, and I'll admit, it's a blow to potential vacation opportunities. What kind of nut job goes to a sweat lodge?" Grant asked, genuinely perplexed.

Lovie and Chase looked at each other in puzzlement at the term "sweat lodge" and shrugged their shoulders.

Marie regretted bringing up the exploitation of old friends for recreational benefit. Grant had ruined her joke by taking it seriously.

"Okay, moving on," she said as she rolled her eyes involuntarily, followed by a sweet smile in her husband's direction to spare his feelings from her previous action.

Sensing he was free to change the subject, Cal interjected. "Grant and I were talking about the Chicken Bowl Kiddie Pool." Lovie and Chase brightened at a topic with which they were familiar.

"Pretty sure I saw Christine Williams craning her old neck over her porch railing to see it in our yard. Unless we do something about fencing it, we'll likely have some authority after us to do it and a fine to pay on top of it."

"Do we have to keep calling it that?" June wanted to know, wrinkling her nose. "I never meant that a stock tank was for our chickens to drink from."

"Do we have to keep saying 'our chickens'?" Grant was doing his best to root that idea out of the household imagination.

Elodie had an answer for both. "I'm pretty sure we do have to keep callin' it that. Sorry, June. And we do have to keep hope alive for 'our chickens.' Not sorry, Grant."

"I love the name Chicken Bowl Kiddie Pool!" Chase piped up as if he were a contributing member. "It sounds funny and fun!"

"Focus, people!" Cal chided. "We need a fence with a locking gate around that big tub o' water out back. An ugly but serviceable chain link will cost about $500 if we install it ourselves. A couple of white vinyl privacy panels to match the garage, with 4' wrought iron fencing with a gate, will cost about three times that but look ten times better. Grant reminded me it's not a budgeted expense for the household, so what do you all think is fair? The stock tank was a gift for June, so maybe it's on us," Cal wondered aloud.

"But we all enjoy it," Marie reminded.

"What if we pay half and divvy up the other half?" June suggested.

"I've been in the Chicken Bowl Kiddie Pool nearly every day since your birthday. I use it more than anyone else. So what if you and Cal pay half, Grant and I pay half, and divvy up the other half?" Marie countered.

"Remind me where you went to college again, Marie," Marcus laughed at her math.

"That's too many 'halves!'" shouted going-into-second-grade Lovie.

"That is definitely too many 'halves,' sweet girl," June patted the top of her head.

"So what if da Van Zants and da Ford pitch in for sand and pavers around da pool? That would help keep da grass clippings out. Could you do dat, El?" Marcus asked.

"Can do, thanks to my summer job," Elodie confirmed.

"It's settled then. I'll order the materials tomorrow," Cal said with relief.

"Are there any other noteworthy items for discussion?" Marie asked.

"I was thinking," began June. "Fourth of July is right around the corner. Do we have any plans, or should we make some?"

"Come to the Faircourt Bike Parade!" Chase fairly shouted in enthusiastic response. He elaborated. "Dad said it used to be just for kids when he was a kid, but now it's for everyone – even old people," he added without malice. "Everyone decorates their bike or scooter. A few rich kids have those motorized cars and drive those in the parade. Some parents rollerblade next to their kids. And moms..." His voice dropped off as a memory rushed back to him.

After a few seconds, Marcus leaned into the gap to draw his feelings out. "What do da moms do, Chase?"

Chase swallowed hard and finished the sentence he'd begun. "Moms decorate strollers for little kids who can't ride tricycles yet." He turned his head to gaze out the front window.

"Did your mom do dat for you?" Marcus prompted.

Chase was drawn back and looked Marcus in the eye. "I guess she did. I don't remember because I was little. But I know she did it for Lovie two years ago, and Dad and I rode our bikes. Last year we all rode our bikes. Lovie just got her training wheels off, and she was wild. Everyone was scared of her." He smiled at that bit of the memory.

"They were not! Everyone was scared of you because you smelled like a rutting goat!" Lovie retorted indignantly.

Elodie emitted a spontaneous laugh, which she judiciously morphed into a coughing fit. Then, when she composed herself, she asked: "Where'd you pick up that phrase, child?"

"Daddy tells Chase he smells like a rutting goat, so he'll take a shower," Lovie answered truthfully.

"Ok," Marcus jumped in before Chase could be embarrassed by his sister's candor. "That's enough about goats. Chase, would you show us how to decorate for da Faircourt Bike Parade? We've never participated in a bike parade and don't know what we're doing, but we don't want to look like we don't know what we're doing, ok?"

"We always go to Dollar Town to get streamers, flags, and fake flowers. If you want to use balloons, tie them on with string. Tape doesn't work. You can't decorate wrong, but the best bikes always have a ton of stuff on 'em. Oh, you should wear red, white, and blue clothes too."

"Well, I'm game to be in da bicycle parade," Marcus declared. "Anyone else care to join Chase and me?"

"I will!" squealed Lovie.

Marie, June, and Elodie looked among each other for an answer to their mutual conundrum. Nobody in the household owned a bicycle, including Marcus, who'd just committed to participate.

Grant leaned over and whispered something to Cal, who nodded in affirmation.

"We're all in!" Grant confirmed, to the delight of Chase and Lovie. Then, to the surprised women, he said in a low tone: "Not to worry. I've got an idea for us."

# CHAPTER FORTY-ONE

Marley slipped her arm through her mom's as they began an evening walk along the beach. It had been their practice to stroll along the water's edge after an early dinner when the sunbathers and body surfers had retreated to the boardwalk's restaurants and amusement rides. It was their last day in South Carolina and their last chance to wash their hair in the evening ocean breezes.

They both wore sleeveless knit maxi dresses they'd bought for $15 at a bargain souvenir shop earlier in the week. Marley's solid bright pink perfectly complemented her long, black, curly hair and caramel skin – a beautiful blend of her biracial genes. Ava's dress was Bermuda grass green with 1" ivory polka dots. As a fair-haired redhead, she'd been partial to green all her life. Both women carried their sandals in their free hands. They walked on the sand, wetted and hardened by intermittent waves, and lifted their skirts when the waves neared their feet.

"This place is medicinal," Ava asserted, taking a deep breath of salt-smelling air. "Did you notice I haven't cried once in five days? That's a record for me."

"As a matter of fact, I noticed. Didn't want to jinx it by pointing it out. I'm happy for you, Mom," Marley rejoiced with her.

"I feel like we've traded places over this last week. You've been mothering me instead of me mothering you. I want to say I'm sorry about that, but I don't want to lie to you. I know you understand when I say: 'Mothering can be exhausting!' I just flat out didn't have the energy for it. And honestly, it was comforting to let you coddle me a bit," Ava confessed.

"I understand. I only have one child, and that boy can wear me out! It's not that Ethan's demanding. I've realized a lot of the exhaustion comes from the expectations I have of myself. I want to do everything right, and that pressure takes a toll. But, looking back, I can see that you wanted to do everything right for us girls, too."

"All we can be is the best we can be, and nobody's best will ever be perfect. So if you've done your best, rest easy. Why is it so uncomplicated to say this to you and impossible to say it to myself? Rhetorical question. I know it's a self-diagnosis," Ava confided. She missed avoiding a splashing wave that soaked the bottom of her dress. With no need to spare it, she gave up further effort.

"It's not the end of the world if these get wet," Marley noted and let go of her own hem. They walked a little further in contemplation and disregard of the waves.

"I wish I had taken more walks with you girls," Ava spoke at last. "I wish I had spent more time preparing my heart for the possibility of life without you. In my wildest dreams, I never thought it could happen again. That God would put me – in my 60s - through the heartache of abandonment again. He's gotten me to the point where I can stand on wobbly legs and say with the Psalmist: 'It is good for me that I have been afflicted.' I know this trial has knit your dad and me closer together – that's one positive result. I just wish it hadn't knocked me down so hard. I would have liked to have been more steady on my spiritual feet. If someone had presented this to me as a hypothetical situation a year ago, I'm sure I would have been confident in my ability to walk through it like a field of wildflowers. I guess that's one of the lessons: God knows us better than we know ourselves. He knows when the hurts we think have healed have not. He knows that to make us deal with ourselves is a severe mercy, but mercy nonetheless."

"Mom, I want to understand what you're saying, and I kind of do. But I don't understand what can be under a healed hurt that's so bad the whole thing needs to be excavated again. That part sounds vague."

"Well, for me, it was anger," Ava explained. "I didn't even know I was angry deep down. But it was quick to surface when your sisters rejected us. Everyone interpreted my tears as sorrow. And there was sorrow, to be sure. But there was a lot, I mean A LOT, of anger in those tears, too. God showed that to me, and Satan exploited it. He threw gasoline on those flames and brought me to some very dark places, of which I think you'd be better off not knowing the specifics. So even though I wasn't aware there was festering in my old wound, God knew it was there. And by faith, I believe this heartache with Mia and Marit will be for my good. I can already see some outlines of good. Does that help you understand?"

Marley stopped and dug up a half-buried starfish shell. She touched the tentacles underneath to confirm it wasn't alive and swished them in an incoming wave to wash off the sand. Then, she presented it to her mother.

"You can soak this in a light bleach solution for a few minutes and keep it as a memory of this walk together," Marley instructed before returning to walking and her mother's question.

"I understand better now. Thank you for being honest and for the legacy gift you gave me on this walk. I wish I had a better gift to give you than a starfish shell."

Ava looked at Marley quizzically. "What legacy gift?" she asked.

"You've shown me an acknowledgment of God's goodness and trust in His wisdom in the deepest pain of your life. If pain is neat and pretty and handled without some ugly and messy, is it really pain?

Mom, the parts you wish you could change, your desire for more steadiness in the storm, that's what tells you – tells all of us who love you – that your pain is real. The anger is genuine. To bless God in the face of that reality is a legacy of faith that is real. You're not just fair-weather faithful. You're storm-faithful, too, because the storm's not over. The situation with Mia and Marit hasn't changed, but you've changed. Your faith has been tested – is being tested – and here you are. Still standing, even if it's on wobbly legs, as you say. I may need to emulate your example someday, so I'm glad you've given me the gift of an example to follow. That's a legacy gift."

"You're not trying to break my six-day tear-free jag, are you? Because you're about to," Ava teasingly scolded her daughter. She inhaled another deep draught of the ocean air. "This is indeed medicinal. And so are you, my girl. Thank you for this week just for the two of us. And thank you for last week back in Faircourt. This time has been precious and has meant so much to me. You gave me a break I didn't know I needed – and it helped. It helped a lot. But I guess it's time to send you back to Adam and Ethan now."

"It's been good for me too, Mom," Marley admitted. "But can we change roles back for the next half hour because there's something I want?"

Ava laughed. "What do you want, honey?"

"Ice cream!" Marley turned her mother around, took her hand, and led her in a giggling, barefoot trot down the beach back toward the boardwalk shops.

# CHAPTER FORTY-TWO

Ava gasped when she saw it. She and Marley drove up the driveway to drop off their bags close to the back door and were greeted by the sight of the completed construction project around the Chicken Bowl Kiddie Pool. The pool was fitted with a tropical blue liner and set upon a pea gravel base. Seven various-colored PVC Adirondack chairs were arranged around it, and a combination of the garage wall, privacy fence, and black aluminum fence with an integrated self-locking gate surrounded the entire thing. And over all was a deep green shade sail.

"Upgrade!" squealed Ava as she walked toward the fence to inspect more closely.

That's when she spied the pump and filter system that had also been added. Marcus came outside and greeted his family as they admired the addition constructed during the week of their absence.

"This is nice!" Marley voiced her approval to her dad.

"It was a group effort. We started out wanting to address da safety issue and ended up wit da Taj-Ma-Stock-Tank. You've made it back in time for da grand opening tonight after dinner."

"Sorry, Dad. I hate to disappoint, but I'm just dropping off Mom and getting back on the road. Adam and Ethan have run the course of their resourcefulness without me. And I miss them too. So, I'm just going to run inside, gather some things I left in the guest room, and say goodbye to everyone."

Marcus and Ava stayed outside while Marley went to complete her inside tasks.

"I'm not even going to ask what this cost. I'm just going to enjoy it," Ava sighed.

"As it should be," Marcus agreed. "You had a good time wit Miss Marley?"

"Marcus, you wouldn't believe what a mature, compassionate, lovely woman our girl is."

"I've suspected it," he replied as he drew Ava in his arms for the welcome home hug he'd anticipated.

She relaxed her body into his, and put her head on his shoulder.

"Thank you," she whispered. "Thank you for the time away that gave me a little reset. I cried once on the first day – the day we left here - and that was it. Being on vacation is different from real life, and I'll still struggle, but being away with Marley was good for me. I feel it. I know it, even if I can't explain it. Part of it was just feeling happy again for a while. I'd forgotten that feeling, and it was a blessing to renew my acquaintance with it."

"That's exactly what I prayed for while you were gone. I asked God to give you joy to renew your spirit."

He let go of his wife as Marley emerged from the house with a small collection of personal items and Marie's lipstick print on her cheek. They hugged her goodbye, each whispering their gratitude in her ear.

"Give our love to Adam and Ethan!" Ava hollered through the open driver's window as Marley backed down the driveway.

They followed, walking down the drive and waving her down Cedar Street.

Marcus retrieved Ava's bag, and they walked through the back door and into the kitchen to a chorus of 'welcome home!' greetings.

"You're just in time for supper. I made my fried chicken that you like," Elodie revealed.

"THAT EVERYBODY LIKES!" bellowed everyone present.

"Well, I made this, especially for Ava!" Elodie scolded with secretive glee at the collective response.

Ava expressed her appreciation to Elodie before, during, and after the meal. "El, I believe your chicken will be served at the Wedding Supper Of The Lamb!" she gushed. "It is perfection!"

"Oh, go on with yourself!" Elodie reacted with feigned humility.

After a chatty dinner in the dining room, while the men cleared the dishes, the ladies gathered sodas and ice, sunglasses, hats, towels, and flip-flops for the official opening of the Chicken Bowl Kiddie Pool. When all were assembled, they paraded out to the newly fenced stock tank. Ava brought an Adirondack chair to the rim of the tank and stepped into the water. She sat back in the chair so that her legs dangled over the edge of the tank.

"This isn't good. Hand me a towel, please, Marcus," she instructed her husband. When he fulfilled her request, she rolled it up and put it under her knees to protect the sensitive area from resting directly on the rim of the tank.

"Now we're comfy!" she declared.

The others followed her example, including weak-kneed Cal, who almost took a dive. He would have fallen if Elodie hadn't caught him and kept him upright.

"Easy there, Calamity!" she advised.

"Much obliged, El Camino," he responded as he lowered himself into his chair.

"We need a beach ball to float in here for real pool ambiance," Marie suggested once they all settled.

"Then we could play ball!" agreed Grant. "Just kick it across to each other."

"Um, theoretically, that could happen, but I truly hope it won't. Too splashy," June grimaced.

"I know what we need!" Ava enthused. "We need to string some party lights under the shade sail. That would give some real ambiance!"

The group let loose a resounding "NO!" which startled Ava.

"I suggested party lights when we were in construction mode and was quickly reminded that bugs are attracted to lights, and they'd eat us alive. I couldn't disagree," lamented Marie.

Ava nodded, "Fair point."

"You know, we could baptize people in dis," Marcus mused aloud.

"Again, theoretically, we could. But why do that when there's a perfectly good baptismal at church?" wondered June.

"He just misses dunking people," Grant laughed mockingly.

"I suppose I do," Marcus admitted as he turned to June. "June, please forgive me."

Before she could question why he needed forgiveness from her, Marcus lunged for Grant and pulled them both into the pool and under the water. The splash soaked everyone.

Grant's shock had turned to mirth when he emerged from the baptism Marcus had imposed on him. His laughter was contagious, and June caught it. She startled everyone when she stood and exclaimed: "Cannonball!" Then, she did a necessarily modified version and plopped herself in the tank, sitting on her bottom up to her neck in the water.

Not to be left out, Elodie, Ava, and Marie splashed into the tank. Only Cal remained in his chair, shaking his head. "We got kiddies in the pool, alright!"

# Chapter Forty-Three

It looked like the party before the party in the driveway of 306 Cedar Street on the morning of July 4th. The Normans brought their bicycles over, as did Bobby McBride, who couldn't refuse Marcus and Chase's invitation to experience the Faircourt Bicycle Parade. Bobby had participated years ago when his daughter and son were little, with them on their Hot Wheels and Julia with him on their bicycle-built-for-two.

"Had to buy new tires to get the Blue Beauty roadworthy again," Bobby began. "Been a long time since she's been out of the garage."

Blue Beauty was a classic Huffy tandem bike with its original Kentucky blue paint, two-toned wide seats in white and blue, and blue handlebar grips. The forward top tube was horizontal, and the rear was diagonal – conventionally designed for a man in front and a woman in the back.

"Hey! Where're your bikes?" Chase demanded of Marcus.

"Not to worry. Mr. Renniger and Mr. Sherman are on dere way here wit dem. Why don't we have a donut while we wait?" he responded while motioning toward the porch.

Elodie made homemade donuts that morning and set a pile of them on a platter, which she put on a porch side table. They were still warm. Marcus, Bobby, and the Norman family dug into the pile. They were soon joined by Marie, June, and Elodie, who held the door as Ava emerged carrying a tray with single-serving containers of orange juice.

"I wuv da donuts!" Lovie, dressed like a tiny Statue of Liberty complete with a mint green cardboard crown, said with her mouth full.

"We all love the donuts," affirmed June as she patted Lovie's back.

As if the smell of fresh donuts guided them home, Cal's truck, with windows rolled down, pulled up and parked on the Tamarack Street side of the house. Attached to the truck's trailer hitch was a borrowed trailer with a 6-seat golf cart Grant secured on loan from Grassy Fields Country Club. All he had to do was promise to attach a promotional sign for the Club, which they thoughtfully provided, to display in the parade.

"That is awesome!" June shrieked.

Grant jumped out of the passenger seat. "Isn't it? We'll show Faircourt how to parade!"

Everyone came to the roadside to watch Grant unload the cart from the trailer and park it in the driveway.

"All ready to decorate. Who's in charge of decorating?" Marcus asked, knowing the answer.

"I'm in charge. Let's get to it!" commanded Chase as he began giving instructions on distributing and applying streamers, flags, and flowers.

"El Camino, I see only six seats on that golf cart. I've got an extra seat on my bicycle. Would you like to ride with me?" Bobby asked politely.

He'd forgotten to use the nickname Cal said she liked when he saw her at June's birthday party. It hadn't gone well for him then, so he intentionally worked it in for this opportunity.

Elodie looked at him as if he had slapped her. "I would not!" she replied succinctly and moved to work on the opposite side of the cart, away from Bobby and his bicycle.

"Well, I would!" Marie volunteered quickly and enthusiastically. "I've always wanted to ride one of these. May I?"

"Indeed, you may!" Bobby confirmed, happy to have both an escape from the embarrassment of Elodie's adamant rejection and a partner to ride with.

Marie shot Elodie a disapproving glare for her rudeness. Elodie caught the look and dismissed it with a toss of her head.

Marcus and Grant both gave Cal a hairy eye stare for how disastrously his prank on Bobby had played out. He mouthed "Sorry" to them, lowering his head sheepishly.

"Hey, did I see you all had donuts on the porch?" Cal asked as he escaped. Grant followed him.

"It's not us you need to say 'sorry' to," he rebuked Cal when they were on the porch and out of whispering earshot.

"I know. Right now, I'm going to stuff a donut in my mouth so nothing else can come out."

Grant grabbed a donut and a box of orange juice and returned to the decorating committee. Chase was delighting in his roles of "expert" and "boss" – titles the others, except for Lovie, used generously. He moved around the bikes and cart, identifying bare areas to fill and suggesting his preferred material for the remedy. He even inspected the adults' outfits to ensure they were red/white/blue compliant. The only one not up to Chase's standards was Rover, who'd appeared in the driveway to wander around the collection of legs, rub against them, and purr.

"Someone put a flower in Rover's collar!" Chase instructed. Ava removed a white silk daisy from her hair and adorned the cat's red collar.

It took the group just half an hour to transform their various transportation appliances into displays of patriotic portage. Then, when Chase pronounced the job completed to his satisfaction, they all, including Rover seated on Ava's lap, headed off on the cart and bicycles to the parade staging area seven blocks away. Bobby and Marie had a shaky start on the bicycle-built-for-two, wobbling their way down the first block before eventually getting the knack.

Christine Williams watched their activity from her living room window, unnoticed, and seethed at the commotion.

# Chapter Forty-Four

"Chase and Lovie should sleep well tonight," Cal remarked to Micah as they sat in chairs removed from the stock tank enclosure and placed near the far-side edge of the garden.

"No doubt," he agreed.

Cal and Micah were the keepers of the sparkler supply and doled them out to the kids who ran around the home's double lot, alternately waving them like they were directing aircraft on a runway or writing their names in the air with the tiny flares.

It had been a long day for the kids. The Faircourt Bicycle Parade that morning was followed by a ride in Cal's truck to assist with returning the golf cart to the country club where Grant worked and where he treated them to a hamburger and root beer for lunch. After that, they spent most of the afternoon playing in the Chicken Bowl Kiddie Pool, which Micah, June, Marie, and Bobby supervised while consuming copious amounts of iced tea. Finally, for dinner, they all shared a simple supper of grilled hot dogs, chips, and watermelon eaten in the backyard of the household of friends. Now, there was sparkler-fun as the sun sank low. Eventually, the kids were bound to drop into their beds.

Elodie dragged a chair over to join Cal and Micah and watch the children.

"Next week, they're havin' VBS at the church we attend. Would it be alright with you if I took the kids to that?" she addressed Micah.

"What's VBS?" he asked, interested.

"I'm sorry for usin' the acronym. It's Vacation Bible School. It's two and a half hours for five mornings, and kids from all over the community are invited to learn Bible stories and songs, make crafts, play games, and eat snacks. Technically, Chase is over the age limit, but Marcus would love to have him as a helper. He's teachin' the Bible lessons and would love to have an older child to help him 'herd the cats' and keep some order."

Micah was thoughtful. "I don't know. Dahlia and I always said we'd let our children make up their own minds about religion when they were grown. Dahlia was Jewish, but only ethnically and culturally. Her family observed some of their holidays and didn't seem to mind I wasn't Jewish. She didn't discuss God or pray that I know of. I wasn't raised religiously at all. So, I don't know what Daliah would say about this. I don't think I should change our agreement. But I know Chase really connects with Marcus and would probably like to help him. Lovie just likes eating snacks!" he made himself laugh. "Let me think about it, ok?"

"Fair enough," Elodie nodded. She intended to ask the household to pray for a positive response at this week's Thursday Meeting.

Ava and Marcus had the front porch to themselves. The glider was usually the after-dinner territory of Grant and Marie, but they were relaxing at the Chicken Bowl Kiddie Pool with Bobby and June now that the junior splashers were running around with sparklers.

"Long day, eh?" Ava commented as she slipped a freckled arm through her husband's bare brown one.

"I don't know how Chase and Lovie are still on dere feet," he answered as the children began making loops around the magnolia tree with their sparklers.

They watched them silently before Ava recited: "Little children, little problems. Big children, big problems."

"Not in dis case," Marcus disagreed after a few seconds of thinking about it. "For dese little children, losing dere mother is a big problem. And for our big children," he referenced Mia and Marit, "dere problems are so little dey have to put dem under a microscope to make dem seem big."

Ava reached a foot to the porch floor and stopped the glider's motion. She looked open-mouthed at Marcus. "You are exactly right! Yes! You're exactly right," she repeated. She pulled her foot back and let Marcus resume their gentle sway. Then, continuing to gain perspective, she whispered again, "Exactly right."

In the stock tank enclosure, Grant, Marie, June, and Bobby sat in the four remaining chairs with their feet in water warmed by the day's sun and the heat-retaining properties of the metal tank. Grant had gotten up at one point to empty the remaining contents of the purchased bag of ice into the pool. It didn't help except to offer the lowest form of entertainment as they watched the cubes quickly melt.

"Well, we can think cool thoughts," offered Marie pathetically, adjusting the full skirt of her blue and white-striped shirtwaist just above her knees.

"Or maybe you let the warm water inspire you to figure out how to turn this big bucket into a hot tub in the winter," Bobby suggested.

Grant laughed. "Ya know, some warm hydrotherapy in the cold

months might be a medical equipment expense we could deduct."

"I got ya thinkin' about it now!" It was Bobby's turn to laugh.

"El would pour Epsom salts and essential oils in," Grant blurted without realizing he shouldn't bring her name up in Bobby's hearing for a while after this morning's public rebuff.

Marie and June looked at each other, slightly horrified. Bobby met the challenge head-on.

"Does she put salt in your wounds, too?" he asked.

Grant realized his mistake, but it was too late. Marie jumped in.

"Sometimes she does. But she doesn't mean to. I'm not going to say that's true in your case, because, from what I've observed, she's deliberately mean to you."

"Oh yeah, it's deliberate," June affirmed while tugging at her Capri leggings, which were absorbing water on their hems.

"What have I done?" Bobby wanted to know.

"I don't know. I haven't discussed you with Elodie. But if I had to guess, your crime is being a handsome black man who's been nice to her. Now, the rest of us forgive you for that. You can't help how the good Lord made your face, and you're probably a product of how your parents raised you – with decency and manners."

"It's true. We don't hold any of that against you," Grant recovered and aligned himself with his wife's compassionate sarcasm.

"You've probably watched enough football to have heard the adage 'The best defense is a good offense,' right? So it looks to me like El's playing offensive defense," Marie suggested.

"Look at you with the sports analogy," Grant complimented his wife and exchanged a fist bump with her.

"So she's afraid of me?" Bobby puzzled.

Marie paused before she offered the only factual information she would divulge about her friend of nearly 50 years. "She's been hurt."

# CHAPTER FORTY-FIVE

Micah was persuaded to let his children attend Vacation Bible School by their response when he asked them if they were interested. Both were enthusiastic about wanting to see the place they knew their neighbors went every Sunday morning. Lovie said she knew two girls from her first-grade class who attended Grace Fellowship Church and might be there. She missed her school friends during the long summer break.

Chase remarked to his dad: "Mr. Van Zant needs me. He didn't know anything about being in a bike parade till I helped him."

Three days after she'd asked his permission, Micah told Elodie the kids could go to VBS. He had wrestled with preserving Dahlia's continuing influence on their children versus prioritizing their changing needs without her. In the end, Micah reasoned that he and his wife had made their agreement when circumstances were very different. He believed she would support a change if she were somehow aware that Chase and Lovie wanted and needed the sanctuary of an extended family of churchgoing neighbors who cared for them in her absence.

On the first day of VBS, Elodie walked the children to Grace Fellowship Church and timed their arrival 10 minutes earlier than most kids would arrive. It would give Chase a chance to get instruction on his duties from Marcus, and Elodie and a chance to enroll Lovie officially.

When the kids walked through the church doors, they were unprepared for the astonishing décor. The entire vestibule and sanctuary had been transformed into an African jungle. Chase and Lovie were wide-eyed.

Craft paper murals of jungle landscapes adorned the walls, and real fig trees in pots were scattered here and there with stuffed animal monkeys and birds tucked in their branches. Hundreds of feet of emerald and lime green streamers hung from the ceiling, interspersed with lengths of brown paper vines with colorful paper butterflies and beetles attached to them. A small flock of plastic pink flamingos stood at the entrance to the sanctuary, and a life-sized inflatable gorilla was positioned just inside.

At the front of the sanctuary, on either side of the room, stood archery-target deer transformed into antelope with the addition of paper mache horns. A small hut stood on the left side of the central platform. It was covered with pool noodles spray-painted tan to resemble bamboo and had a grass roof made of shredded brown construction paper glued onto cardboard.

But the pièce de résistance was a life-sized paper mache elephant in a semi-circle of large potted trees and tropical flowers placed on the right side of the platform. It was stunning. When Elodie saw it, she concluded it must be the work of a professional paper mache artist, if such a profession existed.

When Chase and Lovie saw it, they gasped, "Woooow."

"Dere's my assistant big-game hunter!" shouted Marcus across the sanctuary.

He was dressed in khaki pants, a brown shirt, a khaki-colored hunting helmet atop his head, and brown hiking boots on his feet. He carried a genuine rifle in one hand and a camouflage t-shirt in the other which he tossed to Chase as he approached him.

"Here, put dis on. You have to look legit," Marcus instructed.

Chase obeyed and put the t-shirt on over the Kentucky Wildcats t-shirt he wore.

"Now that your help has been delivered to you, I'm going to take Lovie to get signed up. See you later, alligators," Elodie said as she took Lovie's hand and led her back to the vestibule sign-in table.

Children were beginning to pour into the church, and a small army of church volunteers wearing jungle green t-shirts greeted them and divided them into age groups. The four and five-year-olds started the morning with a snack in the kitchen, the 1st through 3rd graders went to the fellowship hall set up as a craft room, and the 4th and 5th graders went outside to play games in the field next to the small cemetery behind the church. After rotating through these activities, they all met in the sanctuary for songs and a Bible lesson taught by Marcus. Or, as he would be known this week, "Jungle George."

The week progressed with each age group rotating their starting activity but always concluding together in the sanctuary. Chase's job was to patrol the perimeter of the large room, ostensibly as a "lookout" for wild animals that may creep in, but actually to help keep fidgeters from becoming too much of a distraction to their fellow VBS'ers. Regrettably, Lovie and her two friends from school, Addy and Lena, were the antsiest culprits of the entire assembly, and Chase spent most of his time hovering over them as a cautionary deterrent.

Despite this diversion, Chase absorbed most of what Marcus taught. He learned God created everything and provides for and protects His creation. But, most importantly, he heard the clear gospel message: that sin separates people from their holy Creator and deserves judgment; God sent His son, Jesus, to absorb the judgment we deserve through his death on the cross; Jesus' resurrection proves his sacrifice was acceptable to God the Father; and repenting of our sin and asking Jesus to save us is all we need to be granted forgiveness and eternal life. Then, God will give the Holy Spirit to seal us and help prepare us for Heaven.

As Chase listened to Jungle George talk about how God proved His love for people by sacrificing His only son for them, the words seeped into his bruised heart like butter on a warm biscuit. Before his mother's death, he never considered himself a bad person. But his callous meanness toward his little sister in the aftermath of their loss was evidence his conscience could not dismiss. He knew it was wrong to bully her, and he did it anyway. For reasons Chase couldn't articulate, it simply felt good to vent his anger and frustrations on her. He recalled bruising Lovie several times and then begging or bribing her not to tell their father. It never occurred to him she might run to their new neighbors for refuge, and he'd been shamed when she did.

He felt shame anew in light of learning that the punishment for his sin was born by Jesus on the cross. It was hard to wrap his mind around this thing Mr. Van Zant called "grace." He tried to imagine himself offering to take the consequences for Lovie's sins but couldn't get past the absurdity of the thought. She deserved punishment for her wrongdoings. Besides, how would she ever learn if no one corrected her sinfulness? In that light, he wondered if grace was even a good thing. Then again, maybe God gives grace so punishment doesn't last forever. Chase had a lot to sort out.

When the week of Vacation Bible School wrapped up on Friday, Chase asked Elodie for permission to stay and help Marcus and other volunteers remove all the jungle décor. When the task was complete, Marcus and Chase began a leisurely walk home.

"I really appreciated your help dis week. You spared me several times from having to stop my lesson to remind kids to pay attention so dere neighbors could pay attention, too," Marcus admitted with genuine thankfulness.

"Lovie and her friends were the worst of all!" Chase complained.

"Well, little girls are silly and giggly. I know. I raised tree of dem."

They walked the next block in silence. Marcus was thinking about two of the three little girls he'd raised who wouldn't speak to him now. Chase thought about things he'd heard Marcus say in his VBS lessons.

"How do you know the Bible is true?" Chase asked bluntly, breaking the silence.

"Ah, you're a tinking man," Marcus observed. "Dat's a crucial question to ask because if da Bible isn't true, da gospel isn't true. And if da gospel isn't true, all we have is bad news. Right?"

"Yeah," Chase nearly whispered his reply as Marcus added meat to the bones of his thoughts.

"Dere are a couple of ways we know da Bible is true. Let's tink about one of da ways. Have you studied da American Revolution in school yet?" Marcus queried.

"We studied it last year. I like history!"

"Did you believe da stories your teacher taught from your history book actually happened?"

"Well, yeah. The people – Paul Revere, George Washington, King George the 3rd – they really lived. Lots of history books have been written about them, not just the ones we used in class. Washington is even on our dollar bill!"

"Dat's right. We base our belief in people who existed and events dat took place before we were born on empirical evidence. Since we weren't dere, we rely on da documented witness of people who were. Dat's da same way we know Jesus was real. We have da documented witness of people who were dere – not only dose who wrote da biblical record but in oder history books too."

"Really? I didn't know that." Chase was surprised.

"Really. But not everyone who wrote about Jesus as a real, historical person believed he was da Son of God. To dis day, not everyone who reads about Jesus believes he is da Son of God. So, why do you tink some people read da Bible and believe what's written, and some people read it and don't believe it?" Marcus asked to stimulate application of what he'd learned.

"When you were teaching yesterday, you said God gives people faith as a gift, and they can't brag about it as if they'd worked up that faith by themselves. Is that right? So, the people who believe the Bible have been given faith by God to believe it?"

"You are a good listener and learner! And I have a dollar bill dat can be your dollar bill if you can tell me where in da Bible dat's found," Marcus offered, pulling the note from his billfold as they walked.

Chase thought hard. He didn't remember Jungle George ever mentioning that.

"No clue," he answered dejectedly.

"Ephesians 2:8-9. But dat's ok. You were also trying to do your job while I was teaching." Before Marcus returned the dollar to his pocket, he quickly inspected it.

"You were right," he noted to Chase. "It's got George Washinton's picture on it. Guess what else is on it?" He stopped and pointed out the small print to Chase. "It says 'In God We Trust.'"

# Chapter Forty-Six

"Hey there, Will!" Cal had been sitting on the porch waiting for Will's arrival with their mail.

"Hello, Cal! How are you feeling today?"

"Better than I deserve, and that's a fact. So, say, I know it's last minute, but do you have any plans for this evening? Do you have your boys or anything?"

"No, it's their mother's weekend with them. What's up?"

"Well, I nearly forgot it's our anniversary, and I need to take my Junie out to dinner this evening."

"And you want me to come along?" Will guessed impishly.

"No. Your legs are ugly, and three's a crowd."

Will was wearing postal uniform shorts on the steamy July day. He quickly examined his visible bare legs and frowned. "You don't like my legs?" he asked, feigning hurt feelings.

"Well, the other guys might. You could ask them if you're able to sub for me tonight. We play cards, board games, or dominoes on Friday evenings out at the Garage Cave," he pointed to the garage on Tamarack Street. "It's Grant, Marcus, Bobby, and me – only you'd be me tonight. We also eat snacks and drink ale or wine. Interested?"

"As a native Kentucky boy, I know you mean Ale-8-One and Cheer Wine sodas. Grant told me at church about trying to befriend Bobby and how he punked you all. Sure, I'll fill in for you. What time?"

"We were not punked," Cal said defensively, not entirely sure what the term meant, but game to use it. "We just misunderstood, that's all. You can be at the Garage Cave at 6 pm, and everyone else will come at 6:30."

Will laughed. "I don't know how anyone could replace you, Cal, but I'll give it a go tonight."

Will always hated Friday nights without Sam and Silas. He usually ate Chinese takeout in his apartment and watched television until 10 pm. He would go to bed earlier if he could convince himself that wasn't what sad divorcees did.

After work, Will swung through a fast-food drive-thru and bought himself a 1/3 lb hamburger meal, which he ate as he drove home. Then, he showered, put on a clean t-shirt and shorts, and was about to head out the door when he realized he had forgotten to ask Cal if he should bring anything. He looked through his kitchen cabinets and grabbed an unopened bag of Honey Mustard & Onion Pretzel Pieces. "This could do," he thought and headed out the door.

"Hand over that bag!" Grant demanded when he saw Will approaching with the snack in his hand.

Marcus made a beeline for Will, not waiting for him to enter the Garage Cave.

"With great snacks comes great responsibility, my son," Marcus said as he came alongside Will, put his arm around him, and relieved him of his pretzel pieces.

"I saw it first!" Grant fumed. "Don't be a greedy hoarder, Marcus. You have to share them!"

Marcus clutched the bag tightly to his chest and then held it up in the air by a corner, taunting Grant. "Possession is nine-tents of da law!"

"Gentlemen!" Bobby, who was walking up the driveway, tried to intervene.

"He is no gentleman!" Grant pointed a finger at Marcus.

Marcus was formulating his retort as he stared Grant down, unaware that Bobby had come around his other side. He snatched the bag from Marcus in a flash.

"Well, what do we have here? Hey, I like these!" Bobby declared as he examined the bag.

Will was astounded at the grown-man spectacle he thought more appropriate for a junior high school cafeteria.

"You know, they have lots of these at Dollar Town and Big Mart, just there for the picking," he offered helpfully.

"We're not allowed," Marcus sulked.

"Too much sodium. Too much fat," Grant elaborated in a mock-female voice.

"I'm sorry we got a little crazy dere. It was da deprivation talking," Marcus apologized.

Grant licked his lips like a dog looking at a soup bone and remarked wistfully: "The honey mustard and onion pretzel pieces are the crack cocaine of man snacks. We completed no 12-step program to quit them – just forced, cold turkey, by decree one day."

"So, does this decree say you are not allowed to buy or eat them? Just as a point of clarification," Will asked with a mischievous grin.

Grant and Marcus looked at one other for the answer and came up empty.

"I don't recall da specific stipulation," Marcus reflected.

"Well, maybe putting them in a bowl on the table might help jog your memory," Bobby offered as he tore open the bag and dumped the contents into a plastic bowl.

"Okay! Let's play Farkle," Grant clapped his hands and sat at the card table. His hand was in the bowl of pretzel pieces before the others sat.

"I've played this game before, but it's been a long time. Probably going to need a refresher of the rules," admitted Bobby as he took a seat.

Marcus reached into the box for the instruction sheet and tossed it in his direction. It landed on the table just in front of Bobby.

"Here you go. Sorry, dere are no pictures," Marcus ragged him.

"Oh! We trash talk at men's game night in the Garage Cave," Will observed.

"Well, you don't think we're going to trash talk with the women in the house now, do ya?" Grant retorted. Marcus let out a chortle.

"No, I don't. Just getting the lay of the land here, that's all," Will answered, bemused. He took the last seat at the card table. "

Grant was ready to play and threw the dice to start the round, which determined who went first. "Three. Rats!" he said and passed the dice to Marcus.

"So, you think it's okay to do out here what you wouldn't do in the house in front of the ladies?" Will prodded.

"Here we go!" muttered Bobby as he noted Marcus pushing away the dice and settling back in his chair. He didn't mind, though. Marcus reminded Bobby of his late maternal grandfather, who always said things that made him think. It often caught him off guard, and for that reason, he was slightly unsettling company. Bobby had to be on his toes around Marcus, but he respected him.

"We do," replied Marcus unapologetically, speaking for himself and Grant. "What do you see on dat wall over dere?" he continued, nodding toward the workbench where Cal had mounted a pegboard and arranged his handsaws, hammers, screwdrivers, files, and pliers.

"Tools," Will answered with a shrug.

"And what are dose good for?"

Will thought about how best to answer the simple question before replying, "Making changes to things. Hopefully, improvement."

"Exactly. This Garage Cave is also our tool shed where 'iron sharpens iron, so one man sharpens anoder' as it says in Proverbs. Generally speaking, men do dere sharpening on each oder differently dan women do. We provoke, and we're blunt."

"And we mock. Don't forget the mocking," Grant reminded.

"They do that!" Bobby, who'd been coming to game night for several weeks, chimed in.

Marcus continued. "Now, Marie and Elodie could hang with us out here. Dose women can provoke at an expert level and take it like a man, too. Am I wrong, Grant?"

"Nope. My girl is tough as nails," Grant affirmed. "But that doesn't mean she doesn't need a strong man. Can you imagine her with a weak one?"

They let the question hang in the air for a minute. Imagining it.

"She'd run him down like a cheap battery!" Bobby laughed.

"Yes, she would! But she's wise enough to know that would be a disaster. No woman loves a man she doesn't respect. And no man loves a woman who doesn't respect him. Marriage flourishes when men are tender yet strong. So, my Marie supports my God-given masculinity and my Garage Cave recreation."

Will sat back in his chair and exhaled deeply. "I think I traded my ex-wife's respect for a quiet house so I could study. I just did what she wanted me to do."

"I traded my son's respect for less than that – for nothing," Bobby muttered, surprised at how spontaneously the admission sprang from his lips.

Marcus' inner pastor wanted to probe Bobby's comment, but he felt a stronger compulsion to remain silent. It wasn't a strategy he employed often, but he learned long ago that you sometimes let the fish run with the line until they're tired of running. Then they're easier to bring into the boat.

# CHAPTER FORTY-SEVEN

"Good mornin', Calypso!" Elodie said brightly as she swished into the kitchen in a cherry-red short-sleeved top and matching skirt. She spied and headed toward an open box of Danish on the island.

"Mornin', El Camino," Cal returned Elodie's greeting. "Do you have any special plans with Chase and Lovie today?" he asked as he looked up from his phone.

"We're goin' to the library to return some books and check out others, but that's all I planned. Maybe dip ourselves in the Chicken Bowl Kiddie Pool after lunch. Why do you ask?"

"We could maybe use Chase's help. I got an email here from Will. It says Ed and Jane Brewer from church are moving to Colorado to be near their kids. They're looking to re-home their flock of chickens. "

"Shut up!" El yelled excitedly.

"Their coop comes with the birds," he added.

"Get out!" she howled, forgetting the danish.

"Why should Cal shut up and get out?" Marie wanted to know as she entered the kitchen, adjusting the waist tie on her pink satin bathrobe. She'd heard El's loud commands as she was coming down the hall.

"Sit down, Marie," Elodie commanded her.

Marie sat at the table with Cal, and Elodie sat beside her.

"The Brewers are movin' and need to re-home their chickens – aaaand the coop," El explained.

Marie flew to her feet again. "Shut up and get out!"

"That's what I said," Elodie grinned.

"Will sent this email to our Sunday School class last night, and I just now saw it. Those birds may have already been claimed," Cal tried to curb their excitement.

"Please lend me your phone," Marie extended her hand to Cal expectantly. He handed it to her.

She fumbled around for a minute and handed it back to Cal.

"Could you please call Grant for me? I can't find his name," she said with a tone of exasperation since she was in a hurry.

"His name is 'Lawnmower Man' in my phone," Cal answered matter-of-factly. He pressed the contact and returned it to her as Grant's phone rang.

"What's up, Shermanator?" Grant answered from the first tee at the country club.

Marie rolled her eyes. "This is not 'Shermanator,' this is your wife," she replied slightly gruffly before remembering the reason for her call.

Elodie looked at Cal. "Shermanator?" she mouthed to him before making a face of mocking disdain. Cal shrugged.

"Sweetheart, I have wonderful news! The opportunity to have chickens and a coop – all for free – has been dropped in our lap like a blessing from above. Is there a chance you might approve of freeeee chickens and a freeeee coop?" She turned her back to Elodie and Cal and stepped away from them. She whispered into the phone, "It also comes with an evening of freeeee favors." When Marie wanted something from Grant, she was not opposed to sweetening the deal.

Cal and Elodie could not hear Grant's response, but they'd heard Marie's offer despite her attempt to conceal it. Marie was listening to Grant, but she turned around and made a thumbs-up sign to her friends sitting at the breakfast table.

"Don't worry about it. It doesn't matter. The girls will take care of it," she spoke into the phone. "Thank you, thank you! You're going to love the fresh eggs! See you later," she added and hung up.

"Okay, Cal, what wacky name is Ed Brewer under so I can call him to see if the chickens are still available?"

"He's under Ed Brewer," Cal stated, mystified why she would think otherwise. He got up to rinse his coffee mug and cereal bowl and put them in the dishwasher.

"Would we be able to collect them today?" Marie asked him.

"We could get them this afternoon if we can get Marcus and Chase to help. We'll need Grant too, but he'd need to skip playing golf this afternoon."

"That won't be a problem," Marie assured demurely.

In another two minutes, she hung up the phone with Ed Brewer and announced, "The chickens are ours!"

"Oh, Ava and June will be happy about this, too," Elodie rejoiced with Marie. "We're gonna be able to work some quiche recipes into the dinner menus! Does Grant like quiche?"

"It's not a favorite, but he'll eat it if there's nothing he considers weird in it. Onions, peppers, and sausage will be acceptable," Marie answered.

"Well, that's just an omelet," Elodie frowned.

"How many chickens are we getting? Is it five or fifty?" Cal interrupted, seeking clarification.

"Oh, Grant asked the same thing, and I'll tell you what I told him: It doesn't matter. Whatever the number, we'll deal with it. They're free! If there are 50, we'll send the larger lot of them to freezer camp. I'm going upstairs to change clothes and figure out where to put the coop!"

"Freezer camp?" Cal asked. "Who knows anything about killing and processing chickens? I sure don't, and I don't think Grant or Marcus do, either."

"We'll learn how on the internet! There's nothing you can't learn on the internet," Marie made it sound easy.

Cal boldly asked her one more question as she turned to go: "Why do women use their charms to get things from their men?"

"Because you've trained us to," Marie answered flippantly, practically skipping out of the kitchen.

Cal frowned and looked at Elodie.

"Oh, don't you frown at me! I've got neither man nor charms," she insisted as she took a gigantic bite of her Danish to emphasize the latter.

# Chapter Forty-Eight

Chase opened the front door and walked onto the porch. He'd seen the Van Zants, Rennigers, and Ms. Elodie walk past his house on their way to church and waited until they were further down the street before he came outside. Still wearing his pajama pants, he sat on the front steps and watched the group turn the corner onto Sycamore Street. He wished he were going to church with them. It had been a couple of weeks since VBS and Chase still thought about Jesus. He'd been trying to behave better but still felt anxious about his sin. Even though he didn't hit Lovie anymore, he still really wanted to sometimes. For no reason.

He could hear his neighbors' chickens squawking from their coop behind the Garage Cave garage from his seat on the steps. He'd helped relocate them there from Mr. Brewer's house. There were eight of them – white leghorns that looked exactly alike, which made it impossible to give them names. On the day they brought them home, they all stood before the coop, looking for small distinguishing features among the birds. Mrs. Renniger said she could order poultry bracelets online – various colored zip ties with individual charms worn on their little chicken ankles – to solve the problem of being unable to differentiate the birds. Mr. Renniger threatened to fling himself off a cliff if that happened, and Mr. Van Zant offered to drive him to the quarry. Mrs. Renniger reached out and pinched a bit of Mr. Van Zant's upper arm flesh until he hollered.

"Owwww! Dat's going to leave a mark!" Marcus bellowed.

"Oh, how could you tell?" Marie snipped.

Chase cringed when he heard her say that. He didn't think it was racially sensitive, like he'd learned at school. But then he heard Mr. Van Zant come back with: "Da same way you can tell when you've got a whitehead!" and they both laughed.

He wasn't sure if they were laughing at each other, at themselves, or both. The exchange was confusing to him. Either they had a lot to learn about racial sensitivity or, perhaps, he did. The end of the matter was that the chickens wouldn't get bracelets or names.

As he sat, he noticed Christine Williams across the street fussing with her roses. She appeared to be pulling bugs off them and putting them in a jar. Probably Japanese beetles, Chase surmised. One evening, he'd heard Mrs. Renniger talking to Mr. McBride in her driveway about Japanese beetles devouring her raspberry bushes and his Knock Out rose bushes. Now they both had bag traps in their yards that were filling up with shiny green bug bodies.

He continued to watch Christine Williams. After she finished pulling bugs off the rose bushes, she began arranging some large cloths over them. It looked to Chase like the mosquito netting they used for a game at VBS in lieu of a parachute. He'd lived kitty-corner across the street from Mrs. Williams his entire life. Still, all he knew about her was that she didn't like people, she entered her roses in the Kentucky State Fair and always won a prize, and she didn't give out candy on Halloween, but if she did, she could afford to give out massive chocolate bars.

He knew the latter fact because her bank statement got delivered to him once – stuck to the back of his Highlights magazine. He was too afraid to walk up her porch steps and put it in her mailbox, so he ripped it up and hid it in the trash. But before he did that, he opened the envelope and looked at its contents. Chase discovered Mrs. Williams was filthy rich, but he couldn't tell anybody without confessing how he knew, so he kept the information to himself.

"Hey buddy, pancakes are ready," Micah called out from the front door. "Lovie's already drowned a stack in syrup and is digging in."

Chase didn't make a move to come inside. So, Micah walked onto the porch in his plaid summer bathrobe and sat beside his son. "Pancakes are ready," he repeated.

He followed Chase's gaze to Christine Williams, working in her yard across the street in a sweater even though it was already hot outside. He presumed Chase's mind was occupied with questions about that dreadful woman, so he wasn't prepared for the question that came.

"Dad, is Momma in Heaven?" Chase asked directly.

Micah did not have an answer on the tip of his tongue. Instead, he found himself watching old Ms. Williams' movements, as his son was doing while gathering thoughts unrelated to her.

After a few moments, he responded: "Son, if there's a Heaven, I'm sure Momma's there."

"You don't believe in Heaven?" came Chase's quick follow-up.

"I want to. Sounds like a nice place. But I don't believe in Hell, which makes me iffy about Heaven if you want the truth."

"Dad, would you be mad at me if I believed differently than you?"

At this point, Micah was uncertain about delivering more of the truth. He wanted to blurt out an emphatic, "Yes, I'd be mad! I thought you'd be branching off into your own opinions when you go to college, not while I'm still trying to teach you my values, not while I have to do this without backup from your mother, and not when you make it obvious I don't know everything I need to know."

He was slightly aggravated his son was thinking about existential questions at age 12-almost-13 when his biggest questions at that age were how to get his older sister's friends to let him hang around them. Then again, at Chase's age, his mother was still alive. So was everyone close to him. Micah had never been to a funeral until he was 17 and his paternal grandfather passed from cancer he'd battled for two years.

"No, I wouldn't be mad," Micah half-truthed. It was dawning on him the questions likely came from his exposure to that Vacation Bible School he'd let Elodie take the kids to. Maybe he'd been too yielding. Or maybe it was what Chase needed. He wasn't sure. Micah thought he'd ask Shelby what she thought the next time they spoke. He missed her living in Faircourt. Despite her success in keeping him at bay from her high school girlfriends when he was a kid like Chase, they were great friends.

"But," Micah continued, "I will be mad if Lovie eats all the pancakes. So let's go stake our claim on the rest, ok?"

"Okay, Dad," Chase said, following Micah into the house. He felt he'd laid the groundwork necessary for asking in the not-too-distant future, permission to go regularly to Sunday church with the neighbors. He was sure his dad had as good as said he could believe what Mr. Van Zant believed.

Christine Williams had heard her neighbor's muffled voices and only allowed herself to look in their direction once they'd turned their backs to her. "Humpf," she grunted, turning back to her roses and her determined war against the vile Japanese beetles trying to blemish them.

# CHAPTER FORTY-NINE

It was Lovie's second Thursday Meeting. Elodie encouraged Micah to take Chase for a "Man's Night Out" and volunteered to keep Lovie through the evening. It was no trouble for Elodie since Lovie clung to June like a barnacle on a boat bottom every chance she got, and June welcomed it.

"Marie, any update on Liza?" June inquired as Lovie tucked herself under June's left arm.

"She's done with her chemo treatments. David said she was beginning to put some weight back on, and they were happy about that. She has a scan and blood test scheduled for next week. Her sisters have been encouraging and helpful, and Liza's spirits are good. Thank you for asking about her," Marie answered gratefully.

"Good, good," June murmured. "I'm praying for her and David."

"Thank you so much," Grant sighed. He'd borne this family burden in stoic silence – frightened by it more than anyone, including Marie, knew. He told himself he couldn't talk to David about it because of his son's demanding work life. The truth was, when he mentally put himself in David's shoes, he choked up. How could he encourage David on this dark path when he had no confidence in his own ability to walk it? He was ashamed of his selfish, secret prayers that God would take him before Marie.

"Is there anything in the Garage Cave we could use to make a lemonade stand?" Elodie asked.

Marcus, Cal, and a relieved-that-the-subject-was-changed Grant exchanged looks considering the question.

"Dere's our card table," Marcus offered.

"You starting a business, El?" Grant teased.

She looked at him over the top of her glasses, which wiped the smirk off his face. No one in the household, save maybe Marie, could withstand that withering glare. Lovie saw it and instinctively snuggled deeper into June's side.

"Look what you've done," Grant deflected from his reaction with an accusation. "Scared the child!"

"Scared me too!" admitted Cal.

"She got all of us," Marcus chimed in.

Elodie shook her head and snorted at them, amused and triumphant.

"Because clarification seems necessary, though it shouldn't be, I'm teachin' Chase and Lovie about runnin' a business this week. Thought a lemonade stand might be a vehicle for that lesson," Elodie explained slowly in consideration of her audience.

"I bet Cal could shift together a little lemonade stand from his pile of spare wood under the workbench, couldn't you, Cal?" Grant asked without waiting for a reply before he continued. "But you probably need to value that resource as a capital expenditure for start-up, along with inventory and associated cost of goods sold." Grant was animated now. "I can start you a spreadsheet!" He was on his feet to retrieve his laptop from his bedroom upstairs. They heard him muttering about cost accounting and profitability as he walked away.

Elodie sighed deeply. "He's gonna' ruin this. It's just a little lesson on handlin' money, really."

Lovie mimicked Elodie's sigh.

"Oh, let the poor man make a spreadsheet. He lives to be helpful with numbers," Marie urged. She knew it was also crucial for Lovie to learn that sometimes you allow things to make someone else happy. So she leaned over and whispered in Elodie's ear, "You don't have to pay any attention to it."

"Is it just lemonade you'd be selling, or would you like some home-made cookies to go with it? Lovie told me about peanut butter chocolate chip cookies once, and I've been meaning to try them," June suggested.

Lovie pushed away from June and looked up at her with open-mouthed amazement. June was offering to make her momma's cookies.

"I'll help you!" Lovie answered the question before Elodie could refuse.

"We are, apparently, diversifyin'," El replied in acknowledgment, placing a hand to her forehead, which was throbbing now.

"What does that mean?" Lovie looked at June.

"It means we're making the cookies, Sweetie."

"Grant's spreadsheet just got more complicated. He'll be pleased," laughed Ava as the sound of his footsteps returning down the stairs grew louder.

"Are we done here?" Grant asked as he entered the room, eager to start on the lemonade stand business plan.

"Almost, pal," Marcus answered. "Just one more item for discussion."

Grant took his seat. "What's up?"

"I'd like to invite Pastor Jefferson and his family for dinner some weekend evening. Is everyone good wit dat? I know it's extra work for da ladies to have six more people for a meal. Any dates dat don't work? Last time he was here officially, Marie was absent."

"We don't mind. We love guests!" June answered for the women as she gave Lovie a little squeeze to let her know she was also loved as a guest in this house.

"I've no traveling plans," Marie added.

"Our schedule is likely more open than theirs. So go ahead and invite them and ask when works for them," Ava concluded the discussion.

"Alright. Tursday Meeting is adjourned. Lovie, glad to have you, as always. Your behavior was impeccable," Marcus complimented her.

She looked up at June, and before she could ask, June said: "It means you were perfect!"

Lovie smiled shyly. As the adults stood up and began side conversations, Lovie dreamily and barely audibly said what she was thinking, and no one heard: "You are my best friends."

# Chapter Fifty

Chase broached the subject of being allowed to go to church on Sunday mornings with the neighbors during "Men's Night Out" with his dad. Micah was prepared, having consulted with Shelby about his son's burgeoning spiritual interest. She'd suggested that he and Lovie go with him for support and to see precisely what flavor of Christianity Chase was taking in. Micah was not ready to go that far for himself and Lovie. He justified allowing Chase to go without them by reasoning that he could have one-on-one time with Lovie each week while Chase was at church.

Of course, Marcus was thrilled when Chase asked to go to church with him that Sunday. Chase walked to church with the Van Zants wearing blue jeans and a short-sleeved button-down shirt of blue and green plaid that he wore untucked. Ava, who walked with Marie downwind of Marcus and Chase, asked her: "Is he wearing cologne?"

"Hatchet Body Spray, if I'm not mistaken. It's always on grandson Grant's Christmas list," Marie affirmed knowingly.

When they got to the church, Chase spotted Silas in the vestibule. Marcus didn't need to figure out which Sunday School class Chase belonged to. Silas took him to class and brought him back to the sanctuary when class was over.

Chase was about to wedge between Marcus and Ava in the pew until Marcus corrected him.

"I always sit next to my wife in church now dat I can," he explained. "You're welcome to sit on my oder side if you'd like."

"I'm sorry. I didn't know," Chase apologized, embarrassed, as he changed his trajectory.

"How could you know dat, silly?" Marcus tousled his hair and lightened the moment for him.

Chase was still self-conscious. He didn't know what else he didn't know – this being his first time in a regular church service. However, he was confident it wouldn't be like Jungle George leading VBS.

He smiled as he looked down the row and saw Ms. Elodie, the Rennigers, and the Shermans. He felt part of their big, familiar family, and that helped. He had no idea they no longer sat on the same row but did so today to support him. Silas' dad, Will, turned around and waved to him from several pews in front of them.

A bearded man playing a guitar stood up front and directed them all to stand and sing songs with words projected on the giant screen above him. That part was the same as VBS, except the songs were different and unfamiliar. Chase tried to wing it on the first song and ended up starting the chorus a note or two before everyone else. A redheaded, freckle-faced little girl clutching a rag doll in the pew in front of him turned around and laughed in his face. Her mother jerked her back around. After that mortification, he sang with lowered volume and deliberately lagged a quarter beat.

After the singing, a tall black man dressed in a short-sleeved, lime green shirt and navy slacks stood where the song leader had stood.

Marcus whispered to Chase: "That's Pastor Jefferson. He's going to preach the sermon. I like him, and I think you will too."

Marcus thought it helpful to plant a seed of kindly disposition to the pastor as a professional courtesy.

Pastor Jefferson had recently begun a series of sermons in the book of John, and this week he was preaching in the first half of chapter 3. Chase was riveted by the story of the man who came to Jesus with questions. He had questions too. Pastor Jefferson told his congregation what Jesus told Nicodemus: whoever believes in Him may have eternal life. Chase believed. He thought he did. But how much – how hard - did he need to believe? He'd ask Mr. Van Zant on the walk home. And so he did.

"Chase, it's not about you working up a strong faith; it's about Jesus' powerful work on da cross. Any faith we have is a gift from God. Do you remember dat from our VBS lesson? Of course, we'll never trust Jesus or love Him as much as He deserves. But da fact dat we trust Him and love Him at all is evidence dat we belong to Him. Does dat make sense to you?" Marcus explained as they walked.

"Yes, I think so. God gives us enough faith to believe and be born again. But Pastor Jefferson said we need to repent. That means being sorry for your sin, right?"

"That's part of it. Repenting means your sin makes you sad and sorry for it, but it also means you're willing to fight not to repeat your sin. Anyone can be sad and sorry if dey have to face negative consequences for dere sin – like if you steal something from a store and your dad makes you take it back. Wouldn't all your friends at school also feel awful and embarrassed in dat situation? But not everyone would never want to do it again. Some of your friends might tink it's a trill and couldn't wait for dere next opportunity. True repentance means you're both sorry and sick of it."

"I'm sorry and sick of being mean to Lovie. I don't like myself when I'm mean to her. Dad says I'm supposed to help him protect her. So I'm letting both of them down. And now I know Jesus sees it when I'm bad, too. Ugh!"

"Dat's a solid theological response to sin right dere: 'Ugh!'" Marcus laughed before turning serious again. "Salvation isn't complicated, son. It sounds like you have da necessary ingredients: faith and repentance. Have you prayed and told Jesus dat you're trusting Him for salvation from da punishment of your sin – da sin you now despise?"

"Not yet, but I will," Chase assured him.

"Well, tell me when you do because I want to celebrate my new broder in Christ," Marcus requested as he tousled his hair for the second time that day.

Chase laughed. "Dad's gonna think I got caught in a wind gust," he said as he attempted to finger-comb his hair back into place.

# CHAPTER FIFTY-ONE

"Bad news," Ava informed June, walking in the kitchen back door, returning from the grocery store to get peanut butter and chocolate chips for making cookies with Lovie.

"Nope. Not taking bad news today," June joked dismissively.

"Tell that to the oven with a burned-out heating element."

"No!" June whined.

"Afraid so. I went to preheat it, to make a frozen pizza for lunch, and it made a loud 'pop' and gave up the ghost. Cal's already ordered the new element, but it will be a few days before it arrives."

June sighed dramatically. "The grand opening of the Cedar Street Lemonade Stand is supposed to be tomorrow. I'm going to have to borrow an oven. Say!" she brightened. "I wonder if Bobby will let me use the Italian work-of-art in his kitchen!"

Elodie looked up from the Sudoku puzzle she was working on at the kitchen table. "I smell a saboteur. Do we know where June was before breakfast? She's been bidin' her time for a chance to use that man's fancy stove. She probably knocked out our oven 'cause she got tired of waitin'," she accused June with a wry smile.

"Cal knows where I was before breakfast – in bed with him!"

"Hmm," Elodie answered while she pretended to look around the room. "He's not here to corroborate your claim."

"June, ignore the actual words coming out of her mouth. That's just her way of asking if she can go to Bobby's house with you." Ava knew where Elodie's button was, and she mashed it hard.

"Don't think so!" Elodie said as she closed her puzzle book and retreated from the kitchen to the living room, where Chase and Lovie were watching an episode of Perry Mason with Marcus.

"Well, I'll go with you then. I'd like to see this Italian stove," Ava lied. She couldn't care less about the stove. She would make herself do this.

Since the night Bobby discovered her naked in the backyard two months ago, she'd only slightly interacted with him on the 4th of July. They'd only been in the same general vicinity. They hadn't actually spoken to one another, and that fact bothered Ava now. The situation felt like a wounded animal staring at her and pleading that she put it out of its misery. She felt a surge of bravery and was ready to face her shame and move past it.

June, aware and understanding more than Ava realized, appreciated the offer to accompany her and readily took her up. For her part, June was uncomfortable going to a single man's house alone, even if he was a friend of the household.

"What about Lovie?" Ava asked.

"Well, if he says yes, one of us can run back here and get her."

June gathered all the ingredients she needed into a large canvas tote bag while Ava retrieved two large cookie sheets. On the way out of the house, Ava stopped in the living room, whispered where she was going in Marcus's ear, and gave him a peck on his cheek.

"Ooooooo," Lovie drew attention to the display of affection.

Ava and June dodged raindrops as they hustled across the street to Bobby's house.

"You must have seen us coming," June panted as she climbed the porch steps.

Bobby was already standing at the open front door and beckoning them inside.

"I did! Come in, ladies! To what do I owe the pleasure of your visit?" he asked cheerfully.

Ava and June stepped into the narrow center hall.

"I have a favor to ask. The element in our oven burned out, and I promised Lovie we'd bake cookies to sell for their lemonade stand tomorrow. Could we use your oven?" June appealed.

Bobby's expression turned from pleased to pained – like the cloud obscuring the sun outside had settled inside him and covered his cheer. He opened his mouth to make a reply, but no words came, so he closed his mouth and heaved a deep sigh instead.

Ava and June looked to each other for non-verbal confirmation they'd stepped on some emotional landmine of Bobby's. There was no opportunity to go off on a side huddle and formulate a plan though that was their instinct. They both regretted being so presumptuous of an affirmative answer that they brought their supplies. Ava, following years of her husband's example, waded in.

"We're sorry. We didn't mean to upset you. Would you like to talk about it?" she asked gently.

"Well, I wouldn't *like* to, but I suppose I should. Come into the living room and have a seat."

The ladies abandoned their supplies discreetly next to the front door. They followed Bobby into the living room, arranging themselves on the navy sectional sofa that dominated the space. Ava and June sat next to each other on one side, and Bobby sat diagonally across from them on the other.

"The stove is waiting for my son, DeShawn. It was his dream to become a chef. He always enjoyed cooking in the kitchen with his momma. Julia and I saved for two years to buy that stove for his high school graduation present. We didn't quite have the money to order it sooner, and it arrived two months after his graduation. We gave him a picture of it in a card, and he was excited knowing it was coming. Unfortunately, he never got to use it."

Bobby fixed his gaze on his shoes and continued. "Two weeks after commencement, he and a buddy got the stupid idea to rob a gas station. The buddy didn't show up, and DeShawn went ahead by himself. He brought his pellet gun. The old late-shift attendant didn't know the gun wasn't real – he had a fatal heart attack on the spot. DeShawn cleaned out the till and ran. Course, he got caught and got 25 years for armed robbery and manslaughter."

With the hardest part spoken, Bobby again looked at his visitors. "Julia wanted the stove in the kitchen when it finally came. She said we'd keep it for him, and it would keep us looking forward to the day he came home to us. She had me put the old stove on the back porch, and she used it there until she got sick.

Sometime after she passed, I got rid of the old stove. I use a toaster oven for anything I need to bake and a hot plate to make spaghetti. But I kept the new stove because she wanted it there. It's still waiting for him.

DeShawn's been in prison for 19 years and never let his momma or me see him. Not once. Got another six years to be released - if I live to see it. I dream about him sometimes, and in my dreams, he's still an 18-year-old boy, not the 37-year-old man he is today – the man I don't know."

"I'm so sorry, Bobby. I can't imagine your heartache," June sympathized.

"She can," Bobby nodded toward Ava. "I know your heart is torn up over your girls, and I understand," he said, looking directly into her eyes.

"I had no idea," Ava responded, grateful the subject had been broached but never imagining a context like the one Bobby shared. "It's hard on the heart to have children you raised and loved reject you, no matter their method or reason for doing it. I'm sorry too, Bobby. So many years…" her voice drifted off in disbelief at how long he'd borne his sorrow.

"I just want you to know I never judged you, Ava. I never saw anything but a mother grieving over children lost to her. My Julia grieved hard and ugly over DeShawn. She wasn't as upset about his going to prison as she was that he refused to see us. She said that put her in a prison too. Said she couldn't escape it and the cancer. But you're going to escape that prison your girls locked you in, and nothing's gonna beat you, Miss Ava."

Ava got up from her seat and motioned for Bobby to stand too. She took two steps to reach him and hugged him from her heart. In the end, he'd made his story about her – deliberately kind and reassuring. She vowed that someday she'd be as generous to someone ashamed of their hurt.

When she released him, Bobby turned to June and said: "You can ask me for anything else I own, but not the stove. I just can't. I'm not trying to be a jerk; I'm just trying…" He choked. Lost for words.

"You're just trying to protect that stove since you couldn't protect him," June finished the sentence for him with acute insight.

"Truth is, I could have protected him, June. The kid who didn't show, his dad was watching him that day and knew something was up. He kept his nappy-headed boy home that Saturday night. Where was I? Why didn't I keep my boy at home? Instead, I let my boy run free to land in prison."

Bobby had never admitted his guilt to anyone except Julia. He didn't know why it came pouring out now other than the awkwardness of refusing June's request to use his oven. Still, he wished he hadn't spoken so freely. He loathed feeling so vulnerable.

# Chapter Fifty-Two

June and Lovie baked cookies in the Norman's kitchen in an oven, which June discovered too late, ran hotter than it was set. The first batch burned around the edges and was not fit for selling. Chase and Lovie claimed them for their family, saying they didn't mind breaking off the edges and eating the still-delicious middle bit. Minus the first batch of 18 cookies, they finished with three dozen cookies to sell with the lemonade.

Cal was reluctant to dig into his stash of extra wood to construct the lemonade stand. It was good wood he'd paid a pretty penny for at the lumberyard. He asked Grant and Marcus if they had any idea where he could get free pallets to use for making the stand. Grant did. It happened that the previous week, the golf course had several pallets of Bluegrass/Bentgrass sod delivered to renovate a fairway, and the empty pallets were still behind the maintenance shed waiting to be disposed of.

Cal and Grant brought four pallets home in Cal's truck and, after disassembling them, constructed a lemonade stand that surpassed any-one's expectations. The base was a three-sided rustic stand with gaps between the boards. The countertop was made of tightly joined boards that overhung the base by 2 inches and provided a way to grip and move the frame. Attached vertically to the back side of the countertop were two long thin boards connected by a wide plank, which Cal grudgingly gave up from his scrap pile. He used leftover yellow paint from the

Renniger's bedroom on this canopy feature and hand-lettered the word:
LEMONADE.

Marcus and Chase retrieved the stand from the Garage Cave on Saturday morning. As they hand-carried the load, step by step, across the backyard, Chase shared: "Mr. Van Zant, I want you to know I did what we talked about. I prayed to Jesus. I repented and believed."

Marcus was jubilant. "Chase! I'm so happy you did dat. So now you are my neighbor *and* my broder in Christ. Have you told anyone else?" he quizzed.

"I told Lovie, but not my dad. Not yet. But I will," Chase answered honestly.

"I'm glad you told Lovie. And of course, I'm glad you told me!" Marcus beamed.

They reached their appointed destination and positioned the lemonade stand near the road in front of the lilac hedge that separated the Normans' side yard from their neighbors' driveway.

June, Marie, Ava, Elodie, Micah, and Lovie let loose a chorus of approving oohs and ahhs as they saw Cal's rustic yet beautifully-crafted lemonade stand for the first time. Then finally, it was 10 am and time to open for business. Grant had suggested this starting time to take advantage of Saturday morning chore-doers who might need a refreshment break from their labors.

June and Elodie departed to get the cookies and lemonade. Ava retrieved paper napkins, and Micah got the cash box with five dollars in change. Marie went to the house garage and rummaged for June's birthday party decorations. She found the jute ropes decorated with white, teal, and yellow fabric scraps and brought one back to the lemonade stand. She tied one end to the top of the canopy and zig-zagged it across the frame and around the base. It was the perfect cheery touch. Standing back to admire her decoration, she thought: "Who could resist stopping here for lemonade?"

The group of friends retreated to their porch to encourage from a distance and avoid crowding the sales area. Elodie stayed with the Normans to observe how Chase and Lovie implemented the lessons she'd given them the previous week on business management and customer relations.

In just 5 minutes, they had their first customer. Bobby McBride had finished mowing his lawn and saw the lemonade stand being decorated by Marie. He walked over, sweaty in his khaki shorts and tank top, and bought a lemonade ($1) and two cookies (50 cents each) for $2. Then, he handed Lovie $3 and asked for 50 cents change. Lovie was confused and looked at her dad.

"He gave me $3, but he only owes $2. So I should give him a dollar back, not 50 cents, right?" she puzzled aloud.

"I'm giving the pretty little saleslady a 50-cent tip!" Bobby corrected. "Add that in there."

Lovie smiled at him and handed him 50 cents from the cash box while Chase poured a "get-your-money's-worth" cup of lemonade, and Micah wrapped two cookies in a napkin.'

"Thank you for your business, Mr. McBride!" Lovie thanked him as she'd been coached to respond to customers.

"You're very welcome, Miss Lovie," Bobby responded with a wide smile.

Bobby's patronage set the business in motion. Customers came reasonably steadily. Most were people driving Saturday morning errands who pulled over to give the kids with the cute lemonade stand some business.

Chase looked across the street and saw Christine Williams standing on her porch, hands on hips. He muttered to no one in particular: "She should come over and buy some cookies and sweeten herself up. Probably needs to buy a cookie factory with all her money to get sweet enough."

Although she was standing behind him, Elodie heard Chase's musing. Since Lovie and Micah were busy with a customer, she engaged with his comment.

"What do you know about 'all her money'?" she asked, making conversation.

Chase froze. He didn't realize he'd spoken his thoughts aloud. "Everyone knows she's got tons of money," he answered, unsure if he was guessing or fibbing.

"Not everyone knows that. I didn't," Elodie retorted and dropped the subject as a new customer stepped up to make a purchase.

They sold nearly all the cookies within 45 minutes and had made $26 when a police car pulled up in front of the house.

"It's a perfect day for a lemonade stand," the officer said to the Norman family in a friendly voice as he exited the vehicle.

"Yeah, it is!" agreed Chase, who began pouring lemonade into a cup in anticipation of another sale.

"But I'm afraid I will have to ask you to close up shop."

"What?" Micah exclaimed, startled by the request.

"There's been a complaint about the cars pulling over being a safety hazard. I hate to do this, but you'll have to take this down."

Micah didn't argue, but he looked across the street at Christine Williams' house. Following his father's gaze, Chase understood where the obvious blame lay.

# Chapter Fifty-Three

A rare Saturday night NASCAR race in the living room engrossed Grant and Cal. Marcus joined them, trying to find his inner redneck and connect with it as his friends had. He lasted 20 minutes before he fled to the study and closed himself in.

"Let's have a girl's game night!" suggested Marie as the ladies enjoyed the summer evening air on the porch.

"No, let's not do that," Elodie groaned.

"Why ruin a lovely evening?" Ava pleaded.

June, always taking up for the underdog, threw her support behind Marie. "Come on, girls! Let's do something Marie wants to do. It's not like we have plans."

Elodie looked to Ava and then over the top of her glasses at June. "You'll see. We're all gonna regret this," she said as she reluctantly stood and moved inside the house.

They regrouped in the kitchen, where Marie retrieved a deck of cards from the junk drawer, and Ava divided a box of caramel corn into two bowls for the four of them to share. They sat at the kitchen table, which was more conducive for playing cards than the large dining room table, and farther away from the NASCAR noise in the living room.

Marie shuffled the cards by dividing them into two piles and fanning them into one another with the speed and smoothness of a 70's-era Vegas dealer. She repeated the maneuver three more times before dealing the cards out.

"Mind tellin' us what the game is, or is figurin' it out part of the fun?" Elodie inquired drolly.

"Well, the old maid can figure out it's not Old Maid!" Marie shot back as she picked up the pile of cards she'd dealt to herself.

June's eyes widened at the harsh retort, and she looked to see how Elodie would respond.

"Okay, here we go!" Elodie chuckled and picked up her cards.

"We've got seven cards, so we're playing rummy," Ava observed, kicking off her sandals under the table and tucking a leg under her bottom, which, to Ava, was getting comfortable.

"Thank you, Ava," Elodie replied as she arranged the cards in her hand. "You made sayin' 'rummy' sound so easy like even Marie could have done it."

June gathered her cards and tried to direct the conversation, particularly Marie, away from personal hostilities. "Such a shame the kids had to take down the lemonade stand after only an hour," she moaned, trying to stimulate a sympathetic atmosphere.

"Ava, you go first," Marie directed. Then, responding to June's comment, she added: "What *is* that woman's problem?" There was no need to identify her subject.

Ava picked from the draw pile, frowned, and immediately discarded it. "She's not happy unless she's making other people miserable, it seems," she said when she'd completed her turn.

"Chase said it's common knowledge she's a wealthy woman," Elodie added, recalling his comment. "Don't know what that has to do with anything, but it's somethin' I learned today."

"It's your turn, El. Pick up the 5 of clubs or draw," Marie instructed.

"I'm thinkin'," Elodie weighed her options.

"It probably has a lot to do with it," June reasoned. "Have you ever thought about winning the lottery and what you'd do with millions of dollars?"

"Never played the lottery. Never thought about it," Ava declared.

"That's a lie! When we drove from Bloomington to Boston for that women's conference, you bought a gas station lottery ticket in every state we passed through," Elodie recalled.

"That was what, 30 years ago? I'd forgotten all about that," Ava defended herself. "We were so broke in those days," she added, twisting her wedding band as she reminisced.

"You had a dollar and a dream," Elodie chuckled and became distracted by her reverie.

"Can we talk *and* play the game?" Marie demanded.

Elodie picked up a card from the draw pile and pondered where it fit in with her hand. At length, she discarded a 7 of diamonds.

"Ooh, I need that." June grabbed it on her turn and quickly discarded a 2 of spades.

"You might want to be a little less enthusiastic and a little more discrete about what you need in this game," Marie chastised her while picking up the discarded 2 and throwing down a jack.

June pooched her mouth, then continued with the point she was trying to make. "Well, I've thought about what I would do with a lot of money, and it saddens me to say I'd use it to bribe our nieces and nephews to take more interest in Cal and me. When I admitted that, I realized it's tempting to play god with the lives of the people around you because your money allows it. That's probably why God doesn't allow many of His children to have much of it. We'd try to compete with Him."

"Your turn again, Ava," Marie encouraged.

Ava set her cards face down on the table and responded to June. "You're absolutely right. I never thought of it that way. I'd try to play god in people's lives, too, if I had a lot of money. I never considered God's goodness in shielding us from that temptation by only giving us what we need."

Marie sighed loudly, took the clip out of her upswept hair, and re-arranged it, returning the clip. Then she took a handful of caramel corn and began munching on it.

Ava picked up her cards and played her turn. Elodie drew from the pile and dithered, trying to decide if she should keep or discard it.

"Is it shape-shifting in your hand or still the same card you picked up two minutes ago?" Marie barked impatiently.

June shifted in her chair uncomfortably before unconsciously moving a snack bowl between herself and Marie.

"It doesn't appear to be changin' into a card I could use," Elodie concluded and discarded it.

June played her turn like a jackrabbit. She picked up a card and quickly put one down.

Marie did likewise.

Ava picked up a card and held it. "So, if she's rich and thinks she can play god, what do we do about that?"

Elodie and June shrugged their shoulders and shook their heads.

"No idea," June said.

Marie slapped the table with an open palm. "I have an idea! Let's focus on what we're doing here!"

Ava rolled her eyes and shot Marie a dismissive look, but she finished playing her turn.

Elodie refused to be bullied and pretended to agonize over which pile to draw from. Once again, June tried to fill in the awkward gap.

"I guess the only thing to do is pray," she suggested.

Elodie pulled a card from the draw pile and discarded a 7 of hearts from her hand. "Gonna pray this game is over soon," she muttered.

June picked up the 7 of hearts without commenting that it strength-ened her hand. She discarded a 2 of hearts.

Marie grabbed the 2 of hearts and spread her hand on the table. "Rummy!" she proclaimed triumphantly.

Ava, Elodie, and June rose from the table. "Congratulations," June offered weakly.

"Where are you going? We've only played one hand!" Marie was incredulous.

Ava walked behind Marie's chair and hugged her friend's neck. "That's all we can take, girl!" she said, adding a peck to Marie's cheek.

The three ladies left the kitchen, and Marie, seated alone at the table with the abandoned cards and remaining caramel corn.

June whispered to Ava and Elodie in the hall: "I can't wait never to do that again!"

"Tried to warn ya," Elodie stated matter-of-factly.

# Chapter Fifty-Four

"Love you both!" Ava yelled and blew kisses, dressed in an emerald t-shirt, matching bandana, and khaki capris.

"Have a great day!" shouted Marie, wrapped in a royal blue shirtwaist dress, both arms waving.

"Make good friends and good choices!" June hollered in black Capri leggings peeking underneath a paisley turquoise tunic.

"Be kind and act right!" Elodie bellowed, a breeze catching the orange-tiered gypsy skirt she wore, topped with a purple, short-sleeved blouse.

Lovie cheerfully waved back to her loyal, colorful fan club and blew them kisses before stepping up on the yellow bus that would carry her to her first full day in the second grade.

Chase kept his head down. He'd turned 13 the previous month and was going into eighth grade. Although he loved his neighbors in the confines of their homes and church, he didn't want the bad publicity that could come from having a troup of senior citizen ladies give him a public send-off on the bus route.

The ladies waved as the bus pulled away from the neighborhood stop in front of Bobby McBride's house and continued waving as it rolled past them down Cedar Street. Then, when it made a right turn on Maple Street, they turned toward the house.

"Well, El, what are you gonna do with your weekdays now that your summer job has ended?" Ava inquired.

"Don't know what I'm gonna do with the other days, but today I'm treatin' myself to a pedicure. There's a reason I haven't been out to the Chicken Bowl Kiddie Pool – my feet look like a raptor's."

"Hey, that sounds like a fabulous idea. Mind if I go with?" Marie requested.

"Me too. I could use an hour of feet maintenance," Ava appealed.

"What about you, June? You want to make it a party of four?" Elodie invited.

"I don't think so. Cal's looking a little peaked today, so I think I'll stay home and keep an eye on him," she responded.

Elodie pulled her cell phone out of her skirt pocket and called Towne Nail Bar to let them know she was bringing two friends. They let her know, in turn, that she'd have to move her 10 am appointment to 3 pm in order to be serviced simultaneously. Elodie happily confirmed them for 3 pm.

"That works out because I have dinner duty tonight. Couldn't make a 3 o'clock appointment and have supper on the table at five, anyway." June felt confirmed in her decision.

"What's for supper tonight?" Marie wanted to know.

"Homemade Chinese food: sweet and sour chicken over brown rice and stir-fried whatever-comes-out-of-the-garden vegetables," June informed her. "I'll throw an ear of corn in the microwave for Grant. I know he won't touch the veggies that touch each other," she giggled.

"Sounds delish! And thanks for thinking of my guy," Marie acknowledged.

At 4 pm, June was taking the thawed chicken breasts out of the fridge in preparation for dinner. Cal and Marcus were watching The Beverly Hillbillies in the living room, and Grant was seated at the kitchen table nibbling on a pre-dinner appetizer of grapes. He complained to June that it had been a long hot day on the golf course.

"You don't have to justify your snack to me," she told him. "Enjoy it!" she added as she moved to the sink to give the chicken a good rinse.

June froze for a second when she glanced out the kitchen window above the sink and caught a flash of red floating in the stock tank. She screamed at the top of her lungs: "Lovie!"

Grant was up from the table in a flash as June hollered: "Lovie's face-down in the water!"

Grant flew out the back door with June a few steps behind him. He rushed to the gate, opening and flinging it so hard the latch broke against a support post. Grant stretched across the tank and grabbed Lovie, yanking her out of the water and into his arms.

She immediately yelled in his ear: "Owww! You hurt me!"

Realizing she had been floating purposely and was alive and ok, Grant plopped her down on her feet without his characteristic regard for being gentle. She rubbed the arm he'd grabbed as tears of pain and remorse at being caught gathered in her eyes.

June was now in the enclosure with them, and she stood over Lovie, panting, and yelled at her: "You know you are not allowed to come in this pool without asking one of us! What were you thinking?"

"Ms. Elodie told me I could," Lovie lied.

"Ms. Elodie is not home!" June shrieked back at her, with tears of fear and anger gathering in her own eyes. Then, in one adrenaline-fueled swoop, June grabbed Lovie's other arm and smacked her on her bottom with an open hand.

"Go home!" June yelled, and Lovie ran, squalling out of the enclosure, through the lilac hedge, and back inside her house.

June collapsed in one of the Adirondack chairs and ugly-cried tears of stress and relief, her chest and shoulders heaving. Grant seated himself next to her and took her hand to comfort her.

"It's ok, June. Lovie's ok," he said soothingly.

Marcus and Cal, who'd heard the yelling, made it out the kitchen door in time to see wailing Lovie high-tailing it through the hedge in her red polka-dotted bathing suit.

The next thing Cal saw was his distraught wife seated next to Grant. He limped over and sat in a chair on her other side, and Grant transferred her hand to her husband's.

"We thought Lovie had drowned in the pool. But she was just floating, face-down, by herself," Grant said, releasing a long and deep sigh.

Marcus was standing just outside the enclosure. "Dat is not good," was all he could say.

"Cal, I spanked her! She scared me to death, and she lied to me, and I thrashed her bottom. In anger!" June confessed through sobs.

*"Dat is not good either,"* Marcus thought without saying it out loud this time.

"I would have done the same thing," Cal assured her, not needing every fact to believe it.

"What did she lie about?" Marcus asked.

Grant answered for June: "She said Elodie told her she could swim in the pool."

"Oh," Marcus processed the events with a shake of his head. "Let's go inside," he suggested when he noticed June's breathing beginning to steady.

Cal stood and swayed a bit before taking hold of June's shoulder as she was still seated. They had grown accustomed to pretending this didn't happen to him, so June stood and leaned on Cal just a bit so he could feel like he was supporting her instead of the other way around. Once inside the kitchen, Cal sat June, who had not fully recovered her composure, at the kitchen table.

"Guys, could we finish making supper for her? She's had a shock," Cal petitioned his friends.

"No problem! What are we making?" Marcus agreed.

"I was making sweet and sour chicken and stir-fried vegetables," June answered, forgetting to include the brown rice.

"Great!" Grant chimed. "Italian chicken over spaghetti it is!" seizing his opportunity to adjust the menu more to his tastes. Nobody but him would care this evening.

# Chapter Fifty-Five

Thursday Meeting was somber as a tax audit. It had been three days since the incident with Lovie in the Chicken Bowl Kiddie Pool, and they hadn't seen a hair of either Lovie, Chase, or Micah in that time. It was unusual not to have at least a casual sighting and "hello" exchanged. The entire household felt the tension of their absence.

"I feel so bad," June sniffled. "I don't know what possessed me to hit her. I've never spanked a child in my life! And now she probably hates me. I'm sure her daddy hates me, too." June began to weep softly and openly.

"Well, I spanked all three of my girls when they were kids and…" Ava's voice dropped off as she recalled the current state of her relationship with two of the three.

"Yeah, never mind," she concluded and tucked a leg under her bottom.

"Perhaps we should address the situation directly and talk with Micah," Marcus proposed.

"It's been a pretty strong relationship to this point," Grant noted in support of the suggestion.

"But now the honeymoon is over," sighed Cal.

"Not so fast, Calculator. I had eight weeks with those kids, five days a week. We love them, and they love us. That's a true fact! " Elodie refused to give up.

"Maybe we just need to give it more time. Maybe they need to be mad for a while, and then they'll cool off," Marie counter-proposed.

"No!" Ava reacted with passionate objection, putting both feet on the floor. "That saying, 'time heals all wounds,' is a crock of baloney! The passage of time degrades, not builds. Relationships dissolve; they don't magically improve without effort. Over time, people cement themselves in their hurt and justify their estrangement. Eventually, everyone's just numb to the pain and can ignore it. The saying should be 'time numbs all wounds.' But numbness is not the same as healing. Ask me how I know!"

No one had to ask.

"But I don't know how I could face Micah," June continued to cry, her light blue tunic now darkly splattered with fallen tears.

"I could go over there and talk to him," Cal offered.

Everyone in the household loved Cal, but he was no one's first choice to be their spokesman or ambassador, including June. He'd readily admit he wasn't his own first choice for the task. Cal had always struggled with a deep desire to say the right thing and a chronic inability to pull it off. He admired others, lately and particularly Marcus, who fearlessly and successfully navigated emotionally charged situations. Nevertheless, he was willing to try it for June's sake. Besides, he couldn't delegate this one to Marcus. It was his wife who'd tanned Lovie's hide.

With no objection to his offer, Cal mustered his confidence and said, "I'll go over there tomorrow evening." Then, a second later, he added: "You all better be over here praying while I do!"

"Now that we have a game plan for the neighbors next door, what are we going to do about the neighbor across the street?" Marie asked, her tone not concealing her disdain for the woman.

Grant responded by pursing his lips and blowing air through them the way you'd tickle a toddler's belly. No one was sure what he meant to articulate by the gesture, but they accepted his expression as input.

"Since Grant has so eloquently summarized his thoughts on da subject, I'd like to boldly suggest we not burn her house down around her." Marcus generally saved mocking Grant for Friday nights in the Garage Cave but was too emotionally spent to exert the required self-control.

"Do we not have to do that?" Elodie whined, bouncing one leg crossed over the other, agitated.

"Christine Williams brings out the unsanctified Marie," Marie confessed candidly. "It's one thing to be hateful to adults, but it's another level of vile to be spiteful to children. I've never had an enemy before, but she and her god complex are my enemies!"

"Ah, so you were listening to our conversation when you were badgering us at cards the other night," June engaged.

She had stopped crying when they'd stopped talking about Lovie's family.

"I heard what you were saying, but I wasn't ready to be sympathetic. I wasn't finished being angry with her. I'm still not!" Marie heard herself and was not pleased. She determined to lower her voice and her vitriol.

Grant studied his wife for a moment. She was ordinarily forbearing and thick-skinned. He was not used to her being angry to the point of declaring an enemy. He thought through her mindset audibly and biblically: "You're angry. That's ok. Be angry, and don't sin. You have an enemy, and that's ok. God has enemies, too. How does Jesus command us to treat our enemies?"

Marie lowered her head, looking down at her bare and newly pedicured feet. Then, she answered softly: "Love your enemy."

# CHAPTER FIFTY-SIX

Marcus hated to make the call, but he did. He phoned Bobby at his auto dealership to cancel the evening's Garage Cave game. Although he didn't have to – Bobby wasn't the prying sort of neighbor who'd ask for a reason – Marcus briefly explained the incident with Lovie, the apparent fallout, and that the household would be home praying. At the same time, Cal would attempt to make peace with Micah.

"Oh man, I hate to hear that. Poor Miss June!" Bobby sincerely expressed his regret over their situation.

"Of course, you'd be welcome to join us in prayer at da house if you'd like," Marcus invited.

Bobby decided this was the time to make his position clear so there'd be no similar invitations forthcoming.

"Marcus, I understand your household is religious, and that's cool. But I'm not the praying kind." Then, to underscore the matter, he added: "God's done nothing good for me."

"Ok. I understand. We'll see you next Friday night den."

Marcus put his cell phone on the study desk and leaned back in his chair, letting Bobby's last comment sink deep into his mind. It revealed that Bobby believed in God but held Him to a trivial standard of goodness. He was grateful Bobby, albeit unknowingly, gave him that window of insight.

At 6:30 pm, Cal and the rest of the household gathered in the living room for prayer before he proceeded to the Norman's. Cal led them. He asked God to give him words, wisdom, and winsomeness.

"Cal, you prayed like you were preaching a three-point sermon," Marcus observed without disparagement.

"Well, I listened to a three-point sermon on peacemaking this afternoon to study up. Maybe I learned something," he chuckled.

Cal set off on his mission while the others continued to pray. His plodding gait would take him four minutes to reach the Norman's front door. Cal was back on their front porch in ten minutes. The friends anxiously greeted him at the front door.

"Guess they weren't home," June droned dejectedly as Cal stepped inside the hall.

"Oh no, they were home, Micah answered the door. The good news is that the kids seemed happy to see me. The bad news is Micah was not so much."

"What did he say?" His wife was eager to know details, as they all were.

"Well, he didn't say anything until he shooed the kids into the kitchen. Then, the basic gist of what he said is that he's pretty upset about Lovie being 'assaulted.'"

"Assaulted!" June gasped and wilted on the antique upholstered hall bench.

"That was the word he used," Cal reported with regret. Then he turned to Marcus and continued. "That's not all. He's also not happy about Marcus' influence on his son. It seems Chase has been witnessing to his dad, and it's not going down well with him. When he'd spoken his piece, he closed the door. I didn't get two words in besides 'Hello, Micah.'"

Marcus sat heavily on the bench next to June in the designated place of woe. But the old bench gave way under his impact and weight. He and June landed on the floor in a heap of misery and shock.

Elodie let out a snicker before she could restrain herself. The others glared at her.

"I know! I know! So inappropriate, I know!" she chastised herself in place of an apology.

Standing closest to the collapsed, Grant and Ava extended their arms to help them to their feet as Marcus showered June with profuse apologies. Since she had neither propriety nor solutions to offer, Elodie retreated wearily up the staircase to her room. Marie followed her.

Elodie's room was at the end of the upstairs hall, directly across from the Van Zant's. Its location in the house afforded it one window that overlooked the backyard and one with a view of Tamarack Street and the side of Bobby McBride's house beyond.

The door was closed, and Marie knocked gently.

"Come back with a warrant!" El answered in a tone familiar to Marie as not totally opposed.

She opened the door, passed through it, and replied. "I heard 'come in.'"

Marie saw her friend had draped herself, face up, across her king-sized bed, so she lay down on her side next to her, propped on her right elbow.

Elodie's room was wrapped in cool tones of purples and blues – just as her previous apartment had been and just as the 'Elodie Room' in the Van Zant's former parsonage had been. The walls were a frosty-purple lilac color which Elodie accentuated by always having a lilac-scented air freshener plugged in an outlet furthest from the door. The bedding was a set of plain white sheets topped with a handmade quilt, made and gifted by her mother - a kaleidoscope of purples and light to medium blues on a background of white muslin. Elodie called it her 'forget-me-not quilt' because the colors were reminiscent of the flower and because her mother had made it the year before she was promoted to heaven.

Elodie inherited the furniture from her maternal grandmother, Rosie, who had purchased it new in 1936 with wedding-gift money. It was an art deco satinwood and oak waterfall set with a highboy chest of drawers, a single nightstand, and a spectacular vanity with an oversized, round beveled mirror. Not that the original headboard would have fit her king-sized bed, but it pained Elodie she didn't have the complete set. Unfortunately, Rosie sold the head and footboards and one of the nightstands, from necessity, when her husband went to war in 1942 and was killed within six months.

Marie breathed in the lilac fragrance. "I feel like I'm lying in a bouquet," she sighed.

"Next to a stinkweed," Elodie lamented her failure in the downstairs hall.

"That's me too, girl. Nothing in my flesh wants to be remotely kind, let alone loving, to Christine Williams. Like, the needle isn't even off zero on a scale of one to ten. I suck," Marie groaned and pulled her supporting arm in, rolling over on her back. She stared at Elodie's ceiling.

"I thought you were crazy when you spent a week of evenings on that ladder, but now I'm jealous. Want to do our ceiling?" she asked.

Elodie had applied textured appliques of fleur de lis and swirls that covered the entire ceiling using a stencil pattern and joint compound.

"Let me think about it. No!" she answered and quickly returned to the previous subject.

"Then don't love Christine Williams from your flesh. Love her from the Spirit inside you instead. God doesn't say anything about workin' up feelings first. Obey out of your love for Him, not her. Quit your whinin' and do it!"

"It's good that I like lemons because you don't sugarcoat anything. It's one of many things I appreciate about you, El. I mean 'stinkweed'!" Marie laughed and got up from the bed to leave.

Before she did, she grabbed Elodie's foot and tickled the bottom of it - which she knew El hated. "Miss me!" she threw over her shoulder and closed the door behind her.

# CHAPTER FIFTY-SEVEN

It was painful for Marcus to walk past the Norman house on his way to Sunday services without Chase bounding from the steps of his porch, where he waited to join his neighbors on their walk to church. He was not to be seen, and the front door, usually open behind the screen door as Micah made pancakes, was tightly closed. Ava took her husband's hand in hers, hoping it comforted him as they continued down the street.

About 15 minutes after the neighbors passed their house, Micah opened the front door to let the cooler morning air flow through the house. It had been Dahlia's habit to do this every Sunday morning when the weather was mild, and he liked to continue the custom. Five minutes later, from his kitchen table, he heard a woman's angry voice screeching and repeating: "Who did this? Whoever did this is going to pay! Whoooo did this? I'll make you pay good!" He and Lovie hurried to the porch to see what the commotion was about.

Christine Williams was standing in her rose garden having an absolute hissy fit – flailing about and threatening the neighborhood that whoever did this would live to regret it. From his front porch vantage point, he couldn't deduce the crime. He looked up and down the street and saw Bobby McBride had stepped into his front yard to investigate the ruckus. When they saw each other, Bobby began walking toward the road and motioned to Micah to join him in aiding Mrs. Williams, whatever her trouble was.

"Lovie, stay here," he instructed his daughter firmly.

Micah met Bobby in the street and continued with him to the side yard, where a distraught and furious Christine Williams was now pacing aimlessly. Still keeping some distance between themselves and her, the men were close enough to see the problem. A profusion of red, yellow, orange, pink, and white rose blossoms and buds littered the ground at her feet. Someone or something had cut or pulled them off their stems. The only color remaining on the dozen bushes was the green of their leaves.

"Oh, my, Ms. Williams! I'm sorry about your roses," Bobby sympathized.

"Is there anything we can do?" Micah offered lamely, not knowing what else he could say.

"What do you think can be done here?" She snapped before her face softened slightly, worn out by the exertion of her rage.

"Who would do this? Who would come in my yard and into my private garden and do this horrible thing?" She dared them to answer the question she had asked rhetorically.

She seemed unsteady on her feet to Bobby. He opened the small gate of the picket fence that surrounded her side yard garden and approached her.

"Here, take my arm, and let's sit you down on the porch steps," he instructed, not asking or waiting for her permission.

She took his arm, let him lead her to the steps, and sat, pulling a light cotton sweater tighter around her thin frame. Bobby noticed tears lining the rims of her eyes and a fierce determination not to let them fall. He sat down next to her, a little stunned to be doing so.

Bobby had lived kitty-corner from Christine Williams for 40 years, and neither he nor Julia, when she was alive, had ever gotten this close to her. They'd called her "stand-off-ish," which was a polite underestimation. They'd instructed their children, DeShawn and Claire, to keep their distance from her just as Micah and Dahlia had ordered Chase and Lovie.

"Daaaaaaddy," Lovie called from across the street in her lace-trimmed, pink baby doll nightgown.

*"Perfect timing,"* Micah thought. Since he could do nothing, he excused himself: "I have to get back to make the kids breakfast."

He walked back to his house, wondering why he had lied about having to make a breakfast they'd nearly finished eating. He reminded himself he was a grown man who didn't need to make up excuses for anyone, especially not for the nasty woman he was sure was responsible for shutting down his children's lemonade stand.

"What happened, Daddy?" Lovie eagerly quizzed him when he'd reached their front walk.

"Some nut destroyed Mrs. Williams's roses," he answered succinctly.

"Is that all?" She grumbled, disappointed it wasn't something she considered tragic.

He ushered her back into the house to the breakfast table. Chase stood at the kitchen sink, washing his plate and orange juice glass and placing them carefully in the dish drainer. When he reached for the oily griddle on the stove and brought it to the sink to wash, Micah couldn't believe his eyes.

"What's gotten into you?" he laughed and playfully snapped a drying towel on his son's bum.

"Just trying to be helpful," Chase responded.

Lovie gathered the remaining dishes from the table and brought them to the sink. "Here you go, Mr. Helpful. You should pull your sleeves up; they're getting all wet. Doesn't that feel awful? I hate getting wet sleeves when I wash my hands."

"How do you feel about getting your face wet?" he replied, splashing her with a cupped handful of water.

She ran away shrieking as intended, and Chase was pleased.

# Chapter Fifty-Eight

Bobby let Rover out the back door for his evening hunting expedition and noticed his neighbors seated around their stock tank. Some had their feet in the water, and all held soda cans to sip on. He wandered over.

"Hey, Bobby! There are some folding chairs just inside the garage door. Grab one and a soda from the cooler here and visit a spell with us," Grant invited.

"Sure, why not?" he agreed. So Bobby collected the chair and soda, brought them inside the Chicken Bowl Kiddie Pool enclosure, and found a spot to fit himself between Marcus and June.

"I'm afraid y'all missed the neighborhood drama while you were at church this morning," he began as he opened his cherry cola. All eyes were riveted on him, and he continued, "Someone destroyed Christine Williams' roses. I promise you've never heard a woman rant and holler like she did. Micah and I went over when we heard her squalling. Every rose from every bush was lying on the ground. She was so worked up I thought she was gonna have a stroke. Had to sit her down on the porch steps for a bit and calm her down."

"Who would do such a thing?" June wondered aloud.

"Well, that's what she wants to know for sure. Said when she finds out, there will be hell to pay."

Nobody doubted it.

"You sat down with her?" Marie was intrigued. "What'd she say? What'd *you* say?"

Bobby chuckled. "Yeah, I could hardly believe it myself. It was the most words passed between us in the 40 years we've been neighbors. She said her roses were 'priceless'. Or, was it 'irreplaceable'? Said her whole life's work was in ruins. She also mentioned she wouldn't have an entry for the flower show at the fair next week, but it didn't seem to be her main concern, which surprised me. I reminded her that there was always next year. She said nothing about that but gave me a look that almost lit my hair. Thought I smelled smoke! After that, I just sat with her till I thought her blood pressure was down. I asked her if she needed help into her house, and she refused that right quick. Then she went inside her house, and I went inside mine. That was it."

"It was very kind of you to go to her and give her some attention, Bobby," Marie commented.

"Someone's big mad at that woman, though," Elodie whistled.

"Well, maybe the latest victim of her threats wasn't having it," Grant speculated.

They all pondered that in silence for a minute.

Then Bobby asked: "How'd it go with Micah the other evening, Cal?"

"Not like we hoped." Cal had no energy to elaborate.

"Well, maybe it'll get better after a little time goes by," Bobby offered hopefully.

Everyone looked at Ava, expecting a rerun of her 'time heals all wounds' rant. However, like Cal, she didn't have the energy for explanations on this August evening when everything surrounding them felt icky and oppressive, including the weather. Ava needed deeper refreshment than the Chicken Bowl Kiddie Pool or the cold soda provided. So she surprised them when, instead of a lecture, she began to sing in a smooth alto voice: "Praise God from Whom all blessings flow."

The others joined in, and the hairs on Bobby's arms were raised.

"Praise Him all creatures here below. Praise Him above ye heavenly host. Praise Father, Son, and Holy Ghost," they sang, June and Elodie providing lovely harmony.

"Look at that! Goosebumps!" Bobby held out his arms for their inspection. "I haven't heard that since I was a kid in my momma's church. Beautiful! Just beautiful!" he gushed.

The Doxology touched something deep within Bobby's heart that no lecture could have. Ava didn't know it, but she'd just preached a sermon to him.

"Praise is medicine for the soul, Bobby. I just needed a little bit of that balm on my heavy heart," Ava confessed.

"Well, I thank you for splashing a little bit on me," he said, genuinely grateful and surprised.

"That was a blessing to me, too. I've got something I have to do," said Marie as she pulled her legs out of the pool, stood to dry them off, and slipped on her sandals.

"Can't it wait till tomorrow? Are you just going to leave me here?" Grant griped.

"Can't wait. I have to obey the Spirit. Besides, Elodie won't bite you in front of all these witnesses," Marie shouted over her shoulder on her way to the house.

Marie went to her bedroom and retrieved her laptop from her nightstand and her wallet from her purse. She settled into her leather recliner near the foot of the bed, opened the computer, and searched for "florist near me." There were two choices in Faircourt: Faircourt Florist and Say It With Flowers. Since her mission was to say it with flowers, she chose that florist and clicked on their website.

She looked through the categories of arrangements: Wedding, Funeral, Birthday, Get Well, and Thinking of You. "Ah, that one should do," Marie thought. She clicked through the category options and settled on a medium-sized bouquet of assorted pastel flowers in Victorian styling with trailing ivy and ribbons. The last option before payment was an option to print something on an accompanying card.

Marie ruminated for a minute. The only thing that hung her up was how to sign the card. She suspected the recipient might toss the gift in the street if she knew who had sent it. Perhaps it would be better if sent anonymously. It might help the person focus on the message instead of the messenger. Marie didn't need any credit or thanks. She just needed to obey Jesus' words: Love Your Enemy. A smile crossed her face, and she typed:

*I heard about the destruction of your flowers. I hope these poor substitutes will comfort you, not because they replace what you've lost, but because they come from someone who loves you and cares. With kind regards, LYE*

She took her credit card from her wallet and filled out the payment screen. She hit "submit" and smiled again. Obedience felt good.

# CHAPTER FIFTY-NINE

The chickens may have been Marie's doing, but Elodie had made them her babies now that her summer job tending human children was done. Even after the late-morning egg collection was completed, Elodie would make one, sometimes two, more trips to the coop to visit the birds and have a talk. They'd cluck, Elodie would cluck a response, and they'd cluck again.

The chickens and their conversations amused Elodie. She'd forget the Garage Cave windows above the coop were open, and all the clucking, chickens and hers, could be heard by whoever might be in there. She'd been overheard by Cal and teased about it more than once. Elodie didn't care and was not dissuaded from her talks with the chickens.

This evening, as she came to the coop to see how the birds were getting on and what they had to say for themselves, she heard voices wafting from the Garage Cave over the pen.

"It sure is good to see you; we've all missed you," said Marcus' familiar voice.

"It's his second day coming over after supper for an hour or two. He makes a little pocket money, and I'm weeding out 40 years of stuff I'd likely never touch again. He climbs around and gets stuff down that's piled high. I'd probably break a hip trying to do it," Bobby explained.

"Must be a dusty job. That explains the long-sleeved shirt. I always questioned seeing boys wear shorts in the winter and long sleeves in the summer," Cal laughed.

"Yeah," Chase muttered, self-conscious of his clothing now. "Guess I'd better get to work," he said, walking back across Tamarack Street to Bobby's garage.

"I'll be along. Go ahead and start loading what we got for the dump in the S10," Bobby shouted after him.

He turned back to Marcus and Cal. "Had a nice talk with the boy while we worked yesterday. He misses you all, too. He's not happy that his dad won't let him go to church or see you. Pretty mad about it, actually. He doesn't care that Grant tore up Lovie's bottom. Says she deserved it."

"What?" exclaimed Cal. "Grant didn't spank her. My June did."

"I know! That's why I'm telling you this. It seems Lovie told her daddy it was Mr. Renniger. She must have thought she was protecting Miss June by blaming him."

"Dere's a big difference between a spank a grown man can dish out and one from our little old June, who adores Lovie," Marcus reasoned. "Ah, dat's why he told Cal he tought she'd been 'assaulted.' He believes it was Grant."

"When I went to his house to talk to him last week, he never gave me a chance to talk. He never heard our side of what happened," Cal recalled.

"Some people don't want to know what dey don't know, and dey'll shut you down if you're a tret to their security. I'm sure Micah doesn't want to believe Lovie would lie to him, so whatever she said is the gospel truth, even if it's not. He'd rather separate from us and have his children separated from us dan upset his narrative. And dis way, he gets to demonstrate he's dere protector. It makes Micah feel good, even if it's not good dat Lovie gets away wit lying and Chase suffers the loss of people he loves," Marcus counseled.

"So, what do we do? You know June is distraught," Cal fretted.

"I don't know at dis moment. My first tought is dat Lovie will have to confess. She's got to be missing June too, and in her heart, she knows she did wrong. Tank you for telling us dis, Bobby. We appreciate it."

The men continued their conversation while Elodie walked around the far side of the Garage Cave and crossed the street toward Bobby's garage, where Chase was loading boxes into the truck. The men could dither about what to do, but Elodie knew Chase could also tell his father what happened; but only if Chase knew the truth. So she proposed to tell him.

"Hey there, stranger," Elodie greeted him.

Startled by her voice, he turned around toward her, holding a large box in both hands. He'd pushed up his long sleeves to get some relief from the saturated August air and exposed forearms that Elodie could see were covered in scabby scratches.

"Good grief! What happened to you?" she asked.

"Oh, Rover got a little rough. We were playing."

Elodie looked over the top of her glasses at him. "Boy, do I have 'fool' written on my forehead? Rover doesn't play. And if he did, after the first scratch, you'd have the sense God gave you not to keep on. So, I'm askin' you again, what happened to you?"

Chase put the box on the ground and unconsciously looked across Cedar Street at Christine Williams's house. Elodie followed the glance and sighed deeply.

"Come sit here, Chase." She sat on the open tailgate of the truck, and he sullenly followed.

"Why'd you destroy Christine Williams' roses like that?" she asked with less volume than her previous inquiry.

"How'd you find out?" Shocked, Chase genuinely wanted to know.

"Boy, you told me! You told me part when you lied about Rover, and you told me the other part when you looked at her house over there."

"Oh, are you going to tell my father?"

"No, I'll be there when you tell him, though."

Chase exhaled nearly every bit of breath in his lungs and closed his eyes, imagining and dreading the scene he saw play out before them.

Elodie let him be for a moment. While his eyes were closed, she waved her arm and captured the guys' attention in the Garage Cave just 20 yards away. They walked over to where she and Chase sat. Hearing the approaching footsteps, Chase opened his eyes, which quickly filled with the fear of impending doom.

"Can I ask why you did it? I know there's a reason," Elodie asked, confident the men would catch up on the context. She could tell they'd already noticed the scratches as their eyebrows raised in concern.

"I don't know why. I was just so mad. First, she called the cops on our lemonade business. Then Lovie made trouble, and both of us got punished. After that, I couldn't go to church, and I couldn't..." his voice broke with emotion. "I couldn't be friends with you anymore. I was just so angry." He looked directly at Marcus and sobbed, "I'm probably not even a Christian anymore after what I did."

Marcus gently took hold of both his shoulders and looked into the boy's face. "Chase, remember dis: We don't become Christians or stay Christians based on what we do. We become and we stay Christians based on what Jesus has already done for us. He has lived the sinless life we are incapable of. You have repented and believed, so God has sealed you as His own. It's not within our power to undo dat seal. He will be faithful to His word to keep us and bring us to Heaven someday, even dough we are unfaithful to Him by our sins. We confess our sins and receive forgiveness and restoration of fellowship with God. Chase, you will always be His child."

Elodie put her arm around the boy and pulled him into her side. He relaxed against her, relieved to know he would not be rejected by her or any of the neighbors he loved in spite of the awful thing he'd done.

After a moment of reassuring affection, Elodie addressed the reason she'd approached Chase in the first place.

"Mr. Van Zant is right – we all sin. Your sister has sinned, too. She told you and your dad it was Mr. Renniger who spanked her, and that wasn't the truth. Mr. Renniger pulled Lovie out of the pool, but it was Miss June who spanked her, cause she thought Lovie was dead and because she told her a lie. Miss June didn't mean to; she just lost her mind over Lovie cause she loves her so much. So we're gonna go tell your dad what you did, and Lovie's gonna tell him what she did."

Chase brightened the faintest bit. Misery did indeed love company. Elodie hopped off the tailgate, and Chase did likewise.

"We're gonna get June to go with us. Why don't you guys get Ava, Marie, and Grant and pray on the porch?" Elodie suggested as she and the boy walked away.

Bobby scratched his head. "How did she know what Lovie told her dad? Thought I was the only one who put that together," he wondered aloud.

Marcus and Cal shrugged their shoulders and shook their heads. They returned to the Garage Cave to close the overhead doors before going to their prayer assignment. As they headed toward the house, Bobby shouted, "Can I come?"

# Chapter Sixty

Although he could have walked into his house, Chase stood on the front porch at the front door with Elodie and June while waiting for his dad to answer their knock. When Micah opened the door, Lovie, who was with him, sidled past him as soon as she set eyes on June. She folded her arms around Miss June and buried her face in her tummy.

"Micah, Chase has some show and tell for you," Elodie announced with determination before Micah could say a word.

Micah looked from Elodie to his son, who held out his arms.

"What on earth?" Micah exclaimed.

Chase lost most of the bravery he'd felt from having Elodie and June by his side. Then, ashamed, he hung his head and confessed, "Dad, I'm the one who pulled all the flowers from Mrs. William's bushes."

"Ooooo," Lovie loosed her condemnation of her bother's action from Miss June's side.

June bent down to her level and asked, "Don't you also have something you'd like to tell your daddy?"

Lovie looked confused.

"About who really gave you the spanking," June cleared her confusion. Lovie looked at her feet and said nothing. June stood to face Micah.

"I saw Lovie floating face-down in the stock tank from our kitchen window and feared the worst. Grant ran outside with me, and he pulled Lovie from the water. When I realized she was just playing, I was relieved but also furious. I asked her who had allowed her to go into the pool by herself, and she said that Elodie did – which wasn't true because Elodie wasn't home that afternoon. I was angry at being lied to, and I was pumped with adrenaline. I swatted her backside. I didn't decide to do that; I just reacted, and it was wrong. I was wrong to spank in anger, and I ask your forgiveness and Lovie's forgiveness."

Micah leaned back against the door frame as if he were exhausted and needed the support.

"Lovie, do you forgive me?" June asked her. Lovie nodded in affirmation, confirming the new version of events Micah was processing.

He took a deep breath and began, "She also told me Elodie gave her permission to play in the pool. And yes, Mr. Renniger grabbed her arm, pulled her out of the pool, and spanked her because he didn't like her. I hear myself say that now, knowing it can't be right. I'm very sorry I didn't come to you to hear your side of what happened. But now that I know you were terrified Lovie was drowned, I understand your swatting her backside. I've never spanked her, but I believe I might have in that situation."

Micah shifted from the doorframe, looked at both his children, and scolded them sharply. "I do not appreciate being lied to either. I want both of you to go to your rooms right now. I'll talk to you later. But believe me when I say you do not want me to talk to you right now."

Micah made way for them to pass through the doorway, and the sound of their quickened footsteps up the stairs reverberated in the entrance.

"I'm really embarrassed," Micah admitted, looking down at the scuffed brown loafers on his feet. "I know it was stupid of me to hear only one side of the story. I guess I only wanted to believe there was one side. I made a fool of myself for it."

June sympathized. "Nobody wants to think their kids aren't telling them the truth. I was stunned Lovie would lie to me, so I can't imagine how you feel."

"Micah, your other friends are next door on the porch. Why don't you come over so they can hug your neck, and we'll all put this behind us?" Elodie invited.

Elodie, June, and Micah walked around the lilac hedge and greeted the friends on the porch. El was surprised to see Bobby among them. In fact, so was Bobby. He felt like something tight inside him broke loose when he heard the Doxology sung last Sunday evening. It was strange and bewildering. Unidentifiable.

His desire to join Marcus and Cal in their household prayer meeting surely wasn't from a desire to pray himself. Yet, he was curiously drawn to engage with and observe these neighbors. Moreover, he was puzzled why their first response was to pray about a difficult situation when prayer didn't seem to work any better for them than it had for him as a child. At least, it hadn't worked the last time they prayed for reconciliation with the Norman family.

But now, Micah was coming up the sidewalk, not two minutes after Marcus had prayed to God, asking Him to soften Micah's heart and restore their household relationships. Bobby could still hear all their "Amen"s ringing in his ear. He watched as the Rennigers, Van Zants, Shermans, and Elodie all took their turn to accept Micah's apology and either shake his hand or hug him. The word that kept going through his mind as he watched the scene unfolding was "incredible." He wondered why "incredible" God-orchestrated events like this never happened in his life.

Micah looked like he was about to take his leave to deal with the kids at home, but he stopped to address another issue.

"Marcus, I owe you a special apology. I was jealous of Chase's growing admiration of you. He respects you and looks up to you. I know he loves me, but I wanted everything he had to give, which was selfish. I'm sorry. I want to be the kind of man who admits when he's been wrong. I must be if I want my children to admit their wrongs too."

"The loss of Dahlia is a disorienting gut punch. So, I understand da impulse to hang on tightly to what you have left, and I accept your apology," Marcus replied.

"I'm at a bit of a loss to know what to do about Christine Williams' rose bushes since Chase confessed to destroying them. Am I supposed to haul him over there and make him apologize?" Micah was asking for guidance.

"Oooh, no, no, no," came the answering chorus of everyone weighing in on the question in vehement unanimity.

"Micah, if it were anyone oder dan Christine Williams, I'd say 'probably so.' But since we know her proclivity for legal action and her resolute trets against whoever did dis, I don't tink you need to invite dat. None of us standing here would put it past her to call Child Protective Services and get dem involved. You've all been trough enough trauma. I recommend disciplining your son privately so he knows you take it seriously but leave room for grace too. Talk to him about his anger and constructive ways to deal wit it," Marcus advised.

"Thank you. I'll do that," Micah smiled with relief. "Have a good evening, everyone!"

Bobby walked down the porch steps and walkway with Micah, turning left toward his home as Micah turned right toward his. Bobby shook his head and whispered to himself: "Incredible."

# Chapter Sixty-One

Elodie and June had moved their chairs as far back as possible until the fence prevented them from going farther, but they were still in the splash zone.

"Hey! Have fun but remember we're tryin' to stay dry over here," Elodie admonished the Jefferson boys, who were splashing about in the Chicken Bowl Kiddie Pool.

Her words had an immediate effect, and Kayne, Taj, and Dakari simmered their boisterous play. However, the efficacy waned over subsequent minutes, and the ladies decided their next best course of action was to cover themselves with the boy's beach towels.

The boy's parents, Jonathan and Kesha Jefferson, the Rennigers, Cal, and Van Zants looked on from seats closer to the house where they'd just finished a Labor Day picnic lunch. By staying close to the house, Kesha could listen for 2-year-old Jalen, who was napping in his Pack-N-Play set up in the kitchen near the open window.

"Labor Day is my third favorite holiday behind Easter and Christmas," Kesha declared.

"Really? Not Mother's Day? I always loved Mother's Day when Grant and our boys spent the whole day making a fuss over me," Marie responded, surprised by Kesha's choice of a third favorite holiday.

"Nope, not Mother's Day. Labor Day!" Kesha insisted. "Labor Day is the celebration of the end of summer, which I am delighted to see go.

So the next day, tomorrow, I'll send the boys to school, put out my Fall decorations, make a pot of beef stew and Jonathan's favorite carrot cake, and start dreaming of wearing my sweaters again."

"What a coincidence! I've got the same things planned for tomorrow," Cal joked. "Except I'll also roll myself in pumpkin spice."

"That's funny," Jonathan chuckled.

They all looked toward the sound when they heard a nearby vehicle door slam. Bobby was getting home from a busy sales day at the used car lot and automatically waved to the crowd in his neighbor's back-yard. However, his bright smile faded when he recognized his neighbor's guests. He turned and disappeared quickly through his back porch door.

Marcus noticed that Jonathan's smile had also disappeared. "You two enemies? You're clearly not friends," he stated the obvious.

Jonathan looked uncomfortably at Kesha, who nodded her encouragement for him to provide an answer.

"We used to be friends," Jonathan began sadly. "Actually, I'm best friends with his son, DeShawn. I spent a lot of time in that house as a boy. Mr. and Mrs. McBride were very kind to me. But something happened..." he trailed off.

"DeShawn's in prison now. We know that," Ava filled in.

"Yeah, he's in prison now, and I'm not. I should have been, though."

"You're the buddy who didn't show up!" Ava quickly connected the dots.

"That's me," Jonathan confessed. "Mr. McBride blames me for being a bad influence on his son. He knows I'm a pastor in town, married with kids, and enjoying everything DeShawn hasn't gotten to enjoy. I try to keep a low profile around him, so it's not in his face."

Ava grew animated. "Jonathan, he doesn't blame you! He blames himself! He said your father kept you from going out that night, and he blames himself for not keeping close enough tabs on his son."

"Really?" a light flickered in Jonathan's eyes.

"You said you are best friends with DeShawn. Is he *still* your best friend?" Ava asked excitedly.

"He is. I see him every other weekend at the prison in LaGrange and have since he's been there. He's a serious Christian man now and has been for years. He loves Jesus and leads a men's Bible study twice a week. Our church provides its materials. DeShawn is a voracious reader, and there's not a single book in my study that he hadn't read before it arrived in my office. He's a bigger theology nerd than you or I, Marcus."

"But why won't he let his father visit him?" Ava wanted to know.

Jonathan looked puzzled. "I don't know that he won't. When De-Shawn first went to prison, he was ashamed of himself. Yeah, at that time, he probably didn't want his parents to see him there. He was still a teenager. But then his mother died, and he didn't even know she was sick. He thought they were done with him if they wouldn't tell him she was sick or give him a chance to say goodbye. So, he never reached out. But he's not a kid anymore, and I know he misses his father."

"Jonathan, you have to tell Bobby this!" Ava was adamant.

"It's a big ship to turn around. Been going in the same direction for almost 20 years," Jonathan sat back in his chair and shook his head.

"Look at those boys in the pool! If Kayne were in DeShawn's place, how long would you want his best friend to wait until he told you Kayne missed you? One more month? One more day?" She didn't wait for him to answer, and she didn't speak to him like he was her pastor. Instead, she spoke boldly from her mother's broken heart, commanding: "Get your feet moving to that house. Now!"

So, Jonathan moved. He walked to Bobby's back door - the door he'd used a thousand times with DeShawn when they were teens - and knocked. From their vantage point in the backyard, the others saw a few words pass before Jonathan stepped through the door and into the house.

"Um, um, um. So much wasted time," Kesha lamented, observing and shaking her head slowly.

"We don't know that, Kesha. In fact, we know the opposite. People waste time, but God never does," Ava objected respectfully. "As far as we know, Bobby isn't a believer, and DeShawn became a faithful believer in Christ while in prison. Maybe God used DeShawn's separation from his father's influence to draw him to Himself. And what if God used the long separation to soften Bobby's heart so his son could be an influence on him? We know any pain in the life of a believer is never wasted because God's word promises us that in Romans 8. All things work together for our good – even prison. And after walking alongside Marcus in ministry for 35 years, there's one thing I've consistently seen: the deeper and longer the suffering, the more beautiful the work of God."

Serendipitously, Ava's words to her pastor's wife, based on the sure promise of God's word, preached a sermon to her own suffering heart. The wailing baby of grief she'd been holding began to quiet.

# Chapter Sixty-Two

Grant and Marie swayed gently on the porch glider, appreciating the sharp crispness still present in the late morning air of this overcast Saturday. It was mid-September, and the maple trees up and down Cedar Street were already tinged on their outermost leaves with red and orange.

June extended her quiet time, and they could hear her playing *It Is Well With My Soul* reverently on the piano. They understood her need to declare her faith. She and Cal received confirmation from Cal's oncologist this past week that Cal's cancer was back. He was spending a lot more time sleeping these days, as he was right now.

Ava and Elodie were in the kitchen, already working on this evening's dinner. Green peppers were still pouring out of the garden even though it wasn't being tended with the rigor of early summer or given much attention at all. Ava said peppers thrive on neglect, and she appeared to be right on that score. There were still tomatoes and basil to be gotten from the garden, though not matching the profusion of the peppers.

Elodie had purchased a cheese-making kit and was turning store-bought whole milk into mozzarella curds by the pound. Tonight's dinner would be stuffed peppers, Caprese salad, and potato rolls made from leftovers of last evening's mashed potatoes. There might also be cake or pie if Ava and Elodie could agree on one or the other.

Marcus was busy in the study this morning. He was filling in for

Jonathan and preaching tomorrow at Grace Fellowship Church, not because Jonathan would be out of town, but to give him a much-needed break. Marcus finished his sermon two days ago but was still tinkering with it. It had been nine months since he'd preached his last sermon at Delaware Street, and he admitted to a few butterflies. Teaching as Jungle George at VBS wasn't the same level of pressure as he felt expositing the Word of God to the assembly of saints.

Lovie poked herself through the lilac hedge, walked up her neighbor's porch steps, and plunked herself down in a chair. "Guess what!" she encouraged Mr. and Mrs. Renniger.

"You're joining a circus to become a clown!" Grant teased.

"Nope."

"You just set the world record for eating live goldfish," Marie guessed.

"Eww. No! Those are bad guesses."

"Then you must tell us," Marie chuckled.

"Aunt Shelby is here! She came last night, and her moving truck is in the back of our driveway. She didn't like her job in Nashville and wanted to come back to Faircourt. Aunt Shelby missed me, Chase, and Daddy, and she's going to live with us for a while."

"That's wonderful news. I know you missed her too," Marie rejoiced with her.

"I hear Miss June is playing the piano. Can you tell her my news when she's done? And tell her I'll come to visit her later. I have to help Aunt Shelby unpack now." And Lovie was off, back through the lilac hedge.

Honk! Honk! Bobby's red S10 passed in front of the house, and Jonathan waved from the passenger window as they drove by. Grant and Marie knew they were headed to LaGrange to visit DeShawn. It would be Bobby's first time to see his son since he went to prison nearly 20 years ago. When Bobby told his neighbors about Jonathan's visit to him on Labor Day, he couldn't stop smiling or contain his excitement. He kept repeating, "It's incredible! Just incredible!"

"I'm so happy for Bobby. I hope it goes well today," Marie wished out loud.

"No reason it shouldn't," responded Grant, pushing a foot into the porch floor to continue their gentle sway.

"Hey, y'all!" Will greeted them as he came up the walkway from the sidewalk to deliver their mail. "What's with the moving truck next door? Tell me they're not leaving Faircourt!"

"They're not leaving Faircourt. Micah's sister, Shelby, had moved to Nashville at the beginning of the summer, and it didn't work out. So she's going to be living with them. I hear she's single and gorgeous," Marie informed him with a sly smile.

Will reddened. "I have nothing against single and gorgeous women," he said, handing Grant the household mail.

"Oh, don't forget, Marcus is preaching tomorrow," Grant reminded Will as he turned to continue his route.

"I'll be there, anyway!" Will pledged, grinning.

They watched Will disappear down the sidewalk, obscured by the vast magnolia.

"We've heard Shelby is single? Have we also heard she's gorgeous, or were you embellishing her resume?" Grant chided his wife.

"Just trying to give a brother some encouragement. Man! It's been Grand Central Station here." Marie changed the subject and fiddled with the gold chain bracelet on her wrist.

"You're not kidding! And look who's across the street, probably still mourning her lack of a prize from this year's State Fair," Grant speculated.

Christine Williams was in her rose garden inspecting a few late blossoms that had emerged. Recently, she derived less pleasure from them than she had previously. That they had been ravaged, and that she had lost control over both the roses and her very self, to a certain degree, had been devastating but instructive. She longed to find something less vulnerable to give her devoted attention. But the old roses were her last link to an old memory, and in tending one, she tended the other.

She sniffed and turned away from the recovering bushes, heading into the house through the backyard route and out of Grant and Marie's sight.

Christine stopped before reaching for the back doorknob and pulled something from her black fine-wool sweater pocket. It was a small card she frequently referred to and had laminated to prevent wear or damage. It read:

*I heard about the destruction of your flowers. I hope these poor substitutes will comfort you, not because they replace what you've lost, but because they come from someone who loves you and cares. With kind regards, LYE*

For her life, Christine could not figure out whose initials were L.Y.E. or if Lye was a nickname she should recognize. She resigned herself to living with the mystery and the incredible wonder that whoever it was, the poor fool loved her. She carefully returned the card to her pocket, and a slight smile crossed her face as she remembered being loved a long, long time ago.

Thank you for reading Redeeming The Time, Faircourt Friends Series Book One, my first novel. I sure took my sweet time getting it to print. I've been interested in writing since I won a local newspaper's essay contest in the 6th grade. But then came adulthood with marriage, children, college (yeah, I did it the hard way with three little kiddos), and then careers to navigate – mine and my husband's.

Along the way, I took the opportunities afforded me: writing my own women's Bible studies for classes at church and then for a program on Christian Television Network. I even, boldly and unsolicited, offered to write a religion column for free for a small city newspaper. To my shock, they took me up on it; and then paid me after I proved myself. I felt like a queen getting $30/per column. You betcha.

When everyone's life came to a grinding halt in 2020, I got two wild-hair ideas. One was to make something useful from the crop of dandelions in my yard that threatened my sanity. The other was to combine my passions for discipleship and writing into a fictional novel. The result of the latter, you hold in your hand.

If you enjoyed this story a lot or a little, would you consider doing me the great honor of leaving an honest review on Amazon.com? I'd love to continue these characters' journeys, and your input would greatly help.

1. If you inherited an unexpected windfall like the Van Zants, what would you do with it? What guards could you put in place to ensure you "set not your heart" on the riches?

2. Why do you think Micah didn't get saved when his neighbors helped him scrape and paint his house? He knew they were demonstrating their love for him.

3. Elodie respects Bobby for not pretending to be something he's not to get what he wants (her,) but she's clear about only being his friend. She also sees that Audrey is interested in Micah and warns her away. What's wrong with 'loving people to Jesus' when it comes to romantic interests?

4. After Marie's first volunteer meeting for Joe Jacob's campaign, she comes away "loving Joe's positions on the issues, but not loving some of his methods." If methods matter, how do you decide if something is shrewd business or deceptive manipulation?

5. We see edgy Five evolve into feminine Audrey Rose since coming to faith in Christ. Were there any outward transformational evolutions in your own testimony? What's the most important

transformational evidence?

6. From the outset, Marcus sees Beulah Francis' bequest as a test and struggles with it. How quick are you to see heavy circumstances as tests from the Lord that you desperately want to pass?

7. DeShawn and Claire mend their estrangement by a simple recollection of childhood history. Do you think that's enough? Would you recommend family counseling? Why or why not?

8. What do you think about Shelby's purchase of a memorial stone and plot for her aborted twins?

9. DeShawn described Tom Farmer's gospel presentation style to Shorty as "Heavyweight Combat Evangelism." Are you for or against that style, and why?

10. Name as many positive things that came out of Elodie's passing as you can recall. Why do they matter?

# FAIRCOURT FRIENDS SERIES

**AVAILABLE NOW**     **AUGUST 2024**

# COMING 2025